PRAISE FOR CHRISTOPHER FOWLER

'Fowler writes devilishly clever and mordantly funny
novels that are sometimes heartbreakingly moving.'
– Val McDermid, *The Times*

'Christopher Fowler is an award-winning novelist who
would make a good serial killer.'
– *Time Out*

'An imaginative fun house of a world where sage minds
go to expand their vistas and sharpen their wits.'
– *New York Times Book Review*
on the *Bryant & May* books

'Fowler repeatedly challenges the reader to redraw
the boundaries between innocence and malevolence,
rationality and paranoia... He has the uncanny ability
to invoke terror in broad daylight.'
– *The Guardian* on *Demonised*

'His sentences zip along, wonderfully funny
or moving – sometimes both.'
– *The Independent* on *Paperboy*

'The climax is truly spectacular... this would
make a great piece of cinema. It has everything
that you could ever want from a thriller.'
– *The Eloquent Page* on *Roofworld*

ALSO BY CHRISTOPHER FOWLER

Roofworld
Rune
Red Bride
Darkest Day
Spanky
Psychoville
Disturbia
Menz Insana
Soho Black
Calabash
Plastic
Breathe
Paperboy (Autobiography)

BRYANT & MAY
Full Dark House
The Water Room
Seventy Seven Clocks
Ten Second Staircase
White Corridor
The Victoria Vanishes
Bryant & May On the Loose
Bryant & May Off the Rails
The Memory of Blood

COLLECTIONS
The Bureau of Lost Souls
City Jitters
More City Jitters
Flesh Wounds
Sharper Knives
Personal Demons
Uncut
The Devil in Me
Demonised
Old Devil Moon

ALSO BY CHRISTOPHER FOWLER

HELL TRAIN

CHRISTOPHER FOWLER

SOLARIS

First published 2012 by Solaris
an imprint of Rebellion Publishing Ltd,
Riverside House, Osney Mead,
Oxford, OX2 0ES, UK

www.solarisbooks.com

ISBN: 978 1 907992 43 8

10 9 8 7 6 5 4 3 2 1

A CIP catalogue record for this book is available from the
British Library.

Designed & typeset by Rebellion Publishing

Printed and bound by CPI Group Ltd, Croydon, CR0 4YY

'There is little chance for a
person to exercise the imagination
today in this complex, programmed
society we have.'

Peter Cushing

'For a while,
we really were a family.'

Christopher Lee

For Kim Newman,
who unwittingly set the
train in motion.

CHAPTER ONE
THE SCRIPT

IT LOOKED LIKE a house from a horror film, and it was.

As the red MG bounced along the narrow country lane, Shane Carter cleared condensation from the windscreen and Down Place appeared before him like a slightly down-at-heels fairytale castle.

The damp A-Z in the glove box had been missing the page he'd needed most. The secluded track that led away from Windsor and the A4 had been un-signposted and a devil to find, but at its end appeared an extraordinary bow-fronted 17th century mansion that sat by the banks of the Thames, surrounded by elms and willows, encircled by curlews and crows and geese. Its crenelated battlements had received a fresh coat of white paint some while back and the building had been renamed Bray Studios—apparently Hammer was once again looking for ways to save money, and had turned it into a sound stage.

Lately the grand house had stood before cameras so often that it was a wonder cinema audiences didn't greet it as an old friend when they watched unsuspecting victims clatter up its drive, peering nervously at its darkling windows, framed against thunderstruck skies. He'd heard that Hammer was good at this sort of thing, re-dressing buildings so that they could be used over and over again.

7

He took the approach slowly, savouring the appearance of the building through his windscreen. Bernard Robinson, the studio's production designer, was a master at using the mansion's rooms for each of his films, lightly making them over with new drapes and furniture. Staircases were covered and corridors cut in half, gardens were sown with gravestones and transformed into cemeteries, bedrooms became morgues and libraries, cellars and mausoleums were turned into laboratories and surgeries. Within a few hours, an ordinary sitting room could be reshuffled, ready to go before the cameras as a Gothic asylum. The men and women who worked at the Hammer Film Studios made small marvels.

But Hammer, he'd also heard from friends over at Universal in Los Angeles, wasn't the studio it had once been. The writing was on the wall. The horror boom was coming to an end. Kids were getting wise to all the old tricks. They were laughing instead of gasping. Even the critics had stopped throwing up their hands in horror, and were dismissing the films within a few bored lines.

Shane drove his rented MG into the gravelled courtyard, respectfully avoiding a spray of stones, and ratcheted up the handbrake. He swung his leather briefcase from the passenger seat and headed for the building's main entrance.

Only in England, he thought, tilting his head. Hollywood had the brash frontage of MGM, but one of Britain's leading film studios—at least, now that Rank appeared to be gearing down production—had found a home within an old country house. And not—he liked this part—through any sense of heritage or its own inflated self-importance, but simply because it was cheaper to be based here, and its bosses could motor from their Knightsbridge homes in under an hour. *Out here it feels like 1935,* he thought, *not the Fall of 1966. The world is changing, but not in jolly old England.*

For a working studio, the place seemed oddly quiet. There was no sound other than the patter of falling rain and the

racket of crows. There was no-one to meet him in the chilly wood-panelled reception hall, so he made his way to the first floor. Security was non-existent. Here he was greeted by an awkwardly tall young woman who rose from her desk to shake his hand with excessive vigour.

'You must be Mr Carter, such a pleasure to meet you. We're enormous admirers of your films. Please do come in. I'm Emma Winters, Mr Carreras' assistant. You're a little earlier than we expected. Can we get you a cup of tea?'

He had heard it was rude to refuse tea in England. 'Thank you,' he said, sitting down. Odd that she used the plural when mentioning the company, as if they were an ordinary English family and he had simply come for an afternoon visit to their house. It made a refreshing change from schlepping through the backlot to the icebox air-conditioning of Hollywood studios, exchanging false pleasantries with men who wished him dead.

Walking around the oak-beamed room, he found himself standing before a set of framed monochrome photographs, each one featuring a familiar face. Peter Cushing as Doctor Frankenstein, Christopher Lee as Dracula, and beside these kings of horror a royal gallery of character actors and starlets: Nigel Hawthorne, Andre Morell, Ingrid Pitt, Veronica Carlson, Barbara Shelley and the ubiquitous, endearing Michael Ripper, who seemed to play every servant and innkeeper in the Hammer world, here seen in a ludicrous piratical costume in *Devil Ship Pirates*. Shane imagined walking into the studio canteen and finding them, all these familiar faces assembled in the morning, ready to start work on another mummy, werewolf or vampire film.

Shane had grown up on the monster movies of the nineteen fifties and had eventually worked as a script editor on Roger Corman's Edgar Allan Poe adaptations for AIP, who copied the idea of reusing lush widescreen sets and creating a stable of stars from Hammer. In place of the avuncular Cushing they had the eye-rolling Vincent Price, and for Hammer's straight man, Francis Matthews, they had chosen the newcomer Jack Nicholson.

Like Hammer, AIP employed a regular roster of directors, lighting cameramen, set designers, makeup artists, prop-builders and wardrobe mistresses to give their films a distinctively familiar look. The two studios were virtual mirror-images of one another, so it made sense to come here, especially since he was out of Corman's company now. He'd complained about the studio's cost-cutting techniques once too often, and found himself to be less irreplaceable than he'd imagined.

He'd been meaning to take a trip to England to see his sister, who had married an English architect and was living in Hampstead, and had hit upon the idea of calling on Hammer to see if there was any chance of finding work with them. It was a notoriously closed shop, but he had talked to an old girlfriend who worked as a stenographer in Wardour Street, and she had put him directly in touch with Michael Carreras, who seemed to be the most senior production executive, although nobody could remember his actual job title.

'My dear fellow, so sorry to keep you waiting!' Jovial and rubicund, with heavy black glasses, a shock of thick greying hair and a black moustache that made him look slightly disreputable, Carreras was nattily dressed in a grey striped suit and silk tie, and strode cheerfully toward him with an outstretched hand. In the other he was holding a fat cigar. 'We've been having a bit of a to-do with the censor this morning—but when are we not?'

'I've heard a few stories about British censorship,' said Shane. 'We have the same kind of problems, I assure you.'

'Yes, our chief censor John Trevelyan is a lovely man, utterly starstruck although he'd be the last to admit it, but we're forced to play a rather absurd game with the board. They're forever on about the amount of blood we use, the viscosity, colour and so on. John absolutely refused to budge on *Plague Of The Zombies*, and he's been getting twitchier than ever lately. Ministers are probably breathing down his neck. So I've been looking at some revised sequences.'

'What are you working on?' asked Shane, following Carreras to his office.

'It's been a busy year for us. We finished *Frankenstein Created Woman* a couple of months back and should be wrapping *The Mummy's Shroud* next week. Having a bit of difficulty getting the final sequence right. How to crush a mummy head. We've been experimenting for weeks. We've made quite a mess of the workshop, I can tell you. Come on, grab yourself a seat. Has anyone offered you tea?'

'Yes, thanks.'

'Jolly good.' Carreras seated himself opposite. 'We're trying to produce four horrors a year, but scheduling is always tricky and right now we seem to have a full stable and no riders, as it were.'

Shane was unfamiliar with such oblique sporting metaphors, and Carreras was forced to translate. 'Everyone's here, raring to go. Freddie Francis is itching to direct something new, Peter and Chris are pretty much twiddling their thumbs—Peter's in Whitstable, but that's just a few hours away, and we've some lovely girls lined up for the screamers; the female roles. Alas, there's no script. Hence my pleasure in seeing you today.'

Have I misheard? Shane wondered. *Am I being offered the chance of a job just like that?*

'I don't know whether you're familiar with any of my work,' he began. 'I haven't had a chance to update my CV.'

'But of course,' said Carreras. 'We're huge admirers of the Poe adaptations. All those lovely rich colours, quite startling. Roger's a man after our own hearts, frightfully clever at cutting corners and making money.' It sounded rather a backhanded compliment. 'I'm never quite sure where those films are meant to be set—Italy, possibly? The set designs seem to be Verona meets Vegas.'

'I was really only a script doctor on those,' Shane admitted. 'But I wrote a couple of other films that I'm kind of pleased with.'

'Ah yes, *Edge Of Night* and *The Creature In The Lighthouse*. Both jolly good, I thought. Shame you had to show the creature in that last one.'

Shane was amazed that anyone had heard of them. They had shown in a handful of cinemas, and only in the less particular states. He was pretty sure there had been no international distribution. 'I agree, we should never have revealed him,' he said apologetically. 'The lighting was too bright. And Laurel Canyon makes a crummy substitute for the Spanish coast. You could see the joins in his rubber suit. I still cringe in the last reel.'

'Oh come now, my dear fellow, you're being too modest. We spent years scraping by with the most frightful monsters. We've always been bailed out by clever sets and lighting. We reuse absolutely everything, make no secret of it. Roy Ashton, our make-up man, has pulled us through by the skin of our teeth, although I felt he never really got *The Gorgon* right. All those silly rubber snakes bobbing about. A shame, because I thought it was a terribly good script. Then we have the benefit of James Bernard's marvellous music.'

'And actors who can lift the flattest dialogue,' Shane said, adding hastily, 'not that the dialogue—'

Carreras raised a hand. 'I know, dialogue is sometimes our weak point. It rather lacks poetry, I feel. Freddie would shoot scripts without any dialogue in them at all if he could. I'm sure he thinks it just gets in the way. That's why he's so marvellous with suspense. There's no-one to touch him when it comes to constructing a tense sequence. But I'm the first to admit that he has a bit of a tin ear when it comes to conversation. And we've another problem.'

'What's that?'

Carreras exhaled smoke and studied the ceiling. 'Come now, you're an insider, I'm sure you've heard things.'

'Well, I did hear you've kind of become victims of your own success. Spawning imitators and the suchlike.'

'God, yes. So you probably know about our biggest rival, Amicus.'

'Didn't they do *Dr Terror's House Of Horrors* a couple of years back?'

'Yes, and they had quite a success with it. Terribly flat, some of the stories, awfully hammy acting, but an appealing idea. We rather foolishly loaned them some of our brightest stars. Milton Subotsky has some very fixed ideas about how such films should work. He makes them very cheaply.'

'Right, the portmanteau thing.'

'Purely an economic expedient, I assure you. If you shoot four or five stories of about fifteen or twenty minutes each and link them together with a wraparound segment, you don't need your stars to attend the entire shoot, just the portion in which they appear. Very easy to schedule, and of course you can pay most of them cash in hand at the end of the week. But you know—' He made a sour face, 'handing out grubby fivers in an envelope and gluing the resulting footage together in the editing suite, that's not at all our style. We like to think we're several cuts above that. Then there's Tony Tenser's little company, Tigon. Using our business model but shooting on real locations to save a bob or two. Some of his stuff is quite good. We're having to look to our backs a bit more than we used to.'

'But you still lead the pack.'

'Yes, but for how much longer? The truth of the matter is, we've run out of monsters. Frankenstein, Dracula, the Mummy, Dr Jekyll, the Phantom Of The Opera, the Wolfman—well, that one never really flew in my opinion, although Ollie Reed was terribly good in *Curse Of The Werewolf*—but you can't keep doing them forever. I do feel we're rather stuck in a rut.'

'Surely there are other Victorian horror classics that haven't been filmed?'

'Yes, but this is 1966. Nobody wants to see films based on the kind of books their grandparents used to read. The Beatles have changed the playing field somewhat. Milton has this idea that a teenaged horror film would make money—he's touting around some dreadful treatment involving an undead pop group—but we're committed to a more polished product. What do you think of our films?'

'I guess I've always thought of them as fables. They have a kind of graceful quality.'

'Exactly so. Have you ever read proper fairy tales? I mean Hans Anderson, Grimm and the suchlike. They're incredibly gruesome, birds plucking out eyeballs, girls cutting off their toes to fit slippers. The only reason why John Trevelyan allows us to get away with so much Kensington Gore is because we bring a bit of class to the proceedings. And of course we're usually careful not to set the stories in England. It takes the edge off all the nastiness if you set your tale somewhere on the other side of Europe, where most cinemagoers have never been.'

'Why don't you take something from your rivals and add new monsters? Do it in the style you've become famous for.'

'Easy to say, dear chap, rather harder to pull off I fear.'

'It's something I've been thinking about tackling for a while now.'

Carreras removed the cigar from his mouth and examined the end to make sure that it was still aglow. 'Really? What do you think, then? Is this sort of thing up your street? It takes a certain kind of mind to come up with it. Would you be up for the job?'

'You mean write a script? Would I? Hell, yes.'

'Nice to hear a bit of keenness around here. We're a close-knit band, but it can get a tad oppressive at times. In each other's pockets, as it were. There's one snag, though.'

'What's that?'

'We have a couple of projects in development and two films set to go between winter and spring, but Peter and Chris like to be at home for Christmas, so we tend to shut down around then. Which leaves us with nothing right now.'

'I'm not working on anything in particular at the moment,' said Shane. 'I could start immediately.'

Carreras checked the production calendar on his desk. 'Well, it's Monday now, so if we said Friday?'

Shane was puzzled. 'For what?'

'The finished script.'

'Five days?' *Four and a half if you count this morning,* he thought, panicked.

'Then we could get it off to Freddie and the cast over the weekend, get some feedback—we'd have to submit it to John at Soho Square in advance of shooting, just to make sure we don't waste any time covering sequences that have to be cut out, although you might like to include a few extra-gruesome scenes for him to get his scissors around—let him think he's guarding the nation's morals. Then we take it over to the artists in Wardour Street to see what they can come up with in the way of marketing. We like to get the posters sorted out first, just to get everyone on the same page. Often our artists will come up with something quite outrageous that ends up in the film. Oh, and there are the Americans to keep happy, but if they like the idea they'll give us approval over the phone.'

'But what about the budget?' Shane asked, slightly appalled by the casual air of the entire enterprise.

'That's already fixed. You don't have to worry about stuff like that. You just have to write the bloody thing, and then we'll tell you the bits we can't do.' Carreras sucked noisily on his cigar. 'Listen, you don't have to decide right now, leave it half an hour or so. Have another cup of tea. I'm sure Miss Winters can rustle you up some biscuits, or Mrs Thompson runs a jolly good canteen if you'd prefer something more substantial after your drive.'

'I'm staying with my sister and her family, I don't really have a place to work.'

'Well, there are some decent pubs in the area, a couple of lovely places over at Shepperton, the King's Head and the Red Lion. All the writers use them. You could stay in any one you fancy, so long as it's not more than ten pounds a night. And I think we can spare you an office.' He strode to the door and opened it. 'Miss Winters, can we accommodate Mr Carter somewhere?'

Emma Winters had repainted her lips and loosened her auburn hair. He suddenly saw that she was modelling herself on the starlets covering her office walls. Perhaps she dreamed of auditioning for the company one day. Her legs were a little thick, but there was something dramatic about her eyes. She suddenly shot him a stern look. He wondered if she could read his mind. 'What do you need, Mr Carter?' she asked.

Shane thought for a moment. 'Well, access to research materials.'

'We've a decent library, and of course you could take the screening room if you'd like to reacquaint yourself with some of our past pictures,' she offered. 'There's a spare office next door, and I'm sure we have an old Imperial lying around. That is, you do type?'

'Of course.'

'Because some of our writers prefer longhand and it makes things so much more difficult.'

Shane felt as though he had slipped through the looking glass into a land where films were made on nothing more than polite handshakes and good intentions. He turned to Carreras, who was glowing, thoroughly pleased with himself. 'Is there any particular subject you had in mind?' he asked.

Carreras thought for a moment. 'Well, it should have all of the Hammer trademarks, I suppose,' he said. 'An exotic setting, young lovers, fearsome creatures, a dire warning, rituals and curses, and dreadful consequences. Supernatural apparitions are always good—they give the lighting boys a chance to show off. We like rules; don't go up to the castle at night, that sort of thing. There'd have to be something for Christopher. He's terribly tall and grave, doesn't really handle comedy roles, but he has a wonderful presence. He's a terribly good baritone, but we've never found the right singing role for him. The rest is mostly atmosphere, and we can supply that by the bucketful. You know the kind of stuff, swirling fog, upturned caskets, villagers lost in the woods, fainting ladies in low-cut corsetry.

Plenty of blood of course, although you'll have to run those parts by me. I have a pretty good idea of what will get through.'

'Did you have any thoughts on the subject matter?'

'Well, Peter and I were talking about that the other day, and we rather liked the idea of a train,' said Carreras finally. 'Think you can manage that?'

'I'll start today,' said Shane.

'THE LIBRARY,' SAID Emma, pushing open a wide oak door on the ground floor to reveal a room rather like a gentleman's club, panelled and lined with bookcases, with a pair of red leather wingbacked chairs arranged before an immense fireplace.

'It looks like the spot where Jonathan Harker first met Count Dracula,' said Shane, amazed.

'Oh, it probably was,' said Emma vaguely. 'I'll have the typewriter brought down to you, and we'll get you some new ribbons. Please call me if you need anything. Anything at all.'

She gave him a secret smile—was she flirting?—and quietly closed the door behind her.

Shane pulled up the library steps and checked the bookshelves. They were remarkably well stocked. Some of the more arcane volumes on witchcraft and devil worship might come in useful. He reached up higher. Wedged above one stack of hardbacks were several board games: Ludo, Monopoly and something called 'Hell Train.'

He carefully disentangled the battered box and took it to the table.

CHAPTER TWO
THE GAME

SHE WAS AT home by herself and had grown dangerously bored.

Her mother had gone to the bakery, and had probably stayed to talk with Mrs Malik. Whenever the pair got together they gossiped for the best part of an hour. She had no idea what her mother talked about; recipes, husbands, the new priest with the sea-coloured eyes who had taken over St Peter's. Her father was at work in the foundry, doing whatever it was that the men did there. He would not be back until after dark. He was never home until late, and when he came in he smelled of iron filings, fire and sweat.

Which left her alone, looking out of the window at the torrenting rain. She had brushed and braided her blonde hair into plaits, and had played Pelmanism with a deck of cards, but the Queen Of Spades was missing from the pack and spoiled the game. Her mother had a jigsaw that showed a colourful painting of London Town, but too many of the pieces were missing.

She looked around the overstuffed sitting room. The air was still and dead, hardly ever disturbed. On the dresser was her sister's death-book, its open pages tilted upright. She had died of tuberculosis at the age of five, and for the final photographs

her little corpse had been dressed in her best clothes and sat among the family who loved her. There was her mother's music box, with its stiff-jointed ballerina that came to life at the turn of a key, spinning around to the sound of the *Emperor Waltz*. There was a puzzle book, but most of the puzzles had been completed long ago, even though the answers had been printed in pencil and repeatedly rubbed out.

She remembered there were other games in the attic, old ones that belonged to her poor mad grandfather, and despite the fact that she wasn't supposed to go up there, she recalled that her parents kept the brass key on top of the kitchen dresser. It was difficult to reach, so she dragged over a chair and climbed upon it, standing on tiptoe until her fingers could close over it. She would only take a little look, then replace the key so that her mother would never know.

The house was tall and gabled, with a long, narrow attic full of cobwebby wonders. There was no light up here, but she knew where everything was. Behind the crimson dressmaker's dummy and the butterfly net, next to the two old armchairs, reversed on top of each other like a giant clam, she found the games: four colourful cardboard boxes covered in plaster dust.

The first was a compendium of the games boys liked, blow-football, snakes and ladders, draughts and jacks. Nothing of interest there for her.

The second was a box of magic tricks with a cover that depicted a moustachioed man pulling a white rabbit from a shiny top hat, but its instructions had long been lost, and besides, most of the magic tricks required weeks of practice before they could be performed.

The third was something called 'Strategic Invasion,' and appeared to involve arranging armies across a map of Russia—what a boring idea for a game!

But the last—and by far the largest—box was the most promising. For a start, the lid was tied down with a length of twine, and a card was attached that read: DO NOT OPEN.

She carefully carried it down to her bedroom, lowered herself onto the rag-rug and studied the lid. The painting showed a Victorian train with a cowcatcher and a roaring Devil's face and red horns, and billows of fire coming out around it like angry breath. The elaborate script beneath the picture read: 'Dare You Board The **Hell Train**?'

It seemed odd that she had never noticed the box before. Solemnly arranging herself before the game, she slipped off the twine, removed the lid and took out the playing board. Carefully unfolding it, she laid it flat and began to remove the pieces from their containers.

There were no dice, no counters, and there was no rulebook, but the more she studied the layout the more it seemed self-explanatory. She set the passengers—little painted lead figures carrying valises—at the station which was, curiously enough, named after their own town of Chelmsk, and even shared the same brick chimneypots, the same town square, the same great foundry at its centre. In fact, the entire layout of the board looked like her town in miniature. Perhaps its designer had lived locally, and had glanced out of his window for reference while he was painting.

The board was slotted with a mechanical railway track running through neat illustrations of idyllic countryside, marked with half a dozen little stations.

Around the base of the playing area ran a curious caption.

'*When the Devil was summoned to Earth, he built a train to take the Damned to Hell.*'

A rather severe motto to place upon a child's game, even she could tell that. Her mother would most certainly not approve of her touching the game, which made it all the more exciting. What harm could come of it?

She looked back in the box. What else was there?

With great care, she removed the largest, most detailed and most beautiful piece—a clockwork train. Its name was engraved on the boilerplate: *ARKANGEL*. She peered in at the

exquisitely detailed carriages, their seats and lights and luggage racks. Then she connected the six cars together, including third, second and first class compartments, the last with a section of private suites and a little observation deck at the back.

She picked out the least spoiled players—they were made of lead and had lost some of their enamel painted finish—finally settling on two handsome young men and two beautiful ladies in hats and bustle skirts—one blonde, one dark—and placed them on board the train, in the first carriage. They would be a husband and wife, and a pair of young lovers.

There were two odd little fellows left over, so she set these in the second carriage, a fat little man who had something wrong with his right leg; the lead had got squashed, destroying his foot. She decided he should be a salesman with a sample case. The other was a man in a top hat and mutton-chop whiskers, carrying a tall box. He looked as if he'd be a showman of some kind.

Sparks flashed around the wheels of the *Arkangel* as she wound up the engine with a tin key. Then she set the train down on the slotted track and let it embark upon its journey.

She watched in fascination as the train chugged around the board, making little steam-engine noises, through pretty painted countryside scenes decorated with cherubic angels, over sunlit bridges and through rainbowed ravines.

The train came to rest at a station, and seemed to be waiting for her to do something. She found a little tin ticket machine that dispensed cards, and, turning its handle, withdrew the first one.

It read: 'Piety.' But what to do with it?

At the end of the platform was a signal box with a slot in its roof, into which she inserted the card, and a moment later that changed the points. The train set off once more.

It was beautifully made, but what was the *purpose* of the game?

The clock on the mantelpiece chimed three. Outside, the street was empty and misted with falling rain. When she looked back at the board, she saw that the train was trundling along

the next section of the track, passing a painted banner that read, 'Follow The Rules & Shame The Devil.'

Life, her mother always told her, *is a journey that you must control.*

That's what this is, she decided. *It's a game about life.*

The pattern repeated itself, and at each station she issued another ticket for another leg of the trip.

These new cards read: 'Fair Play' and 'Decency.'

But as the train progressed and the game continued, her luck with the cards turned bad. The next ones were 'Drink,' 'Lust,' 'Violence' and 'Godlessness.'

With each new instruction, the points clicked and the train rolled forward. But now it was heading away from the sunlit country scenes, across to the far left hand side of the board, and she realized that it was moving away from 'The Primrose Path Of Righteousness,' onto a murky branch line fraught with danger; falling trees, a rickety bridge across a ravine, a densely overgrown forest, great black crows, even what appeared to be an erupting volcano. This line was labelled 'The Wicked Way To Eternal Damnation.'

If this was a game about life, it appeared that it was also about death.

That's not fair, she thought. *My passengers have no choice but to stay on board. The decisions aren't up to them, they're just down to fate. How do they know if they're good or bad? Who has the right to test them?*

It was exasperating. Why did games always have to have a moral?

The clockwork engine seemed to be running of its own accord now. Down into the darkest, most sinister part of the board headed the train. The sparks that sprang from its engine threatened to set the cardboard scenery alight. But where was it heading? The name of the terminus on the bottom left hand side of the route had become smudged and was illegible.

And as she leaned closer to follow the train's path, she saw

the *Arkangel*'s wheels really begin to turn as it grew and grew, thundering past her shocked eyes in a blast of fiery steam, threatening to jump the tracks.

The train was getting bigger by the second. With a groan and spit of steel and steam it expanded to fill the room, until it appeared to be thundering out of the fireplace. The pictures on the mantelpiece shook and cracked. The ornaments were shaking. A vase rolled over and smashed. The noise of the engine pounded against the walls, filling her head until she could hear nothing else. The train was thundering across the dining room.

Rectangles of light flashed past on the walls, shaking the pictures from their moorings as the train carriages roared past. The engine funnel was belching coal dust and soot onto the ceiling and over the furniture, the train's bell was clanging wildly, its horn blasting a shrill shriek that threatened to shatter the windows. The wind from its passing sucked all of her mother's music sheets into the air. Caught by the *Arkangel*'s cowcatcher, the piano exploded and was hurled across the room. The great wheels revolved so close to her feet that it seemed they would tear up the floorboards and rip the house in half.

Terrified, she could only watch in horror as the great train roared past her on the start of a journey that, once commenced, could not be halted.

CHAPTER THREE
THE ARRIVAL

THE RIVETS WERE *white gold, fading to crimson and blood brown before they had been fully hammered into place. Iron plate and tempered steel, rods and bolts glimpsed through fire and steam in the cuprous stench of annealing metal. The world of the engines was ever like this.*

The result was a magnificent piece of craftsmanship, but perhaps they were being punished for showing too much pride. One of the workers brought in from the depot had the four fingers of his right hand sheared off in the engine's coupling joint just hours before the dedication ceremony, and the cheap Russian grease they used on the plates infected the wound so badly that by the time the ambulance reached the hospital, his arm was a livid poison sac. Amputation should have caught the contagion, but no; they buried him beside the track less than twenty four hours after the Arkangel rolled out of its shed. No-one pretended the work was easy, but jobs were hard to come by back then and the line brought hope, even if the means of achieving such prosperity also carried lasting shame...

Nicholas Castleford awoke with a start. The memory of his dream blurred and faded like smoke.

He looked out of the window. Greenery, wheat, single track roads, mile upon mile of nothing. Looking at this pastoral scene, it was hard to imagine that the world was at war.

Nicholas had not found the war to his liking. He had absconded to Poland of all places, where he practiced the ancient art of fleecing the locals. Cards proved to be the best weapons in his arsenal, and he used them without mercy, taking huge amounts from stupified villagers who should have known better.

After a trip back to London to deposit more hard-earned cash and to order new suits from his tailor, he'd returned to make a further killing. But this time he had been caught out by a local magistrate and had only just managed to avoid a flogging. With the police alerted, he had made a circuitous route through the nation and across its borders, so that he now found himself on the wrong train, in the wrong country, at the wrong period in history.

Looking out of the window he found the station name to be incomprehensible, but most definitely incorrect. In fact, Nicholas had a feeling that the last half dozen stations had been wrong.

Perhaps the train had turned onto a branch line. Nicholas compared the sign to the railway line in his guide book and saw that virtually none of the letters matched. There were accents and circumflexes all over the place. Why did they have to make everything so damnably complicated? The empire had spread the use of English to most civilised countries, so why the hell had it not reached here?

The battered green train had seen better days, but this was still the most reliable way of getting around the country. Many of the roads had been blockaded, sewn with rolls of barbed wire and planted with rocks. The army was trying to limit civilian access routes across the interior.

The train arrived with a screech of brakes and a squeal of pistons. There was so much smoke and steam and squirting oil

that he thought it might have simply pulled in and collapsed, never to move again. And yet he had barely managed to alight with his bag before it gathered its strength and fled, chuntering and wheezing out of the station.

Nicholas set down his leather suitcase and looked around. He should never have crossed the Carpathian border, not now, not at this time. August 1916, the fragile neutrality ending, the Central Powers on the cusp of invasion. Even a businessman with international standing was not safe in such circumstances. And he was far from that.

Nicholas preferred to think of himself as an adventurer. It sounded colourful, if not quite respectable, which seemed appropriate enough. Although he was a Londoner he had always made his way to foreign climes, accumulating money by gambling, speculating and occasionally stealing. He knew he was heading in the wrong direction, but the choice had not been his to make. He had been escaping creditors, escaping girls, and escaping more than that...

As the smoke cleared he heard nothing but crickets and skylarks, saw no-one on the platform except an elderly man in a stained uniform folding away his green flag. No other passengers had alighted. No-one had been stupid enough to do so.

Nicholas smoothed his slender brown moustaches and looked around: scrubland, tall animated beeches and indeterminate bushes bearing sickly yellow berries. A tree-lined avenue leading away from the station, a dirt road, no tarmacadam. A grey-walled town—possibly abandoned—lay in the distance. Fields and more fields. The rustle of wheat sheaves. A solitary dog barking. No human sounds.

He checked his silver pocket-watch and noted that there was only an hour left before sunset. Had the blasted connection been on time leaving Sofia he might have caught the right train, or at least have arrived in time for lunch somewhere. He wondered what the stationmaster might think of him, a dashing English gentleman, twenty eight, as sturdy and handsome as

one of the new automobiles lately seen in Park Lane, dressed in a black brocade waistcoat, a silver-grey suit and a trilby, far too stylishly attired for this rural retreat. He belonged in London, of course, and acted accordingly, but Nicholas liked to make a fine impression on the ladies of Eastern Europe—sophistication made them so susceptible, and gained access to their husbands' pocketbooks.

He waited for the stationmaster to arrive, and tapped him insolently with his Malacca cane.

'I say, you there. Are you in charge here?'

All he got back was a blank look.

'Ah.' He reopened the dogeared phrase book and spoke loudly. *'De tren mi-a laut pentru a gresit locul.'*

The ancient stationmaster grimaced like a gargoyle. 'We speak English in this town,' he said.

'Where am I?'

'You are in Chelmsk.' The name was pronounced like a gob of spit.

'Well, your train appears to have set me off at the wrong stop.'

'That is no concern of mine.'

'There must be a village, yes? I expect you have carriages waiting.'

'You can expect nothing here.'

'Where are your porters?'

The stationmaster looked contemptuous. 'We do not have porters. Here, people carry their own belongings.'

Nicholas was indignant. 'But I am English! I will do no such thing.'

'Please yourself.' The stationmaster turned to leave.

'Ah yes, your famous European hospitality. Look here, my good man, just tell me the time of the last train back.'

'There are no more trains tonight. And I am not your good man.'

'But I distinctly heard the passengers speak of a train which runs at midnight.'

'There is no such train. You understand? No such train.' The stationmaster spat close to Nicholas' boot, then walked away.

'Extraordinary fellow.' Nicholas sighed and hoisted his own valise. It really was the most astounding inconvenience.

There were no carriages waiting, not even a rustic hack. There was nothing else for it. He was forced to set off up the dusty road carrying his own case, the afternoon sun beating down on the gap between his collar and his brilliantined hair. Removing his hat, he stopped before a tall wooden sign consisting of utterly incomprehensible words. He attempted to look them up in his guidebook, but was finally forced to guess the right direction.

'Ridiculous peasant language,' he muttered, wiping goat shit from his boot.

After a few minutes, he passed over a crossroads. How on earth was he supposed to tell where the nearest village was? Where had the grey walls gone? He knew he should have made a note of their direction from the station platform.

Hearing a ringing bicycle bell, he nimbly stepped back as a girl passed by, dressed in a red dirndl and a white peasant frock, hitched high away from the spokes, exposing her fine tanned legs.

'I say, look out!' he called, and she turned in surprise toward him.

She was stunningly beautiful, with wide blue eyes and corn-sheaf hair that streamed out behind her elegant neck—but it was already too late to stop her, and a moment later she had gone.

It took another half hour to reach the walls of the town. Up close, they were much higher and more forbidding than he had expected. Passing in through one of the great wooden gates, he found himself in a deserted street bookended by big ugly churches that were virtually windowless and were probably always freezing to pray inside. A pack of mangy stray dogs set to barking. One of them limped behind him, looking as if it might try for a taste of his leg.

Somewhere off to his left, a mournful steeple bell rang, as if to warn people away. He looked up at the high grey stone walls, the cobbled thoroughfares, wide and empty, the unadorned houses with closed green shutters.

There was something so grimly utilitarian and military about the scene that he half expected to see Russian soldiers marching around the next corner. Somewhere above him, in the belfry of a dark bell tower, the leathery rustle of bats' wings could be heard. He looked up and saw a cloud of them filling the sky. They swooped down and some brushed against his hair, filling him with dread. He was not comfortable with the things that crawled and flapped through the countryside at dusk. His natural home was in the streets of Belgravia and Mayfair, at the gaming tables, in the pubs, not here where there were only inbred farmers and their sow-faced wives. Where was everyone?

As he reached the corner, a pair of drunk old men staggered past.

'Look here,' Nicholas called, 'is there a hotel? I need a room for the night. I'm from London. You do know London?' He was met with more blank looks. 'The most important city in the world? Glittering jewel of the Empire? Ring any bells? No?'

'It is not safe to be here,' said one of the old men. 'There is a curfew. Have you not heard the news? The army has already reached the next town.'

'When will they arrive here?'

'Tonight, after dark. You must go! *Go!*' One of the drunks waved him away. 'We want no more trouble.'

'Is there a train I can catch?'

In the distance there was the sound of a train whistle. Blast the stationmaster for his lies.

'That was it,' said one of the drunks, unhelpfully. 'There are no more now.'

'But there is one at midnight. I heard tell—'

'Catch that if you want to dance to the Devil's tune.' The

beery old men took one last opportunity to stare at him before bursting into phlegmy laughter and staggering away.

'Cretinous yokels,' Nicholas muttered under his breath, and continued on. Ahead was a great stinking factory of some kind, from which came the smell of smelted ore and the clang of beaten iron.

The foundry had a vast blank stone wall topped with a steep tiled roof, and tall chimney stacks that pumped out oily black smoke. As he passed, he looked through the great rusted iron doors and saw a vision of Hell. Men stripped to the waist in the heat, silhouetted against the furnace flames, shovelling coal and hauling glowing rods from a bank of fire that looked and felt like the surface of the sun. What kind of lives did these men have? How long did it take before they began to cough up black soot and expire? It would be a miracle for any of them to survive into their thirties.

Nicholas considered himself wise beyond his years. He understood how men behaved and how women could be controlled. And yet for one so wise, he often seemed to make the kind of mistakes that required him to get out of town as quickly as possible.

He carried on walking. A soldier in a khaki uniform was leaning against a wall lighting a cigarette. 'Hey, friend,' he called to Nicholas, 'have you seen any men coming over the hill?'

'No, but I hear they aren't far way.'

'Good. We'll have some pleasure from this town tonight.'

'You'll be garrisoned here?'

'You could say that.' He shook his match out. 'We'll drink the place dry. You find good beer in towns like this.'

'Perhaps I'll join you,' said Nicholas.

'You may not want to. After we've had our fill of the beer and the women, we'll bayonet every man who isn't with us and burn these damned houses to the ground.' He took a drag on his cigarette. 'The next time you pass this way, all you'll find is a blackened pile of rubble.'

Nicholas moved swiftly on.

Eventually the street gave way to a leafy lane, and it seemed he was about to run out of houses when he arrived at a picturesque local inn with a well and a cobbled coaching yard.

Nicholas glanced up at the inn sign, which showed a fiery crimson steam train with devil's horns sprouting from its tank. It was running over the severed body of a naked woman tied on the tracks. Using the dictionary in his guidebook, it appeared the inn's name was best translated as 'The Tormented Virgin,' although the wording probably meant something far worse.

Charming, he thought. There seemed to be nowhere else open, so Nicholas headed in through the low porch. He stopped in the doorway and surveyed the busy tavern. With depressing predictability, the locals—all men—immediately ceased their prattling and turned to study him. A couple of them snickered at his outfit. Somebody farted insolently. Determined to remain undaunted, he approached the bar.

'Good evening, landlord. I am in great need of a gin and Italian, please. With plenty of ice.'

The landlord was boozy-nosed, bucolic and rotund, with wild sideburns and a face like a bulldog chewing a nettle. Without bothering to reply, he pulled a cloudy, frothy pint of ale and slopped the pewter tankard in front of Nicholas. To be polite, Nicholas took a sip. It tasted as if a rabid dog had broken wind in it. He quickly set it back down.

'I need a room for the night. A clean one, if you have such a thing.'

The landlord was clearly displeased, but his natural parsimony prevented him from turning away a customer, even one from the city. 'Englishman, you are no friend to us. You cannot stay here long.'

'I'm not asking you to hide me. I'm not ashamed of being English.'

Without removing his eyes from Nicholas, the landlord called over his shoulder. 'Isabella!'

The landlord's daughter—for there was a mercifully faint resemblance within the eyes—appeared in the doorway behind the bar. Nicholas found himself looking at the firm-legged beauty on the bicycle. Too young, too pert and far too innocent, but what a challenge! Perhaps, he thought, she might prove to be sport for a city gentleman craving a little excitement on what had otherwise been a ghastly journey.

'Yes, father?' She briefly caught his attention, but did not smile. She looked as if she had never had much of a reason to smile, and yet she had eyes as hopeful as sunrises.

'Where have you been? Show this gentleman a room.' He turned back to Nicholas. 'If the soldiers ask for you, I will tell them you are here.'

Pushing up the counter top with a strong, tanned arm, Isabella stepped back. 'Follow me, please.'

The room was sparsely furnished, but clean enough. There were blurry photographs of sturdy men posing before train sheds on the walls, but fresh gardenias stood in a vase beside a white china jug and water bowl. Nicholas dropped his bag on the bed and tested the mattress, only to realize that it was stuffed with straw and was likely to give him the worst night's sleep of his life.

'Please excuse the room,' Isabella ventured in perfect English.

'You speak our language beautifully.'

'Our schoolteacher was English.'

'Excellent. I hope he continues to teach you.'

'No, he was shot.'

'We're not all bad, you know. I'm Nicholas.'

'I am Isabella. We have very few visitors here.'

'Well, you're not exactly near anywhere important, are you? I'm amazed anyone finds this place. I'm not supposed to be here. There was a problem with my train home. I'm from London.'

'London.' She tried the sound in her mouth, savouring the word.

'It's the most exciting city in the world. I work there, you know. I have rooms in Park Lane but my family is from Herefordshire. Do you know Herefordshire?'

Isabella shyly lowered her glorious eyes. 'I have never left Chelmsk.'

'What, you've never been anywhere?

'No.'

Nicholas took a step closer. 'Isabella, do you know where a beautiful girl can go?'

'No, where?'

'Anywhere she damn well pleases.'

Her blue eyes widened. He watched in amusement as she fled the room, reddening with embarrassment.

'And you are so very beautiful,' he told her retreating form.

CHAPTER FOUR
THE ASSIGNATION

LONG AFTER ISABELLA had left the room, Nicholas could smell her scent, redolent of wild summer fields and wide blue skies. Of course, there was the novelty of country girls—London women were sharp and sly with their charms, but so made up and used up, and these days it seemed that the fresh ones were seized before their buds had even come into bloom, snapped up by old roués as if they were purchasing opening night buttonholes.

He stepped down the narrow stairs and stood in the shadows, watching her deliver drinks to the saloon tables. The men grabbed at her buttocks and breasts as she passed. Nicholas knew the importance of shielding his cards, but as Isabella returned to the bar, he found himself catching her arm.

'Why do you let them do that to you?'

She looked surprised, as if the thought had not crossed her mind before. 'I have no choice. A woman is nothing here.'

'Can't you get away?'

'It is not possible.' She looked back in desperation at the swaying, braying villagers.

'Isabella, the war will tear this town apart.'

'I know nothing of war.'

'You will soon enough. What time do you finish?'

'I never finish. Father never closes until the last man has gone back to his wife. Most would never leave if they had a choice.'

Nicholas looked at the locals slumped across their tables and imagined conversations that rarely rose above discussions of compost and the comparison of farming implements. 'Then meet with me,' he suggested.

Isabella looked back at the hard drinkers in the bar. One was stamping the caked mud from his boots and throwing it at the cat.

'Isabella, you have nothing to lose, and the world to gain. What is the best restaurant in town?'

'There is only one. It is called The Pig.'

'The Pig. Meet me there.'

She turned back to the bar, her mind in turmoil. 'I don't know how long it will take to get away.'

'It doesn't matter. I will wait for you.'

Nicholas walked through the deserted streets on his way to the restaurant. The sun had set abruptly, without colour, and cones of cold light now fell from the tin lamps suspended over the road. On the way he passed an incredibly wrinkled old woman carrying a reluctant squealing pig. A drunken farmer was slung out of a doorway and fell before him into the gutter, where he was violently and copiously sick. Nicholas watched in growing disgust. *Isabella deserves a better life than this,* he thought angrily. *She belongs upon my arm in London. How fine we would look together, entering the Café Royal!*

He stood before the windows of The Pig. The restaurant was empty except for a snoozing waiter with brown soup stains on his vest, slumped over the bar counter. Upon each bare wooden table was an arrangement of dried wheat, framed around a flyblown severed pig's trotter. The thought of dining here appalled him. Drawing a deep breath, he entered.

It took a minute for the waiter to rouse himself. Surprised by the unexpected appearance of a client, he wiped the table and placed a grubby leather menu before Nicholas. There were

no other patrons in the restaurant. Nicholas studied the dishes with distaste and pointed to an unpronounceable item.

'What is this?'

'It is pig,' the waiter replied.

'And this one?'

'It is pig also.'

Sighing, Nicholas stared from the window and checked his pocket watch.

'WHAT DID HE want?' asked the landlord.

'I told you, Father. He is an English gentleman.'

'There is no such thing. I know gentlemen. They only bring trouble.'

'He was being polite.'

'Polite!' Isabella's father gave her a look of disgust. He touched his daughter gently on the arm, but she drew away. 'All I want is what's best for you. Be happy with what you have. Please, tend to your future husband.'

Isabella looked over at Josef, who was seated with his cronies by the fireside, and hesitated. She loved her father and was keen to obey him, but sometimes her life felt stifling and predictable.

Josef was a handsome man from solid working stock. He was not refined, but his nature was predisposed to kindness. It had long been decided that she would be joined in matrimony at St Peter's. No doubt she would bear the first of his children in the following spring. There would be four, according to the priest: three strong boys and a girl to keep house. This pattern, as predictable as the seasons, was a source of joy in the lives of the other village women, but the root of dissatisfaction in her own.

Filling a tray with beers for Josef and his boorish friends—Ivan and Karek—she set them down before the man she had been instructed to marry. She could see that Ivan was trying to get him drunk again. Jealous of Josef's success with her, he was always undermining his friend.

'The coalition army will destroy the railway station,' said Josef glumly.

'Our comrades are fighting beside them,' Ivan reminded him. 'We stay as their allies, or run as their enemies.'

'I can't leave Isabella here, Ivan. Look at her. They won't leave her alive.'

'Oh, you've got yourself a little firebrand there,' Ivan said in a voice loud enough to carry to her ears.

'I love her,' Josef admitted, drinking deep.

'All the men in town want her. They've probably had her, too.' Ivan slyly caught her eye.

'All except you, Ivan,' laughed Karek, who always had trouble following the conversation. Ivan lashed out, slapping Karek around the ear.

'What did you do that for?' Karek clutched at his head like a scolded child.

'Isabella is keeping herself for me,' Josef assured his companions.

'That old story?' Ivan scoffed. 'You really think that's true? Did you see the way she looked at the fine city gentleman?' He clapped his friend on the shoulder. Isabella stood a short distance away, listening.

'Marry her fast and give her a dozen babies,' Ivan advised. 'No-one will look twice at her then. Not when her breasts are falling to her belly.' He slurped his ale and roared with laughter.

'She will be a fine mother,' said Josef.

'Perhaps she will,' said Ivan. 'But the army will shortly be arriving here. A girl like her will turn soldiers into animals.'

'I will protect her.'

'That won't be enough to save her. You must take her virginity,' Ivan replied. 'Tell them she's diseased. Scar her face. Make men shun her. You must do something so that they won't look twice at her. Take this. Do it soon.' He removed a lethal-looking razor from his leather belt.

Isabella's doubts crystallized at that moment. Leaving the

beer glasses to dry themselves, she ran behind the counter and removed her apron.

'Wait, Isabella,' Josef called, knowing that Ivan had gone too far this time.

'The barrel needs changing,' said her father.

She caught his eye defiantly. 'I shall only be a few minutes.' She went to the back door, but found it locked. The keys were in her father's leather apron. Returning to the bar, she slipped up behind her father and carefully removed the key ring from his pocket. Then she ran for the door.

Isabella had no jacket, but did not dare risk collecting it from her room. She darted out into the courtyard, then stopped, fearful of being followed. Looking back through the dimpled glass, she saw Ivan and Karek raising their tankards to Josef. They had already forgotten about her.

She ran to the restaurant.

She found Nicholas seated before a plate of roasted and sliced pig's head, and sat down beside him. Realising that he was witnessing an assignation, the waiter poured Isabella a glass of red wine and slid discreetly away, keeping watch from the corner of his eye.

'You came.' Nicholas only just resisted kissing her.

'I have to leave.' Isabella looked terrified. 'They spoke of cutting my face. So the soldiers wouldn't—'

'Listen to me, Isabella. Part of your country has joined the enemy. Very soon now it will be hard to know who to trust. It won't be safe for you when the troops arrive here.'

'They want me to bear Josef's children because he will inherit a directorship at the iron foundry. It is the lifeblood of the town.' She cast a longing glance at the railway travel poster on the wall. 'I have seen London in books,' she confided, 'and I have been there in my dreams.'

'You could be there tomorrow. I'd pay your ticket.' She demurred, but he drew closer. 'Why not? What do you really have to lose?'

'I feel so confused.' She touched the crucifix at her neck, apologetic now, almost ashamed of her innocence. 'I am supposed to marry a man from the town, like all the girls.'

'Are you so sure this is the life you want?'

They watched from the window as a drunken villager rolled past, groping at his fat wife's fat bottom.

'Josef is a good man.'

'But he is your father's choice, not yours.'

'No, it's not that...'

'Then come to London.'

'They would never allow me to leave.'

'Opportunity is not a lengthy visitor, Isabella. A chance like this may never come again. You'll never know what might have been.'

Isabella glanced back at the framed picture of the train on the wall. She could see her reflection imposed upon the train. All of her life she had been surrounded by images of travel. Nicholas pressed his advantage.

'Each minute brings you closer to danger. Look at you—what will the soldiers see? A pleasure to be taken and discarded. Life does not run on a track like one of your trains. This may be the only time in your life when you can choose. You are free to go wherever you want, if you believe in—'

'What?'

'—the power of love.'

Seizing the moment, Nicholas drew her face close and kissed her; a long, lingering meeting of mouths. She had watched the girls and their swains at the village fair, but this was different from the way they kissed, from the chaste, dutiful way that Josef kissed; it felt reckless and full of heat.

But she was the first to pull away. According to the priest, all girls had to choose between damnation or paradise. Girls who were promised to one man and dallied with another were destined to go to Hell. But she was curious to see the other path of her life, to know what might yet be. While the other

girls barely thought about their destinies, Isabella's greatest weakness had always been her curiosity.

'Please, Isabella, I want this for you.'

'Don't you see? It is madness.'

'No, the war is madness, and this is the only sane answer for you.' Nicholas believed what he was saying, even though it was not the first time he had used such words on a local girl.

'I cannot leave everything behind and come with you.'

'It is only fear that keeps you here, Isabella. Fear of the unknown. Take the chance.' He kissed her again, touching her tongue with his. 'Take flight with me. We'll pack our bags and catch the midnight train.'

'But my father...'

'They'll all be drunk by now. I will give you the world. Say yes.' He kissed her a third time, deeper than before, and she felt herself slipping under his spell. A new world was opening up at her feet, and she was willing herself to fall.

'Yes,' she heard herself say. 'I know a way out.'

CHAPTER FIVE
THE WARNING

BACK ON THE railway platform, acrid coal smoke from the departing train still hung in the air. A young couple dressed in English touring clothes, a style most noticeable for stripes of inconsistent width, stood beside their luggage, which included tennis rackets, shuttlecocks and a cricket bat. It was a wonder they had not brought picnic tables with them. The man was balding and already running to fat, and wore a blue and white cricket jacket. He could not have looked more out of place if he had been wearing a grass skirt.

'Missed it!' Thomas exclaimed, 'How is that possible?'

Miranda was four years older than her husband, and already developing the shrewish nature of her mother. Her attractive mouth had lately started becoming pinched, never more so than when she thought about money. Her eyes seemed to narrow more suspiciously with each passing day.

'You said they never leave on time,' she accused.

'Damn and blast!' Thomas kicked out at his suitcase. The stationmaster had disappeared. There was no-one else to be seen.

'Thomas, remember who you are! I told you we should have set off earlier. Well, there's nothing else for it. We'll simply have to go back.' Miranda stooped to pick up her valises. She

was perfectly capable of taking care of herself. Indeed, with a husband like Thomas, the skill was virtually a necessity.

'We can't go back, Miranda. Apart from anything else, I've not allowed more money for another room.'

'I told you, we should never have left England,' she said unhelpfully.

'There must be someone around here who knows when the next train is.'

He stumped off along the platform looking patently absurd, and stopped at the ticket office. When he rapped his knuckles on the wooden counter, the stationmaster suddenly rose from behind it, making him jump.

'I say, you there. Look here, are you in charge? The train has gone.'

'Then you have missed it.'

'I expect there's another, yes?'

'There is not another, no. You can expect nothing here. There will be no more trains tonight.'

'But what are we to do? We cannot go back. In case it has escaped your attention, your country is heading for civil war.'

'Then you will have to choose a side, Englishman.' The stationmaster hawked and spat on the floor. Lately, spitting at foreigners had virtually become a national pastime. He slammed his ticket window shut.

Miranda had seated herself on her luggage. It was still hot, and she was perspiring. 'Is there nowhere safe in Europe?' she asked, dabbing at her neck with a handkerchief. 'It's as if the world has gone mad.'

'There's supposed to be another train,' said Thomas, puzzled. 'I'm sure I heard someone mention it in the café earlier.'

Miranda fanned herself. 'When?'

'I can't be sure. Towards midnight, I think. But the stationmaster—'

'But what if the army arrives before then?'

Thomas was trying to think of an answer when some kind

of animal released an unearthly scream from the misting wheatfields beyond the station.

'What on earth was that?' Miranda tried to see.

'It sounded like a pig. Probably caught in a trap.' Thomas unfolded his map and followed the railway line. 'Here we are. Chelmsk—Snerinska—Schlopelo—Blankenberg—Zoribskia, just those stops, then nothing. It makes absolutely no sense.' He turned the map around to show his wife. The part revealing the final destination had been scrubbed away, as if it no longer existed. 'We got into the country, Miranda. There must be a way back out.'

Miranda was exasperated. 'This is no longer neutral territory, Thomas. They are closing the borders.'

'We have to stay ahead of the army.' Thomas shielded his eyes from the low sun, trying to see signs of life, but there were only the endless green and yellow fields.

'And if they arrive here? We could be shot.'

'Then we have to be on the last train.'

'What train? There's nothing on the schedule!'

Her husband firmed his jaw. 'We must have faith, Miranda.'

Thomas touched the crucifix at his neck, and not for the first time Miranda regretted marrying a country vicar. He checked his pocket watch and looked anxiously down the line.

'Can you see anything?' she asked.

Thomas's eyesight was poor, but he could discern a faint glow moving in the shadowed woods.

'Is it the train?'

'No,' said Thomas gloomily. 'I think it's the army.'

The bushes at the end of the platform suddenly rustled and parted. Emerging from them, a filthy boy stepped onto the paving stones. His clothes were ragged and his feet were unshod. His piercing blue eyes held the signs of madness.

Thomas refused to be intimidated by a mere child. He strode up to the urchin and confronted him.

'Little boy, can you understand me?'

The child studied him, then pulled something alive from his wild hair and put it in his mouth. 'We all speak English. There was a teacher here once. We liked our teacher very much.'

'Jolly good. When is the next train?'

'No train.' The boy scratched at his head, looking for more lice.

'I thought there was supposed to be one at midnight.'

'Something comes at midnight.'

'What do you mean?'

'Something that looks like a train.' The boy examined another wriggling bug held between his fingers, then ate it.

'Where does it go?'

'Mustn't look at it. Turn away when you hear the rails sing. Cover your ears when you hear the whistle. At midnight you must run. Hide.' The boy turned to go.

'Wait—'

But it was too late. The child had vanished in the darkening woodland.

'What was the boy saying?' Miranda called.

Thomas could hear the worry in her voice. 'Nothing that made sense,' he told her.

'What shall we do?'

'What can we do?' said Thomas. 'We wait.'

CHAPTER SIX
THE ESCAPE

NICHOLAS LOOKED THROUGH the window of the tavern and saw trouble brewing. Josef and Ivan were standing with Isabella's father. There was much gesticulation.

'Wait here,' he told Isabella, and he went as close to the window as he dared, listening.

'Wake yourselves up, you two,' the landlord was saying. 'Stop the Englishman. And find my daughter. Ivan, sober up and help Josef. It's his wife he'll be losing.'

Nicholas watched as Ivan and Josef left the bar with sudden purpose.

'Come this way,' Isabella whispered. She was holding open a narrow wooden door at the side of the tavern. He slipped inside, and followed Isabella to the foot of the stairs.

'Go to your room and pack your bag,' Nicholas said. 'I need some things. Be as quick as you can. I'll meet you outside.'

Running lightly up the stairs, Isabella darted into her room and stuffed her mother's old cloth bag with a few essential items. When she glanced out of the window, she saw Ivan and Josef burst into the courtyard below. Isabella blew out her candle and descended, leaving through the back door, into the alleyway at the side of the inn.

Outside his room, Nicholas froze as the floorboards creaked. He listened intently, but hearing nothing from the floor below, he continued inside. Quietly and quickly, with an expertise that revealed much practice, he grabbed his valise and the string-tied wad of notes he had hidden under the mattress, and started to leave, crab-walking awkwardly down the back stairs.

At the bottom of the staircase, the landlord and his men were waiting for him. The barkeepers of Eastern Europe kept a keen eye for men who tried to slip out. 'Where do you think you're going, friend?' asked Isabella's father. He tapped a heavy stick in his palm.

Isabella stared through the window helplessly as Nicholas was hauled back into the inn by the drinkers, and was forced to sit on a stool before the open fire. He was surrounded by angry villagers who never once took their eyes from him.

Nicholas considered his options. He had, in truth, been in stickier situations. There had been that time in Valencia with the Mayor's daughter, for a start. They had nearly cut his fingers off. But the door was too far away for him to cut and run. The others in the bar would never allow him to leave.

'There is no time for this,' he warned, trying to rise but held down on the stool. 'The enemy is already inside your walls.'

'Whose enemy?' asked the landlord. 'Not ours. This town was built by the railways. Our families were raised on iron and fire. Our men are engineers and metalworkers, and our women become wives and mothers, not sport for bored city folk.' He had been mulling red wine over the open fire in an iron cup. It was now boiling.

'And you would see Isabella raped to save yourselves.'

'Let's show the stranger our hospitality. Pour him a drink, boys.' Two of the toughest looking farmers in the bar pinned Nicholas down and forced open his mouth. The metal wine cup was red hot and bubbling fiercely. The landlord drew up a three-legged stool and seated himself before Nicholas. *Perhaps,*

Nicholas considered, *this situation is worse than Valencia*. He struggled, turning his head aside.

Outside, Isabella watched in horror, unable to act. She was shocked by the ferocity of men she had known all her life, men she thought she knew. What she was witnessing only firmed her resolve to leave. But there was nothing she could do to save Nicholas now.

The landlord lowered a pair of tongs into the fire and lifted the iron cup, carefully raising the glowing goblet over Nicholas's open mouth. Drawing it close above the fine English gentleman's upturned face, he started to tip it. Behind him, a tough old farmer held Nicholas's arms by his sides.

Kicking out as hard as he could, Nicholas knocked the fat landlord off his stool, upending the scalding cup into the farmer's eyes. The farmer roared, blinded, and fell back. The cup fell on his forehead, branding his flesh. Nicholas seized the moment to make a break for freedom. Grabbing the farmer, he slammed him into the fire, setting his hair alight.

He dashed for the door and barged it open. Seizing Isabella's hand, he rushed from the tavern with the others in pursuit.

The pair ran as fast as they could. Isabella pulled Nicholas aside as Ivan and Josef came around the side of a building and blindly charged past.

The streets were dark and empty, both a blessing and a curse. As they reached the town's outer wall, they saw that a platoon of bedraggled soldiers had began pouring in through the open gate.

'The town has one road in and out,' Isabella warned. 'If we are to survive, we must cut across the fields.'

Panicked, she ran even faster, with Nicholas close behind.

In the penumbral gloom ahead, Nicholas could make out rows of upturned marble tablets, angled among grassy hillocks like rotten teeth. 'Is that a graveyard?'

'Yes. We must go through it to reach the station. From there we can follow the tracks out of town. It is the fastest way.'

As they fled toward the ragged field of corpses, their pursuers

started closing in. Nicholas knew that their valises were slowing them down, but he could not possibly travel without his belongings.

Ivan and Josef were strong country lads and quickly gained ground. Then Isabella missed her footing and fell heavily, pulling him down into the grass.

Moments later, the fleeing couple were seized by their pursuers.

CHAPTER SEVEN
THE TRAIN

THOMAS AND MIRANDA had seen the torches of the arriving army wavering through the treeline, and had fallen into panic.

Miranda wrung her hands and paced back and forth on the platform. In England, she took control of every situation in which she found herself. Here, it was impossible to do so. She had never felt so powerless. 'We don't have the right papers,' she cried. 'They'll see that we're English.'

'We must pray to Our Lord,' said Thomas.

'Is that your only solution? It's too late for prayers.'

'That is a blasphemy, Miranda. Remember, we are all children of God. The conventions of war demand that we be taken prisoner and remain unhurt. No harm shall befall us.'

'And that's it, is it? Abject surrender? Begging for leniency?' Miranda rounded on her husband. 'I do not understand how you can say that, when you know perfectly well that the Central Powers are not honouring the code of conduct set out by the Allies. The newspapers have been full of nothing else, for all that they have been censored.' Her husband's pacifism was increasingly making her angry. The world was fast descending into a fiery pit, and all she heard was the damp drizzle of appeasement. Why did the weak always pin their hopes on compassion?

But Thomas was no longer listening. She had seen him do this a hundred times before, closing his mind to anything he did not wish to hear. With each passing day of her marriage, she was becoming less and less pious. If God had chosen to speak through man, she was fairly sure He would not have picked Thomas to be his mouthpiece.

Something pricked at Miranda's ears. The rails were pinging, softly at first, then more clearly. 'There's something coming,' she said.

ISABELLA TRIED TO free herself from Ivan's grip. Nicholas fought off his attackers, smashing the first man who touched him in the nose with a Marquis of Queensberry jab, only to be viciously kicked in return.

Now another advanced on him with a flensing knife in his right fist. Nicholas brought up his knee and broke the farmhand's arm with a sharp crack.

Josef looked as if he had just realized he was required to fight for his fiancee. Physically imposing but held down by his bulk, he slowly advanced on the Englishman. Nicholas studied his solid gait, his thick arms and bull neck with dismay. He knew that one well-placed punch from the foundryman could render him unconscious. He desperately searched around for something he could use as a weapon.

Too late. Josef attacked. Nicholas had been taught boxing skills at Cambridge, but was not afraid of playing dirty. He kneed Josef as hard as he could in the groin, sending him over, onto his back. Isabella screamed. Josef threw out a hand to grab his opponent. Nicholas was faster, but he slipped on the wet grass.

Josef seized his chance and pinned Nicholas down on an overgrown grave-slab edged with iron railway spikes. Pressing his arm across the Englishman's throat, he began to choke the life from him, bearing down with his full weight. Nicholas could pull his arms free, but this would not help his situation. He tried

to bring Isabella into his line of vision, but could only hear her crying out. Josef pressed the advantage, pushing down harder.

Lights danced before Nicholas's burning eyes. His right hand gripped the grave's iron corner spike, desperate for leverage, and he was shocked when it came away in his hand, rusted through.

As Josef pushed down to break his neck, Nicholas stabbed at the soft flesh of his attacker's throat with the sharp tip of the spike. The pain was enough to make Josef release his grip. Isabella pulled forward and tried to separate them, bringing Ivan with her. Josef rolled onto his back as Nicholas climbed to his feet and found Ivan running at him. He grabbed Ivan's sleeve and spun him around, kicking away his legs to send him sprawling. The foundrymen were strong but slow.

Nicholas grabbed at the sobbing Isabella and pulled her away, snatching up her bag, making a dash for it. He had lost his own valise in the fight, but had thankfully retained the wad of banknotes inside his breast pocket.

The commotion had drawn the attention of the incoming soldiers, who were raising the alarm. More torches could be seen in the town's streets, flickering against the walls, stretching shadows into monsters. It seemed their pursuers were uniting into a single lynch-mob.

Isabella and Nicholas could only stumble to their feet and flee from the graveyard in the direction of the station, the fiery procession closing in behind them. Now luck came to their aid, for a line of trees blocked the revealing moonlight, shielding them from sight as the soldiers swarmed among the cemetery stones, shouting to each other in drunken confusion.

As the exhausted couple passed the church clocktower, Isabella saw that the iron hands were almost at midnight. Ahead, she could make out the low black form of the station building.

'This way,' she called, pulling at his sleeve. 'We must run faster.'

Nicholas had a stitch in his side. The clocktower began to strike twelve, the sharp clang of the bell cleaving through the

clear night air. One more muddy field to cross, with the torchlit rabble weaving toward them.

They reached the misty station and charged up the ramp onto the platform. The single straight track was empty. Two figures were waiting at the platform edge, but it was too dark to make out their features. They were also carrying luggage, and one of them appeared to be wearing a straw boater, something surely no-one but an Englishman would do.

The soldiers had now been joined by other villagers, and were running along the path to the station in a chaotic hue and cry.

Thomas and Miranda turned, astonished by the noise of the pursuit. Just as the simple boy had predicted, the railway lines were singing, then rattling. Miranda could feel the platform trembling beneath her boots, and was suddenly filled with a terrible sense of foreboding. She leaned forward to try and see if there was something coming, but could only make out a black billow of sparkling coal-dust forming in the cut between the pines. The cinders glittered like stars falling to earth.

Then she saw two lamps like tiger-eyes, one vermilion, the other amber, swaying slightly, growing larger. The great stack of the chimney darker than the sky, *chuff-chuff-chuff*ing toward them in great plumes of choking firefly smoke, a gleaming disc of green steel, engine and coal-car and links of carriages, hurtling towards them, as the great train stormed into the station.

For a flickering second, the front of the engine had the Devil's face, an illusion caused by shadows and smoke. Like some great extinct creature recreated in mechanical form, the locomotive thundered and wheezed to a stop with eruptions of stinging cinders and sprays of arterial oil.

Isabella looked into the carriages and froze, some distant demon roiling in her head. 'No,' she said, shaking her head, 'no, not this.' She began to back away, but Nicholas grabbed her hand. He looked into the carriages himself, but they appeared bright and bare, nothing out of the ordinary.

By now, the rest of the villagers had reached the ramp to the platform. The soldiers among them were raising their rifles. There was not a second to waste. Nicholas flung open the door of the first carriage behind the coal car, ready to push Isabella inside. She tried to resist, but she knew that if she stayed behind she would never survive the swarming soldiers. In that brief moment, she was forced to make a decision.

The soldiers opened fire. Bullets sang against the wall of the train. Miranda screamed. The decision was made.

One of the villagers made a grab at Nicholas, but caught a bullet that tore away a quarter of his skull above his right ear, sending him spinning off the platform and onto the track. His blood spattered the wheels. Nicholas froze in shock, covered with gore and flecks of white bone.

There was nothing else for it. Isabella was pulled up the carriage steps. Having come to a halt, the engine driver had seen the commotion on the platform, and was preparing to depart in haste.

At the next carriage door, Thomas and Miranda were fighting to get aboard with their luggage. Thomas was determined to leave nothing behind. For a moment it seemed as if they were not going to make it. With the train releasing its brakes and rolling once more, Isabella threw wide the door and grabbed at them. Their hands reached out and connected, from Nicholas and Isabella to Miranda and Thomas. In that brief flash of life, Isabella felt as if their fates were joined together.

Thomas reached back and pulled the door shut behind him with a bang, just as a bullet flicked his boater from his head.

Nicholas was surprised to find that the rest of their pursuers were suddenly falling away, fighting with each other and the soldiers. 'They're not following,' he said. 'Why aren't they coming after us?'

The four new passengers crowded at the window, watching the tumult shrink away as the train pulled out and the platform receded, and they left the townspeople of Chelmsk to the anarchy of the invading army.

CHAPTER EIGHT
THE CONDUCTOR

THEIR JOURNEY HAD been baptised with blood. Not a good way to start.

Thomas and Miranda had collapsed into the plush velvet seats of the First Class compartment and were struck dumb by what they had just seen. Miranda was trying hard not to cry. Under normal circumstances, they would now have been sniping at each other in the way that English travellers did all over the world, fussing over the luggage, who had been responsible for packing so much, why had they not shipped one of the valises ahead and so on, but instead other questions crowded in. Why had a group of villagers run after them, and why had they fallen back just as suddenly? And where had the other couple disappeared to now? The one who looked English—where had he gone? They glanced around the six-seat carriage and found themselves alone.

'Did you speak to them?' Miranda asked.

'No, but the man was definitely one of us, I'm sure of it. Had it not been for the girl we would never have boarded in time. We should find her and thank her.'

'This dreadful war makes animals of men.' Miranda shuddered. 'What a frightful experience. I daresay our paths

will cross theirs again. Fellow countrymen have a way of finding each other. Show me the map.'

Thomas dug in his tennis bag and produced a creased wad of densely printed paper. 'I looked at it earlier but the last panel appears to be missing. The route goes off the edge of it.'

'Then we are in unknown territory. More excitement.'

'Not too much, I hope,' said Thomas.

Miranda did not bother to explain that she was being sarcastic.

ISABELLA LED NICHOLAS along the ornately decorated corridor of the train. The lower half was clad in polished teak boards, topped with a slender brass rail. Above this, the walls were painted a lustrous deep green, with fitted brass lamps and framed maps lining the way. The air smelled of pipe smoke, dusty fabric, wood shavings and metal polish, but there was something else in the air—a tang of sulphur, probably from burning coal. They passed a decorative silver plaque embossed with the name of the train and a date: *Arkangel—Maiden Voyage, August 1887*.

They were picking up speed now, racing through the lush green countryside beneath a black sky sprinkled with coldly glimmering stars like points of frost.

'That couple,' said Nicholas, 'English, obviously. Perhaps we should find out what they're doing here.'

'There's time enough for them later. First we have to see—'

'See what?'

'There doesn't seem to be anyone else here.' Isabella was anxiously peering in through the compartment windows.

'Of course not. This is the first class carriage. We're in peasant territory. The locals will all be in third. This part won't fill up until we reach a decent city.'

'Oh. I have never been on a train before.'

'Why did you pull back?' Nicholas demanded to know. 'You could have got us killed.'

'I did not want to board.'

'In Heaven's name, why? There's nothing to be frightened of now. You are being borne away from the town with each passing second.'

She shook her head. 'I realized we had no choice.' She would say no more on the subject.

'You are angry with me,' said Nicholas, after the silence between them had grown too long. 'I fought in self-defence, you know. It was him or me.'

'My poor Josef.'

'Come, I'm sure he has suffered worse. Anyway, there is nothing to be done now. Let's find out where we're going.' He took her hand once more and continued along the corridor.

She stopped to point to a framed map on the wall. 'Look, there are four stops after Chelmsk on the route: Snerinska—Schlopelo—Blankenberg—Zoribskia.'

'You must know these towns.'

'No, I have never left my village. On my thirteenth birthday we planned to visit the coast, but we were prevented from making the trip. That was the day they shot the English teacher.'

'What had he done wrong?'

'He tried to run off with one of the local girls.'

Nicholas squinted at the faded map, attempting to follow the blue train line to its conclusion. 'What's our final destination? What comes after Zoribskia?'

Isabella traced the route with her finger. 'The terminal is obscured. Ink has been poured on it. There must be someone on board who can tell us.'

They walked along the rocking passageway to its end, opened the door and stepped across into the second class carriage. Here they found another map detailing the train's route, but this too had lost its final destination. The terminal in the bottom left-hand corner had been scratched out, even more severely than the last.

Ahead, Nicholas could see a dark figure unaffected by the swaying of the train. He approached the motionless man, a tall,

dark-eyed fellow with a long chin, dressed in a blue conductor's uniform with double rows of brass buttons, black silk piping and a round flat cap. He stood in his alcove surrounded by mementoes of his journeys, waiting to be called upon, like a statuette kept in a cupboard. His sea-legs absorbed the roll of the carriage, keeping his torso still and erect, something that probably came with experience.

'I say, are you in charge here?' Nicholas demanded to know.

The figure slowly turned to stare at him, as he might peer at an insect. He had a pair of lethal-looking silver clippers in his right hand. 'I am the Conductor of the *Arkangel*,' he replied in perfect English. He was as pale as ivory. The low timbre of his voice resonated from somewhere deep and far away. Although deeply set in the caves of his skull, his shining black eyes missed no detail.

'Well, what is our destination?' asked Nicholas sharply.

'That must depend on you.'

'Perhaps you didn't understand the question. Where does the train terminate?'

'We need to stay on board until we cross the border,' asked Isabella. 'Is that possible?'

'You will finally come upon a border, yes.'

'Then we'll need tickets to get us there.' Nicholas dug into his jacket and began to count out some notes from his billfold.

The Conductor looked down at the notes in his hand as if being proffered used toilet paper. 'I cannot accept your money.'

'If it is the wrong currency—'

'It has nothing to do with the currency.'

Perhaps the railway did not wish to encourage dishonesty. 'How else can I pay?' Nicholas asked.

'Those without tickets must find another way.'

There were places in Eastern Europe where bills had to be stamped and restamped by teams of clerks before payment. 'Even if this is some kind of local custom, it still doesn't make any sense,' he said. Clearly the man was not of a helpful disposition. 'Wait here, Isabella. I'll be back.'

There had to be somebody else on board the train. Nicholas pushed on ahead and came to the next second-class carriage. Here two of the compartments were occupied with single men. One was grave and correct, in the garb of a decade ago, an aesthete perhaps, or an actor. He sat with his chin on his knuckle staring out at the rushing countryside. Curiously, there was fresh dirt on the shoulder-pads of his frayed jacket, as if he had just been dragged from a grave. The other passenger was a rotund fellow with a caliper on his leg, a man who was clearly falling upon hard times; a salesman, judging by the sample case stowed above his head. Neither of these men would be willing to give up their passage home.

Nicholas continued onwards, searching without success.

The third and final pair of carriages housed the lowest grade of compartment. Here the wooden slatted third class seats were arranged in an open plan, with iron luggage racks large enough to hold suitcases and crates of vegetables. At the far end he found a sleeping peasant couple, the ruddy-cheeked wife collapsed upon the husband's shoulder like a dozing potato. This was more promising.

Nicholas studied the husband and noted his top pocket, from which protruded a pair of unstamped tickets.

Returning to the centre of the train he found the Conductor in exactly the same place, as if he had not moved a single muscle. Nicholas offered him the purloined tickets. The Conductor threw him a suspicious look, but took them all the same.

'I would like to upgrade those tickets to first class,' he explained.

'There is no difference in payment,' said the Conductor. 'Passengers find their own class and sit there, for that is where they are most comfortable.'

'That sounds very… communistic. What is our journey time?'

'We must travel deep into the night.'

'Hm. Not very exact. Do you have food and drink on board?'

'There is no dinner service on this line apart from tea, which you will find in the samovars throughout the train, one per

carriage. Sustenance may be obtained from the porters at the stations, who may be persuaded to come to the train.' He clipped the tickets and handed them back, but as Nicholas went to take them, he found the Conductor holding them tight until Nicholas was obliged to look at his eyes. 'You are now travellers on board the *Arkangel*,' he intoned. 'I must insist that you read the instructions printed on each carriage and pay heed to them.'

The Conductor turned and stepped back into his alcove, his hands dropping to his sides. He seemed quite content in this position, rocking with the bounce and sway of the train.

Nicholas and Isabella made their way back along the carriage. Nicholas stopped before the framed panel of instructions and read:

All Passengers Are Respectfully Reminded:
You Must Be In Possession Of A Valid Ticket
You Must Not Alight At The Stations
You Must Remain Until Your Journey's End

He stared at the notice board in puzzlement. 'How odd to find such a thing, and printed in English too, as if for our benefit alone,' he said. 'But what does it mean? What are stations for if not to alight onto?'

He went to the window and looked out. All he could see was rushing greenery, dark forests, icy stars and the spit of yellow sparks from the wheels as they flinched against the iron rails.

CHAPTER NINE
THE UNKNOWN

NICHOLAS RETURNED TO the carriage, and Isabella went to smarten her appearance. She returned, having brushed the mud from her hem and pinned up her hair, and once more looked like the embodiment of summer. Her youthful luminosity quelled his fears and gave him fresh hope.

'The strangest fellow,' he said, 'talking in bloody riddles. What can he have meant?'

'The Conductor is well known in our town.'

'You know him?'

'No, but I have heard the terrible stories about him. The foundrymen speak of him in hushed voices.'

'Stories? I don't understand.'

'You know how men will talk. They're worse than wives.' Once again she avoided his searching gaze and turned her attention to the window. 'We had no choice but to board. But we are here now, so we must make the best of the situation.'

'What do you mean?'

'I have the gravest fears that—'

Just then, Thomas and Miranda passed the compartment, gesticulating and arguing. Thomas was obviously searching them out.

'Oh, hullo!' he said, his suburban middle class English a faint absurdity in the Slavic atmosphere of the ornate train. 'I thought you must be English. I was saying to Miranda. Thanks for your help at the station. We were rather making a mess of things. Too much luggage. The town…'

'It's been taken. You're civilians?'

'We were on a touring holiday.'

'But this is a war zone,' said Nicholas in astonishment.

Thomas looked affronted. 'I believe it was actually neutral territory when we set out.'

'We were advised not to come,' said Miranda, taking Nicholas' side. 'Everybody said it was a quite preposterous idea, but Thomas is giving up his diocese in Henley-Upon-Thames and taking up a new position in East Anglia. He was absolutely insistent upon making the trip. Butterflies and wildflowers. He's interested in cataloguing them.' She could not have made her lack of interest plainer.

'I knew it was to be the last chance we'd have to take a trip before settling into our new vicarage,' Thomas explained.

'You're safe so long as you keep heading north,' said Nicholas.

'Do you know where we're going?' asked Miranda.

'We're trying to find out, but the maps in the corridors have all been defaced.'

Miranda straightened her hat and checked the lacing on her gloves. 'You must think us unforgivably rude. Our peculiar situation is simply no excuse for poor manners. I am Mrs Wellesley, but you must call me Miranda, and this is my husband, the Reverend Thomas Wellesley.'

'I'm Nicholas Castleford, from London. And this is Isabella.' If he was bothered by the fact that he had no idea of her last name, he did not show it. Isabella doubted he would be able to pronounce it anyway. They all shook hands with grave formality.

Miranda was already wondering about their relationship, and assumed the worst. A cultured Londoner and a local girl, it was probably best not to ask. That was fine. She was an expert

in avoiding subjects. All Englishwomen of quality were. 'What is your destination?' she asked.

'Eventually London,' said Nicholas. 'It may take some time to get there.'

Miranda studied Isabella with mischief in her eyes. 'But surely you are not English.'

'No,' Isabella admitted. 'I had to leave my home.'

'And you're afraid of what you might find.'

'London has long been a dream, but only that.'

Miranda tilted her head, studying the girl. Quite a beauty. 'My dear, life is nothing more than a journey towards our dreams. We give chase to them, then when we pin them down they die—like butterflies.' She gave Thomas a sour glance.

'I think it is time for me to make my own destiny.' Isabella felt lost among these curious English people who clearly preferred to say one thing and think another.

'But of course you must. We are emancipated women, are we not? But I fear for your country, my dear. Carpathia is no longer in a state of neutrality, and those soldiers arriving at the station were in Bulgarian uniforms, were they not? They are fighting with the Turks and Germans. We heard such stories about them in England, about tossing newborn babies on bayonets. The most frightful barbarians, all. Tell me, where is your family?'

'My mother died last year.'

'How sad. What was wrong with her?'

'She was suffering from hereditary disappointment.'

'And your father?'

'I left my father behind.'

'You poor dear.' Miranda took her cold hand and patted it between white gloves. 'Well, I do hope we shall be friends.'

Thomas was peering at the train's fittings with interest. 'This is a Krupps-Henschell Turbine locomotive from 1887,' he said. 'But decorated in a manner that's quite unique. There's something about the style I can't quite put my finger on. I can't imagine what it's doing on this line. Marvellous engines, built

locally, made to last. Lined brass pistons, they never dry out or overheat.'

Miranda gave her husband a look of exasperation. *Less husband than ornament.* 'Arrange a table in the supper car, Thomas. I shall go and find the Conductor.'

'Don't be ridiculous, Miranda, there won't be a supper car,' Thomas replied, but his determined wife had already gathered her skirts and tacked off along the corridor. Miranda had always been formidable. Once, on an outing in Richmond, she had slapped a horse in the face for whinnying at her. He reminded himself of that whenever he thought of answering back.

'There's tea in the samovar,' Nicholas called after her. 'You'll find the Conductor at the centre of the next carriage.'

MIRANDA FOUND HIM in his customary position in the alcove, exactly where Nicholas had indicated.

'I say there, excuse me.' Miranda went to tap the Conductor on his braided epaulette, but something in his bearing stopped her. She lowered her hand and stayed where she was, reining in her tone. 'Could you tell me, if we remain on the train to its end, where do we finally arrive?'

For a long moment there came no answer. 'The *Arkangel* will take you to the border,' the Conductor finally intoned without turning to speak to her directly.

'Yes but which one, Bulgaria or Moldova?'

'The journey's end depends on you alone.'

'Well, that's not an awful lot of help, is it? We need tickets. We have none of your paper currency, but my family can be billed. We are well known in England.'

The Conductor turned to study her now. 'I think there may be another way for you to pay.'

'What do you mean?' asked Miranda.

* * *

BACK IN NICHOLAS and Isabella's compartment there was excitement. Isabella rose and pressed her hands to the glass. 'We're slowing down.'

'According to the map this must be Snerinska,' said Nicholas. 'If it's like the other towns, it will consist of eight churches, a dozen houses and a pig farm.'

The *Arkangel* was steaming into a low, grey-walled station with a rain-stained tin roof. Oil lamps swung in the misty night air, casting swaying pools of yellow light along the platform where passengers waited to board. The travellers had the dogged urgency of refugees; many had their belongings bundled in curtains and tablecloths. Nobody spoke to one another. The crowd was motionless and downcast, waiting for the train to reach a stop.

Nicholas and Isabella opened the window and braved the rush of cold night air, trying to see where they were. The train heaved to with a belch of steam. They were beneath mountains now, and the air was cooler, damper, sharpened with the scent of pine resin.

'Wait,' said Isabella, drawing back quickly. 'I know this place. I've seen it before.'

'But you haven't been on a train.'

'I have seen it in pictures,' she insisted, sitting back down with an air of defeat. 'Perhaps my mother…'

Nicholas and Thomas looked out of the window, checking the station name against the map.

'The signs are in monkey language,' said Thomas, snorting. 'If they can speak English, why can't they write their names in English?'

The huddle of travellers pushed forward to board the train. They were quite a crowd; some unfriendly-looking peasants in mud-spattered smocks, an old gypsy woman carrying a squealing pig, a blind priest led by a choirboy like a character from a Bruegel painting, some boisterous English soldiers, a skull-faced old man in a bathchair, an elderly man in tropical kit dragging a leather holdall and a butterfly net, a sombre hatchet-faced gentleman in funeral clothes.

At the rear was a man with a silk top hat and grey mutton-chop whiskers, fussing behind a porter who was trying to manoeuvre a tall box into place. On the side of the box a yellow painted flag read: 'Professor Io's Marvellous Nightingale.' Further along the platform were poor farmers with faces like shrivelled apples.

The Conductor had deserted his alcove to appear on the step of the caboose, and was turning some of them away, as if he sought only a certain type of passenger.

Isabella opened the carriage door and swung it wide. Her dainty foot hovered over the step.

'Snerinska,' called the Conductor. 'All aboard.'

The sole of Isabella's high-buttoned boot remained above the platform.

The pig squealed at her, frightening her back inside. The gypsy woman grabbed the door just before she could shut it and hissed at her in a gutteral dialect. Then she beetled along the platform to board in the third class carriage. Shocked, Isabella fell back in her seat. Nicholas had not noticed her hesitance about disembarking.

'What did that filthy old hag say to you?' Thomas demanded to know.

'I think… it was part of an old poem, something we learned in the nursery. What do you call it—an old wife's tale. We must not alight.'

'Why ever not?'

'The story.'

'What story?'

Isabella was resolute. 'Nothing. It is nothing. I do not believe in such things.'

'I say, look here.' Thomas shoved down the window and leaned out, pointing. The steam evaporated, revealing an astonishing sight. A tall, slender lady of upright bearing, dressed entirely in crimson chenille, her coat floor-length and laced with spiderweb silk, her face heavily veiled above red

ruffs and frills. Everything about her was a shade of scarlet, even the three pieces of luggage born by a black boy servant.

To Thomas, the lady's appearance in the mist was more than merely startling. As he watched her reach the carriage step he felt an unwholesome heat spread through his body. He was captivated. He tried to stop the boy bearing her valises, but the servant's angry glance warned him away. Instead he reached out to a toothless old woman who trailed adoringly in her wake.

'Can you tell me,' he asked, 'who is that?'

The shawled crone turned one good eye to him. 'That's the Red Countess, of course. Maria Theadora Grudczinska, originally of Austria, from the Hungarian line.'

'I have never heard—'

'There are tales about her that would burn your ears.' She bustled on, anxious not to be left behind.

As the Red Countess tilted her head and whispered something to the Conductor he touched her arm, helping her onto the step. He did the same to an storm-faced army Brigadier, the man dressed like a funeral director and the elderly fellow with the holdall. Many of the others were turned away.

The train seemed to sigh with impatience. There was an argument about tickets. One of the peasants attempted to fasten himself to the carriage window, but Thomas quickly drew it up and slammed the lock shut.

And this is a Christian minister, thought Nicholas, *how fast he is to close the foreigners out.* He had travelled the world and learned much of others' lives, and the only lesson he had learned from Christianity was how many slights were remembered and how little was ever forgiven.

Nicholas glanced down at the sweat-softened map in his hand and felt sure it could not be relied upon. Behind the station at Snerinska he had seen angular green hills cropped with brown mountain rock. The track arced around, heading into the night-shrouded landscape, and there was no way of knowing what they would find there.

'There seems to be some kind of delay.' Nicholas looked out at the passengers who had been denied entry to the train. They stood mutely waiting for the *Arkangel* to leave. He saw two men in black frock-coats pushing a long wooden crate into the guard's van. 'They are loading something on board that looks like a coffin.'

Isabella looked around in sudden anxiety. 'Where has Thomas gone?' she asked.

CHAPTER TEN
THE COUNTESS

THOMAS FOLLOWED THE Red Countess's approach and embarkation, transfixed. He could smell her perfume—cloves and almonds—and some kind of herb.

He stood outside the compartment and watched in fascination as she raised her arms, allowing her coat to be removed and folded. The boy servant carefully spread her dress, allowing his mistress to be seated upright against red velvet cushions. Something about his protection of her lower back suggested great age in her, but she did not stoop and was not slow. Her neck was long and slender, quite unlike a woman of age. Thomas was still unable to discover her features.

As her luggage was stowed in the compartment above her, the Red Countess fanned herself with the crimson-laced edge of her shawl, then settled into her seat. She was surrounded by luxurious fabrics—cotton, calico, cambric, cheviot, chiffon, chenille, crepe de chine, cretonne—and the air became pungent with burned spice. The boy had lit joss sticks in the cabin. As the Countess adjusted to her seat, a white oblong packet fell from her lap to the floor.

Thomas had been drawn close to the open door of her compartment. Without thinking, he stooped and picked up

the packet, which he realized was an oversized deck of cards. Embarrassed, he set it before her on the table.

The Red Countess turned her veiled head toward him and inclined it slightly in thanks. She raised a slender scarlet-gloved hand and flourished at the opposite seat. Unable to remove his gaze, Thomas did as he was bidden.

She deftly opened the pack without removing her gloves. Fanning out the cards, she turned them over to reveal faces filled with strange woodcut images and cabalistic symbols. Skeletons, peasants, radiant suns, cups and kings, beggars and monks.

'They're beautiful,' Thomas whispered.

'It helps to while away the hours. Do you play?' Her voice had the depth of maturity, but the edge of youth. There was something unsettling and decadent about it.

'No. I am a man of God.' He felt compelled to explain himself.

'And cards are the game of the Devil, are they not? They are also the consolation of the lonely.' The Red Countess languidly removed her scarlet kid-skin glove and dropped it on the table. For a moment her hand appeared as an old woman's claw, the liver-spotted skin transparently stretched across tendons. But it must have been a trick of the light, because when he looked again, he saw that the hand was as fresh and youthful as that of a sixteen year-old virgin.

Thomas was puzzled. He studied her young hand and trim figure. The perfumed smoke was making his head swim. 'Surely you cannot be lonely, Countess,' he said.

'I have a past. It allows a woman to know too much.'

'But experience is valuable.'

'The weight of your mistakes can break your spirit. Turn the card.' She drifted her hand across the table. He did as he was instructed. He had always enjoyed the company of strong women.

'You yearn for something,' she told him. 'Youth. Love. Pleasure. These things never stay. Only the cards remain.'

Thomas looked down. The card before him was the dark lady herself, the Queen of Spades, swathed in black, her face a cadaverous mask, surrounding by corpses dancing on a thunderstruck hill.

'It is the card of passion. Feel it. Do not be afraid.' Now her voice had the craquelure of limitless age.

Thomas reached out his hand, and the Red Countess shifted slightly in a whisper of silk, moving forward to touch his fingers.

'Once,' said the Red Countess, 'all men longed for my embrace, but now...'

Thomas's hand reached up for hers.

Miranda appeared in the doorway, out of breath, the buttons of her bodice virtually popping. She had searched the carriage, a feeling of panic rising in her chest. For a moment she had been seized by the absurd thought that Thomas had abandoned her and left the train.

The tableau before her might have been carved from tallow, the stiff-backed Countess reaching out to her husband, his hand meeting hers halfway across the card table.

'No,' she cried harshly, breaking the moment. Thomas turned to look at her just as the Red Countess reached out to him.

Miranda pulled him back. It was suddenly very important that her husband should not touch this woman. Thomas blinked, the spell shattered, for here was Miranda, all sense and planning, huffing inside her corset like a pigeon, urging him to rise.

The Red Countess folded away into herself, impassive. She had no time for men's wives.

'Thomas, I have a solution to our problem,' said Miranda excitedly, barely noticing the presence in the compartment. 'I need you to come with me.'

The Red Countess released him. Thomas gave a curt embarrassed bow and stepped out into the corridor with his wife, annoyed by the interruption. Together they hurried back through the stationary train.

'I think you were exceedingly rude just then,' said Thomas.

'And I think you would do well to stay away from that woman,' Miranda told him. 'Come along, we're to meet them in the guard's van. Smarten yourself. If you made more money, we wouldn't have to do this.'

Thomas did not understand his wife—he could rarely fathom her plans—but brushed at his coat sleeves and straightened his tie. 'I prefer to put my faith in God,' he told her.

Miranda was unimpressed. 'God cannot bring us home.'

As they passed along the dimly lit train corridor, the Conductor turned from his supervision at the door and watched them go. He could see Isabella and Nicholas leaning from the window, watching the embarkation of passengers, and permitted himself a narrow smile. He merely had to bide his time. Isabella stared angrily back at him. The Conductor caught her stare.

'Mrs Wellesley is to be the first,' said Isabella softly.

'What do you mean?' Nicholas asked, following her gaze.

'I meant to say—' She shook her head, confused.

'Tell me, Isabella. What do you know about this train? Why did you not wish to board?'

'I remember no more than... a legend.'

'What is the legend?'

'Oh, Nicholas, we are in mortal danger, and must leave the train. There are dangerous people aboard. People who would see us harmed.'

'What do you mean?'

She tried to brush the clouds from her brain. 'I don't know. I remember something from my childhood—a storybook perhaps, or a game, something that frightened me very badly— but the images disappear when I try to look directly at them. That woman, the one dressed in scarlet, I'm sure I have seen her before. I even remember her servant.'

'Perhaps she once came to your town.'

'No, I have only seen her likeness.'

'Then that is it. A magazine. You shall see many fine ladies in London, I promise.'

Isabella sat back and turned her head to the window. She tried to remember where she had seen the veiled Countess, but nothing further came, other than a creeping chill in her heart.

CHAPTER ELEVEN
THE MONARCH

THE MAN IN the brocade frock coat was waiting for them in the guard's van.

Mr Scheffen was a mortician. Parchment-skinned and beetle-browed, his sparse oily hair was plastered over a dome that seemed too far forward on his shoulders, making him appear stooped even when he was standing tall. He had been brought aboard to supervise the loading of a magnificent coffin, but was anxious to be off before the stationmaster's whistle sounded.

He looked from Reverend Thomas Wellesley to his wife in some amazement. In his striped blazer and cricket trousers, the vicar appeared to be dressed for a boating holiday somewhere in the Thames Valley. His wife sported a fine blue hat fixed with a feathered pin, and had massaged her plump frame into a tightly corseted green jacket. Why did the English abroad always dress as if they were asking to be shot at?

'My dear Madam,' said Scheffen. 'Good sir.' He wetly kissed Miranda's hand, then raised his red eyes to hers. 'Such fresh skin. A pity we all dry out in the end.'

Miranda snatched her hand away. 'The Conductor tells me you are willing to help us earn our passage,' she said, eager to arrange their business.

'The matter is rather delicate. If I may be frank?' Scheffen gave a mirthless smile. 'Among its many duties, the *Arkangel* train delivers the deceased of this region for the Necropolis Company. You may be familiar with us? We have offices in London, at Waterloo Station. We specialise in the shipping of those who have passed over.'

'I believe I have heard of such a thing,' Miranda admitted. 'I've heard it said that there are more dead in London than alive, and that it is little more than a giant grave.'

'Indeed so, Madam. But that is nothing to be feared. The word 'cemetery' comes from the Greek, *koimeterion,* meaning a dormitory or garden of sleep. We all sleep in the end. This coffin is to be returned to its family. I cannot stay with it.'

'Why not?'

'Dear Mrs Wellesley, my place is here, for the war is sure to increase our business tenfold. Beyond this, I am not at liberty to explain.'

'Miranda…' Thomas touched his wife at the waist, but she pulled away. If it was left to her husband they would remain stranded here at this filthy station until the troops arrived to torch it.

Scheffen continued. 'All I ask is that you accompany the coffin. Do not let it out of your sight. One hates to mention a subject so vulgar as money, but in addition to your passage, I can promise you will be most handsomely rewarded.' He stepped aside to reveal the ornate closed mahogany casket with its lid in upper and lower sections.

'A personage of quality and renown,' he replied to Miranda's unvoiced question. 'He was a victim of this terrible war.' He lowered his voice from respect. 'A member of the Carpathian royal family.'

'But where is his final resting place to be if not here?' Miranda asked.

'Miranda, do you really think—'

'A fair question, my good lady, and one which deserves to

be answered. The Prince has family far beyond the Carpathian mountains, in Romania, Latvia and Hungary, in Germany and even among your own great royal Hapsburg family in England.'

'What happened to him? Was it an assassin's bullet?'

'No—a certain delicacy.' His tone fell as he broke a confidence. 'Such gentlemen have different constitutions to you or I. Their blood is of a separate composition. Their veins lie near the surface of their skin. They always feel cold. They are— prone, yes that is the word—to exhaustions of the spirit. They carry dormant illnesses deep within themselves that rise up in times of anxiety. The war was too much for him. A nervous disorder of persistent vigour brought about his collapse. It was felt best that he be returned to those who would care for him in a family vault befitting of his regal status.'

'Miranda—'

'I am getting us home!' Miranda hissed at her husband, shaking free his hand.

Mr Scheffen ran his pale fingers along the polished fluting of the coffin lid. 'A top of the line model. Nothing but the best, by royal decree. Crafted for him on the day he was born. Silk lining hand-stitched by nuns. Blinded themselves finishing that, they did.'

'When I die, I should wish cremation,' said Thomas, 'it is the modern way.'

'Forgive me for saying so, sir, but you won't get a Christian send-off in a pot.'

'My husband is a claustrophobe. He has a morbid fear of confined spaces, Mr Scheffen,' Miranda explained.

'Death is the final remover of earthly fears.' He turned to Mrs Wellesley, who obviously took care of all financial affairs. He could see questions of money in her eyes. 'You'll be paid upon your safe arrival.' The train's whistle blew, ready for departure. 'So long as the casket remains sealed, nothing... untoward can happen.'

'Whatever do you mean?'

But Mr Scheffen had already donned his stovepipe hat once more, and flicked the black plume of its veil behind his bony neck. He hastened to the steps as the Conductor waited to pull them up. The wheels protested and the carriages began to roll.

'Remember. Stay beside the casket at all times. If one of you has to leave, please ensure that the other remains. Never leave it unguarded, even for an instant. My office will wire your recompense in full upon your final disembarkation.'

And with that Mr Scheffen drifted back to the platform and was gone. The remaining rabble of travellers flapped their tickets, anxious to be allowed on board, but were ignored. With a sigh of steam and a groan of steel, the *Arkangel* had hoisted itself once more and began to move out of the station, the unaccepted walking beside it, then running and reaching out to touch the walls, as if they held some talismanic power.

And then the train was gathering speed again, its boiler hot, its smokestack belching cinders, heading from the station into the velvet night.

CHAPTER TWELVE
THE GYPSY

Soon the *Arkangel* was once more racing through countryside as black as tar. No lights showed in the splintered hills. There was only the faintest difference in hue between the treeline and the ragged sky.

Isabella sat beside the window, her hands pressed nervously against her thighs. Every click of the tracks bore her further away from the life she had known.

Nicholas looked at her and marvelled. The way a stray blonde curl fell forward across her right eye, the curve of her slender neck, even the smear of mud on her ankle seemed right. He would make a fine woman of her in London. There were jewels and dresses she could wear, left in his Mayfair rooms by that chorus girl from the Gaiety. 'Please,' he begged her, 'don't be afraid. I know this must all seem so strange, being torn from your home, your family and friends, but it was for your own good. One day, when this terrible war has ended, we'll be able to go back and visit.'

'I can never go back,' said Isabella sadly. 'My father would kill me. Josef would not take me now. In our town, feuds run in the blood and last for centuries. Josef's family will demand retribution. Everything there is ruined for me.'

'Then thank God I am leading you to a more civilized nation.

We will find everything you need, food and clothing and the necessary papers—I have money—and we will board a ship across the channel to Dover, thence to London. You shall have dancing and joy, and no time for regret. There is nothing you need fear. I will protect you.'

'There are things even you cannot protect me from,' said Isabella darkly.

'Such serious words from such a young lady.' He reached across and stroked her chin. 'Let me put a smile back on that delightful face.'

'I don't even know who you are.'

'Then allow me to elucidate. I am an adventurer. I am two years shy of thirty, and have been from Siam to South America.'

'A sailor, then?'

'For a while, yes, in a way. I tired of my father's beatings and ran off to Portsmouth, to board the first steam packet that would have me. I returned to find my uncle had died, and I was to inherit his fortune.'

'How did he die?'

'In the most mundane way possible, mown down by a Hackney Carriage on the Strand. When the war began I decided to play my part and took the King's shilling, enlisting as a soldier, but destroying the lives of others proved not to my liking.'

'What brought you to Carpathia?'

'That is another long and dull story which I am sure to bore you with one wintry night in London, when we have little else to do but sit in front of the fire and yarn,' he laughed. It was probably best to avoid the absolute truth about his past: the whoring, the fighting, the escapes and escapades. The pregnant girl in Nice he had abandoned all those years ago. That night in Constantinople with the belly-dancing twins, the robbery of the brothel and the flight in women's clothes. He was ashamed of his past, but not enough to publicly recant it.

He saw her thaw a little, and the faintest smile began to play on her lips, but at that moment something slammed against the

corridor window. Isabella started as a blemished, hairy face leered at them through the partly open glass.

The old woman wore her wealth about her. Gold teeth flashed, gold earrings shook, the necklaces of dead relatives hung about her sagging breasts. Fixing Isabella with a fierce green eye, she muttered something in old Carpathian, then raised the index finger of her left hand and ran it briskly along her right, before spitting hard at Isabella's feet.

'Get out of here, you filthy old crone!' Nicholas rose and slammed the window shut. The old woman continued to shake her head and stare, but finally shuffled off along the corridor. 'She must have come in from the Third Class carriage,' he said. 'Are you all right?'

Isabella was shaking. 'The gypsy woman was warning me.'

'You could understand her? What did she say?'

'She was reciting what she had begun on the platform. It was part of an old poem, just a line or two repeated, something we used to say as children.'

'Can you remember what it was?'

'I can recall the verse as if I had heard it yesterday:

What you see and what you hear
Upon the train may not be real.
Except to you, who on this night
Will face the test that must decide
Your fate, your life, your very soul,
Before you reach your journey's end.'

Nicholas hated poetry, which seemed to be no more than arranged words. 'That's all very well, but what does it mean?'

'A foolish playground curse, nothing more.'

'And yet you remembered it.'

'That's because our town was built on—' She suddenly stopped herself.

'What?'

She looked back up at him, seeming to see him for the first time. 'Superstition. It was built on superstition, Nicholas, nothing more. Take me to London.'

'You're lying to me. Holding something back.'

'No, there's nothing. In truth, I do not fully remember. But there is something in my childhood, just out of reach—' She forced a smile that only made things worse. 'I am not lying. If I do anything untoward, it is only to protect you. There are things here that it is better for you not to understand. There are—secrets. We are waiting for a sign that it has all begun.'

'What on earth do you mean?'

'I think—there must be an act of self-harm, the taking of a life.'

'I do not understand what you are saying.'

'Somewhere on this train there is another like us. He is in grave danger.'

'Another like us? Please, Isabella, I am trying to understand—'

'I feel so tired suddenly. My head is swimming. As if I may not survive removal from my home.'

'That is because you have never left before tonight.'

'No, there is something more. The train.'

'It is our fortune and your escape.'

'But Nicholas, it is more than a train. It is a compendium of terrors that could unfold into infinity. We are running into terrible danger.'

'Please, tell me what the gypsy woman meant.'

'I cannot, for fear that I will make it true.'

'But these are superstitions, don't you see? Nothing more.' He rose and sat beside her. 'I will let no harm befall you, Isabella. I have not been true to women in the past, I have to admit, but a man can make changes in his life, just as you have made a change in yours. Now banish your fears and try to sleep for a while. I'll find refreshment for us at the next station. In a few hours you'll awaken in a new land, where it seems the very streets are built for your delight.'

'You are so kind to me, Nicholas.'

'You see, there is nothing to be afraid of.'

But as she set her head back on the antimacassar and fell into an uneasy slumber, lulled by the swaying of the train, he wondered what it was that had frightened her so much.

CHAPTER THIRTEEN
THE CHAUFFEUR

In their First Class compartment, Nicholas and Isabella dozed.

In the guard's van, Thomas and Miranda commenced their vigil.

In his alcove, the Conductor set about his paperwork.

And in one of the second class carriages, a salesman who had boarded the train at Snerinska fidgeted nervously. He did not know it yet, but he was about to become a catalyst in the fates of those who had joined the train at Chelmsk.

Franz Urban had only been a salesman for three months, and hated the job. He had no proficiency in selling fishing rods and grousing rifles to the Eastern Europeans, firstly because he worked only to make a wage, and second, because right now the Eastern Europeans had more serious things on their mind than recreational sports.

Digging into his jacket, he found the vial of blue pills prescribed to him in Vienna and took two more, knowing that they would dull the pain in his calipered leg, but they would not be able to lift the terrible feeling of guilt that burdened him. Franz Urban knew there were doctors to whom he could talk about his state of mind, but they charged too much for sessions, and his own doctor was a kill-or-cure man who had no time

for those of a delicate disposition. Indeed, he had heard it said that soldiers were returning from the battlefields with terrors in their heads that made them scream at night, but doctors merely thought them cowards.

With Hannah, his wife, gone, there was no-one to whom he could turn. Franz had taken the position of travelling salesman to earn enough money to escape, only to find that his nightmares were following him wherever he went.

He had certainly not intended to board the *Arkangel*, but it seemed to appear at the moment when his spirits were at their lowest ebb, as if it could somehow read his mind and bear him away. He did not care where he was going, only that he would be free from the dark thoughts that pursued him. For he, Franz Urban, was a murderer. No—something much, much worse.

He looked around the compartment. The man opposite was asleep, and drooling a little. There was something very odd about the train. Franz had never seen anything like it before. He had boarded it at a small branch-line station where only clapped-out local two-car trains usually stopped, and it had not been listed on the platform timetable. It had appeared from the mist like an avenging demon. Then there were the carriages, glorious baroque brass and mahogany interiors from a bygone age. Yet they were populated by the rudest of peasants, farmers with reeking pigs, drunk old women, rowdy soldiers—who were these people, and where were they going? There was no final destination marked on the *Arkangel*'s route. It was all most perplexing.

The war had upended the world. The old order, it seemed, was swiftly dissipating. Behaviour that was unthinkable just two years ago was now commonplace across Europe. Worst of all was the level of hatred engendered in otherwise normal mild-mannered citizens. Friends and neighbours hurled abuse at one another, fights broke out with the spontaneity of brush fires, the streets themselves were unsafe to walk at night— no, in broad daylight even. The new Europe was no place for children to be born into now.

The pills did nothing to assuage his growing anxiety. Hollow-eyed and grey, he fidgeted and finally burst into movement, rising from his seat and hobbling from the carriage, pursued by his fears. Outside, in a cluttered recess off the corridor, he found the Conductor preparing travel documents.

Without looking up, the Conductor pulled down a little circular wooden seat from the wall and bade Franz to settle himself, almost as though he had been waiting for him.

'You must talk to me,' he said, turning the glare of his attention to the salesman.

'I don't understand. I boarded the train...'

'Not knowing where you were headed,' said the Conductor. 'I am aware of this. I have been waiting for you. There is something you wish to tell me.'

Franz was amazed. It was as if the Conductor could see inside him. Or was it simply that he recognised the look of a passenger with no final destination in mind?

The Conductor raised his great dark head and listened to the clacking of the tracks. 'You hear that sound?' he asked. 'With each passing second you are further removed from the source of your terrors. And yet—'

'I carry my terrors within me,' completed Franz. 'They are all around me, travelling on board this train.'

The Conductor lifted a cigarette from his tiny desk and lit it. 'And it is all because of your awful secret, the secret no-one else in the world knows.'

'How did you know?'

'You came to me in order to unburden yourself. Many passengers on this train do so. I can help, although perhaps not in a way that you would wish. What is the nature of this secret?'

It was strange, but Franz felt that he needed to inform this cadaverous stranger about his life. 'You might think me mad if I tell you.'

'I might think you more mad if you don't.'

'I destroyed the world with a single glance,' he said simply.

'That is intriguing.'

'I assure you I am not suffering from any derangement except heartbreak.'

'I do not judge. You must share your burden,' instructed the Conductor. 'I am nothing to you, but you are my passenger and my responsibility. There is a way through your dilemma. Share your burden with me and I promise you that it will transform the journey of the *Arkangel*. Each journey the train takes must begin like this.'

'What must I do?' asked Franz.

'You must tell me of the circumstances that brought you to this train.'

'I have not dared to tell anyone in over two years.'

'And the weight of it is destroying you. You speak and I listen. At the end, you will decide what must be done.'

The Conductor talked in riddles, and yet it seemed to make a kind of sense. Lulled by the swaying walls that surrounded him, Franz Urban began to speak.

'I was not always a salesman. I was born in 1885, and grew up poor in the outskirts of Dusseldorf, but I had no desire to become a farmer, and escaped my violent father at the first opportunity. One day, at an international trade fair, I saw something that changed my life, a Benz Motorwagon of gleaming lacquered metal, and at that moment I knew the world was about to be transformed. I could see that there would be no more need for horses and carts. The piston engine, transplanted into a personal carriage, could become a mode of transport for all the world to use. In America, I heard, the Oldsmobile factory was beginning mass production of such vehicles, so that people of all classes could afford to ride them.

'Of course, I could not afford such an engine or even have access to such a marvel, so I became apprenticed to an automobile engineering firm. Soon I became a driver for the new automobile, a profession few had been able to master. I quickly saw in it a way to make money. I drove the first

Daimler-Mercedes. I was one of the few men in Austria who had mastered this skill, and my services were greatly in demand. I was asked to go to America and train further there. But—'

'—there was a woman,' completed the Conductor.

'Yes, sir. There was a woman named Hannah, with whom I had fallen in love. And, I felt sure, my love was to be reciprocated.'

'To be reciprocated?' The Conductor looked puzzled. 'It was not initially?'

'No. We were separated by our stations in life. Hannah was a Lady-In-Waiting to the Duchess of Hohenberg. High-born and highly strung. She had no interest in a man such as I. And yet, with each meeting, her attention grew stronger.'

'How did she come to meet you?'

'I was delivering cars to the palace. The royal interest in the new automobile was strong. At this time I had the great good fortune to become a chauffeur in the service of Count Harrach, a nobleman of the Austro-Hungarian Empire who was also a close friend to the heir of its throne. A most important personage whom I was to have the privilege of serving.'

'Not bad for a boy who had been expected to become a farmer,' said the Conductor, tapping his ash. 'Did this levelling of the classes endear you more to Hannah?'

'I like to believe that she warmed to me for who I was, and not because of my new position in life,' said Franz coolly. 'Over the next few months, we saw more of each other, and I was invited to walk with her—chaperoned, of course—on several occasions.'

'And you proposed.'

'At the first available opportunity. It was difficult to get Hannah to myself, to find the privacy for such a conversation. As you can imagine, she was usually surrounded by members of the household staff. But one afternoon in the gardens, I was able to separate her from the others and spoke of my intentions.'

'She accepted, I take it.'

'She asked for a period in which to consider my proposal. For the next few nights I was unable to sleep—'

'This is all very romantic,' said the Conductor, impatiently waving smoke from his face. 'Let us assume she accepted and you were married.'

'Indeed, sir, that was the situation. I was wed with the blessing of her family—although some members stayed away from the nuptials, feeling that my parents were below hers in station. We began living as man and wife, and all was well for a while.'

'But something happened.'

'Something happened.' Franz gave a bitter laugh. 'I fear to tell it, for you really will think I am quite insane.'

'I am used to insanity on this train,' said the Conductor, examining the end of his cigarette. He checked his watch. 'I must hurry you. I have to begin my duties, and you must reach the end of your story.'

'Then I shall tell you of my dreadful shame,' said Franz. 'Tell me, do you believe in fate?'

'Most certainly,' said the Conductor. 'Our paths through life are set as rigidly as railway tracks, but we alone have control of the points over which our lives will run.'

'I did not believe in fate before these events, but I do so now. And if, as you say, we control the points of our lives, then the fateful day came when I changed not just my fate, but the fate of the entire world.'

CHAPTER FOURTEEN
THE GLANCE

FRANZ SAT BACK as he remembered, his head lolling with the clatter of the tracks. 'My hours were long,' he said, 'and I was sometimes required to drive great distances for the Count, which took me away from Hannah. Often my trips were for the most trivial of reasons—the collection of a vase, the delivery of a letter, but the job was well paid and I became an expert Mercedes driver. Meanwhile, life in the royal Bohemian household required Hannah to be at the beck and call of her mistress at any time of the day or night, although as the now married Countess Sophie Chotek had herself been a Lady-In-Waiting, she proved a kind and understanding employer.

'Still, in the first few months of 1914 Hannah and I seemed to spend less time than ever in each other's company, a situation that made us both fractious and argumentative. I realise it now, I had been spoiled by my new position. I had been ushered into a world that no-one in my family had ever seen, and still I could not be entirely happy. I see now that the downfall of men hinges on tiny things—in my case a stray glance, a new shoe, a perfume bottle, a pair of scissors. These things were enough to bring about the disaster for which I must now hold myself accountable.'

'You look a little pale,' said the Conductor. 'I think that

perhaps for the next part of your tale we should get you some fresh air.' He rose to his full height and helped the little man to his feet. 'Follow me.'

The Conductor led Franz through the train, passing Nicholas and Isabella, asleep in their compartment. He made his way to the observation deck, where the final portion of the carriage had been cut away to allow air in.

'Breathe deep from the darkness of the forest,' the Conductor instructed. 'I find the effect most beneficial.'

Franz drew a deep breath and smelled, pine, earth, rotting vegetation and something more disturbing, the bitter tang of cordite and tobacco that revealed the presence of troops. He stood against the rushing darkness, recalling the events that had led him here.

'It began with a girl of some seventeen summers,' said Franz.

'There is always a girl,' sighed the Conductor.

'This one was radiantly beautiful, the niece of the Count, and when Elizabeth walked into court it was as if the sun had emerged from clouds. Everyone admired her. Since my wife's employer and the great friend of my own employer had married, I now saw Hannah in the imperial household, although we were rarely able to speak.

'It happened one morning that she emerged into the courtyard as I was bringing out the car, and I saw the young Princess Elizabeth heading our way. When members of the monarchy appear, all employees are required to make themselves scarce, and after a while you become used to halting whatever you are doing and dropping into the nearest doorway. The royals like to move through a world of stillness, uninterrupted by the chaos of life. Hannah saw that the Princess was coming and swiftly found an arch support, stepping behind it, but there was nowhere for me to go.

'In this situation, we are required to simply become statues. I froze and waited for her to pass. But she stopped and smiled at me. What could I do but look back?

'Hannah was a jealous woman, and hated the fact that there had been other girls before her. That night, she accused me of flirting with Elizabeth. I told her not to be so absurd, but she would not be consoled, and cried her way to bed. I see now, looking back, that this irrational behaviour was a symptom of some mental derangement.

'The next morning I discovered that Leopold, the Archduke's chauffeur, had not appeared for work. Nobody knew where he was, so I was asked to take his place. It was well-known that the Archduke liked and respected his chauffeur, so I was asked to do this without informing anyone of the change in personnel, for fear that people should think the Archduke capricious in his favourites. I was to accompany the Archduke to Sarajevo, where he would inspect the imperial garrison. I was to drive a beautiful automobile, a black 1911 Graf & Stift 'Bois De Bologne' Tourer.

'The night before I left, I bought a bottle of perfume for Hannah, Atar Of Roses, her favourite. I meant it as a reconciliation gift, but I found her in a worsened state. She had somehow convinced herself that I was about to leave her for a member of the royal family. I tried to explain the outright absurdity of this idea, but she only grew angrier. I had left the perfume on her dresser while I tried on the chauffeur uniform that had been arranged for me. There was a problem with the shoes—the soles were of new leather, and extremely slippery.

'Hannah opened my gift and, with a scream, smashed the perfume bottle on the floor. I ran in and saw the mess; broken glass everywhere, the overpowering scent of roses, and my beloved wife rending her nightdress and slapping herself between sobs of anger. Fearful that she might cause further injury to herself if she tried to clear up the glass, I began to pick up the pieces. In doing so, the rose oil covered my right shoe. I removed the shoe and left it to air in the corridor, then retired to bed.

'Hannah refused to sleep in the same room, and removed herself to another bedchamber. At 6:00am the next morning I

looked in on her, but she had already dressed and left. I was upset and wished I had been able to say goodbye to her. I did not know that morning that we would never see each other again.

'I admit, as our retinue set off on the state visit, I had guilty thoughts of Elizabeth's glance. Is it man's vanity alone that encourages him to think he may attract the eye of a beautiful girl, even if she is far above his station in life? Stranger things had happened. The Archduke himself had fallen in love with a woman who was said to be far removed from his social class.'

'Time is running short,' said the Conductor curtly. 'You must finish your story and then reach your decision.'

'Why is it so important that you should hear me out?' asked Franz, puzzled by the Conductor's attitude.

'I am not obliged to tell you, sir,' he replied. 'Suffice it to say that the outcome is of the gravest interest to me, as you may come to understand. Pray continue, but do so quickly.'

'Very well,' said Franz, turning back to face the darkness, the wind whipping his hair. 'Now we come to the fateful moment that tore my very soul apart.'

CHAPTER FIFTEEN
THE SACRIFICE

FRANZ LOOKED LIKE a man hunted by his past. He had trouble continuing until the Conductor laid a placatory hand on his shoulder. 'Please,' said the Conductor, 'you must reveal the nature of your burden to me.'

'Very well—where was I?'

'The Archduke's state visit.'

'That's right. The Archduke met me from the train in his blue-grey tunic with the red piping and gold buttons, his moustaches freshly waxed. I held the door open for him and he entered the vehicle in great style. Although there were many who opposed him in the city, there were an equal number of ardent admirers. But I had little knowledge of the city and its factions. I had no idea it was a powder-keg waiting to be ignited.

'While we were waiting to set off I heard him say, "There is an extraordinary scent of roses in here. Are we near a garden?" I looked down and guiltily noted that my right shoe was still covered in rose oil.

'The Archduke had been warned not to travel to Sarajevo. I understand little of politics—to me, the mechanics of an automobile could teach me more about the world than the rifts and alliances of the Balkan states. But I knew Bosnia-Herzegovina

had been declared a part of the Austro-Hungarian Empire by the Emperor, and that it had caused unrest among the Slavic people and the Russian Tsar who opposed it. What I did not know was that assassins lay in wait for us upon our route that day.

'There were six automobiles in our procession, and there were six assassins spread out along the Appel Quay that ran beside the river. These assassins belonged to an organisation called the Black Hand, and each was under instructions to attack us when they saw us approach. Following a request from the Archduke, I rolled back the roof of the car so that the crowds could get a better look at him and his wife, Countess Sophie.

'At around 10:00am the first of the protestors struck, although we did not find this out until later, because it transpired that this man had turned coward and failed to throw his bomb at the procession. Supposedly, there had been a suspicious policeman standing close by, who had unnerved him.

'Fifteen minutes after this, the second assassin hurled a grenade at our motorcade. I saw the small grey object flying toward the windscreen of the car and accelerated, watching as the bomb flew over our heads. It bounced upon the rear of our vehicle and disappeared under the car behind, the third in the procession. The grenade had a ten second fuse, and exploded under the wheels of the automobile, seriously wounding its occupants and peppering a number of bystanders with shrapnel.

'We were travelling at a fairly high speed, and the route was thronged with a heavy number of spectators who, we were to discover, slowed down the progress of the conspirators. The bomb-thrower tried to take his own life by swallowing a cyanide capsule, but the chemical was out of date and merely caused him to vomit. He jumped into the river Miljacka, beside which we were travelling, but the water was a mere four inches deep, and so the police were able to pull him out and arrest him.

'The Archduke decided that we should head for the hospital to visit the victims of the bombing. General Potiorek, who was

traveling with us, said that we would need to avoid the city centre to do so. I understood later that he had a plan that we should continue along the quay all the way to the hospital. Unfortunately, he did not inform me of this idea, and I turned right into Franz Josef Street.

'There was a run-down café there, where a small, sickly lad of nineteen who had been turned down for membership of the Black Hand sat, disappointed and embittered. He thought that the death of the Archduke would magically release the shackles that bound his people to the empire. He had missed his chance to attack our convoy, and had given up when he saw our automobile turn into the street.

'The second I realised that we had made a wrong turn, I put my foot on the brake and began to back up. I admit I was disturbed that there might be another attack, and in my rush I stalled the car's engine, locking the gears. From the corner of my eye I saw the sickly fellow rise to his feet and raise his arm toward us. He was holding a pistol, and used it now to knock a fellow bystander out of his way. I saw all this as if time itself had suddenly slowed down.

'I attempted to reverse more quickly, but the rose oil on my shoe had made the leather sole more slippery, and my foot slid off the accelerator. In that brief moment while the automobile was stilled, the lad took aim and fired twice. His bullets found their mark; both the Archduke and his wife were shot. Franz Ferdinand's neck was pierced and gushed blood. Count Harrach's face was splashed with it. The Count put a white handkerchief on the Archduke's jugular vein to stem the flow of blood. I heard his wife call out, 'For Heaven's sake, what happened to you?' but she had been shot in the stomach, and fell from her seat. We thought she must have fainted, but the Archduke knew what had happened and begged her not to die for the sake of her children. His ceremonial hat slid from his head—I remember there were shiny sapphire feathers all over the car floor.

'I pulled to the side of the road and we tried to remove Franz Ferdinand's tight blue tunic, but we could not find a pair of scissors with which to cut it open. He died before we could get to the wound. The crowd rushed forward, and in the process my leg was crushed.

'When I returned home, I discovered that my beloved Hannah was dead. She had walked into an ornamental lake and lain down in it, breathing the water down into her lungs to take her own life. No-one could tell me if she had heard about the Archduke's assassination before she died, or if her wits had simply wandered after fearing that I would stray.

'The Archduke's chauffeur, Leopold, had miraculously reappeared—there seemed to be some mystery in his absence to which I was not privy—and I was asked to stand down. Later, I understood that all despatches would suggest he was with the Archduke when he died, and I, a lowly mechanic, was erased from history. You see now, sir, the burden I carry.'

'I think I understand perfectly.'

'I am responsible for nothing less than the deaths of thousands—millions for all I know—for just two months after Franz Ferdinand's death, Austria-Hungary declared war against Serbia, and this great conflict in which we now find ourselves began, and it seems it may never stop until all the world is dead.'

'You could argue that the Archduke's assassination was not the only starting pistol for the war in which we are now engulfed.' said the Conductor. 'I believe there were other causes for the commencement of the conflict: nationalism, imperialism, militarism.'

'No, sir, I will not be absolved so easily. The fact remains that if the Archduke Franz Ferdinand had not been struck down, we would not have declared war on Serbia when we did, and thereby set into motion a chain of disastrous alliances that spilt Europe in twain. And his death could have been avoided.'

'I sympathise with your fatal role,' said the Conductor, unlatching the door of the observation car and slowly sliding

it open. 'You saw the day's events reversing themselves, your foot not slipping from the accelerator, the perfume bottle not spreading oil across the sole of your shoe, the glance from the Princess not incensing your wife. A single look was all it took, and now the world has been shifted on its axis. It has taken the road to Hell and damnation.'

'You read my mind,' said Franz, looking down at the racing tracks. 'I have suffered with this pain for two long years. With each passing day the death toll rises, and I think to myself that it could all have so easily been avoided.'

'But that is what fate always makes you think,' said the Conductor. 'That is the role of destiny.'

'Be that as it may, I now find that this is not a burden with which I wish to live any longer.'

'The world does not know that you are responsible for its greatest tragedy,' the Conductor admitted. 'Unless you plan to tell them?'

Franz felt inside his jacket and removed an envelope. 'Again, you read my mind. I have taken the time to write down my true version of the events. Can you make sure that it reaches the right authorities?'

'You know there is a way for you to be absolved.' The Conductor urged him on. 'You cannot change what will be now—you have unwittingly helped me in my own cause by speaking of this—but you can bring your own misery to an end.'

'Yes,' Franz agreed, looking down. 'I belong with the innocent dead.'

'They will take comfort in the knowledge that you have joined them. All you have to do is take one simple step. All this pain can be over in a moment.'

Franz shifted his weight and extended his crushed foot above the abyss. The train was hammering over a raised section of the track. Far below, the black woods fell away to a rock-strew ravine beset by hungry wolves.

Franz turned to look into the Conductor's coal-dark eyes. 'We

humans are weak,' he said sadly. 'One glance from a woman is all it takes to destroy the world of men.' And with that he let go of the hand-rail, falling out of the train. His body tumbled over and over, and was rushed away into the ravine.

The Conductor locked the observation car gate and turned away, smiling faintly to himself. 'An act of self-destruction, Franz,' he whispered with relish. 'A sacrificial suicide is all it takes to oil the wheels of fate once more. Now that your offering has been made, we can test the mettle of our new passengers. How I always love the start of the journey.'

He set off along the carriage, content in the knowledge that the game had been set in motion. 'So,' he said to himself, 'it begins.' Looking toward the guard's van, he sensed that something terrifying had just been woken, and his smile widened.

CHAPTER SIXTEEN
THE SCRATCHING

THOMAS AND MIRANDA sat beside each other. The Conductor had set out two wooden chairs, one on either side of the trestled coffin.

'Well, this is a fine way to travel, I must say,' Thomas complained. 'Separated from the other passengers, in the company of the dead.'

'If you had made better plans, we would not have been reduced to this,' said Miranda. She sighed. 'My mother had high hopes for me. She saw me in the millinery business, running my own company in Regent Street with a staff of young ladies at my command, outfitting the children of the high-born; not married to a country vicar, serving teas, surrounded by colicky babies. Thank God she cannot see me now.'

'Yes, I know all about your mother's plans,' Thomas murmured. 'They were the death of your father. The women in your family have always been strong-willed.'

'Only because the men were weak. My mother is an Emancipationist, but freedom requires capital.' Miranda reached out her hand and pressed it against the cool mahogany of the coffin. 'Royalty, Mr Scheffen said. That's why we must accompany him.'

Thomas recognized the gleam in his wife's eye and feared it. 'What do you mean?'

'He died tragically young. He is to be buried in his family regalia.' She looked back at the coffin with dark shining eyes. 'With his gold medals, his sceptre and sword, a hilt studded with precious jewels. They must be guarded from thieves and brigands. We are in bandit country. It is a task that carries responsibility. This is why we were selected. We are English, after all, and therefore entirely trustworthy.'

The van swayed and Miranda's head, filled with dreams of pomp and ceremony, began to droop. Thomas was left alone to watch the coffin. The train was slowing down. He rose and peered from the only window, little more than a narrow slit. There was a large sliding door, but it was bolted shut—somewhat insecurely, it seemed to Thomas.

A dense billowing fog was sinking down from the surrounding palisade of pine trees to envelop the train. The wheels turned ever more slowly, the pistons sighing like bellows.

The *Arkangel* crept cautiously through the fog. Thomas cupped his hands against the glass, trying to see, but visibility had dropped to almost nothing.

'As silent as death,' he whispered. 'Can't find a thing out there.'

Miranda's chin was touching the green-beaded bodice of her dress-coat. He returned to his seat beside the coffin. The train had fallen silent, but for the creaking of the carriages.

He listened intently, and heard a faint sound. A scratching, like a squirrel scrabbling for a nut, or a rat dying in a wall. He rose once more and tried to trace the sound. There were very few items in the guard's van that might hide a rodent.

There it was again.

It seemed to be coming from inside the coffin. But that wasn't possible. Thomas put his ear to the casket.

Skritch—skritch.

Startled, he jumped back.

'Miranda!' He touched her shoulder and she raised her sleep-filled eyes to him.

'What's the matter?'

'Can you hear something?'

She listened for a moment. 'No, not a thing.'

Thomas hushed her and raised a finger. 'There it is again! Listen…'

She humoured him by listening, but heard nothing. Turning, she saw the murk outside forming dew against the glass. 'It's the fog. It muffles everything.'

'No, inside. You can't hear that?'

She shook her head, genuinely perplexed. 'No.'

Thomas's raised finger tilted down and slowly came to a stop above the casket lid. 'You must be able to.' Back in Henley-Upon-Thames he had occasion to help himself to a nip of whisky, and she usually heard the top coming off the bottle from the floor above. 'It's coming from in there.'

'Don't be absurd. There is a corpse inside.'

'What if he's not dead?'

'What are you talking about?'

'Inside—I could hear him while you were asleep, scratching at the lid. What if he's still alive?'

Miranda stared at her husband as if he had lost what little of his wits was left to him. 'Don't be so absurd.'

'Listen, can you really hear nothing?'

'No. You must try to set aside such fantasies.'

But Thomas watched the coffin in horror, listening for sounds from within. He imagined the casket's silken interior being torn to shreds by broken fingers. Hands clawing away at the lid with cracked and bleeding nails.

Skritch-skritch.

'There it is again!' The sound was clearer this time. A definite double scratch, as if it were caused by fingernails snagging and dragging down the silken lining of the casket. Could Miranda really hear nothing at all?

Thomas stared at the coffin, then reached forward and ran his hands around its lid. The seal was tight, but he could not discover how the top had been locked.

'I wonder what is in the paperwork Mr Scheffen gave you?' he asked.

Miranda looked inside the folder the undertaker had left them. She took out a heavy vellum envelope and broke the seal, tearing it open, tipping out its contents.

'Miranda!' he cried, horrified. 'I meant that there might be some kind of medical note. That is private and not for our eyes!'

'We'll say it was damaged in transit.' She scanned the pages. 'It contains details for a state funeral. Invitations to be edged with black silk. Incense burners and sobbing mourners. Laid to rest amid an angelic choir. The pecking order of the pallbearers. Contents of the casket. Gold chains and the royal Carpathian seal, inlaid with rubies and emeralds.' She rubbed her forehead, overpowered by the images in her head. 'I need to think.'

Thomas continued to stare at the casket. The noise of scratching filled his head. He imagined the inside of the coffin, an emaciated monarch gasping for air.

He clamped his hands over his ears. 'Perhaps it is merely… a rat. That's it, a rat. Or insects.'

As Thomas looked back at Miranda, the scratching suddenly stopped. Had it merely been his overworked imagination? The stress of the war, the disaster of the touring holiday, their escape? Thomas continued to stare at his wife. 'You really cannot hear anything?'

'No, Thomas, only the breathing of the train.'

'Then I alone must suffer this sound.'

Miranda attempted sympathy. 'Perhaps your mind is a little overexercised. Hardly surprising under the circumstances, having to earn our passage home like common travellers.'

But the scratching started up again.

Skritch-skritch.

Thomas watched his wife intently. It was clear she heard nothing at all unusual. He examined the coffin more carefully this time. Under the edge of the lid, a red wax seal ran unbroken.

He looked down at the contents of Mr Scheffen's envelope and sorted through it, finding a second item his wife had missed. Splitting the seal of the tiny rectangular envelope, he tugging the card free and read through it.

'What if he wasn't dead, Miranda?'

'What are you talking about?'

Thomas held up the note accompanying the body and displayed it to her.

'The death certificate.'

'You censured me for looking at the funeral seating plans, but now you examine his private medical records.'

'It says the carrier suffered epileptic fits. Epilepsy! I've heard it can appear as a death-like trance. What if he's still alive?'

'He would have been pronounced deceased by doctors. The casket is tightly sealed.'

'But they are the ones who sealed it.'

'You heard our benefactor. The man inside this casket was declared dead, and the dead do not come back to life!'

Skritch-skritch-skritch-skritch. Louder than ever before.

Thomas was a man possessed. He tried to tear open the lid of the coffin with his fingers, but could not manage it. Then he rose and began searching for something to open it with.

'You are imposing your own fears on this, Thomas,' his wife warned. 'You are afraid that someone else might suffer the fate you dread! Can you not see that?'

'Help me find something that can prise off the lid.'

'What if he died of the plague? A terrible contagion? Perhaps the death certificate lies. Perhaps that is why the coffin had to be accompanied.'

'The mortician knew about his epilepsy. He wanted to cover up the truth. Imagine; a crown prince dissents in time of war, and has to go. A conspiracy. This man died trying to get out. I know, because he is still clawing at the lid.'

Miranda looked at her husband in horror. 'Thomas, this has gone quite far enough. We must do as we are told or we won't be

paid. You'll take some hot tea and pull yourself together. I will find us some.' And she rose to her feet, leaving the guard's van.

Thomas sat miserably alone with the prince's coffin. All was quiet. He tapped the side of his head experimentally, trying to find out what was wrong. Too many years spent in hushed cloisters, too much time passed in guilty denials, a marriage in haste that he now had leisure to regret—were these finally leaving the marks of madness upon him, as they had his poor father? *Is it me,* he asked himself, *or whatever's inside that great mahogany thing?*

And suddenly the terrible noise returned, the loudest yet. As if hypnotised, Thomas approached the coffin.

He saw that it had two slender locks built into the wood, one for each part of the lid, which was divided in two at chest height. He sought the envelope again and turned it out, but found no keys. How were those on the far side of the Channel meant to pay their final respects to their relative if they had not been provided with access? Slowly he bent down and peered through one of the keyholes.

A single red eye, as bloody as a sunset, suddenly appeared on the other side, staring furiously back at him.

Thomas leapt away in shock just as Miranda reappeared with a small tin urn of tea. Had he just imagined what he'd seen?

His wife had a look of steely slyness on her face that he saw whenever she was planning a stratagem. 'I have been thinking,' she said, seating herself beside him. 'A member of the Carpathian royal family. You're right. The royals are not like us. We should check inside, just to be sure. Try and find something to open it with.'

That's the answer, let her see for herself, and then we shall know if I am mad, he thought. They looked for something they could use to open the coffin. Thomas dug into his valise and produced a tiny pocket-knife, with which he tried to pick the lock.

'Get out of my way, Thomas.' Miranda had found a stoker's coal shovel almost as big as herself. She raised the shovel and

wedged the blade into the edge of the coffin lid, pushing with all her might. There was a hiss of air as the wax seal started to crack apart.

'We'll say this was damaged in transit as well, when the train braked suddenly,' she told him, giving the spade another whack. 'Say the casket was insecurely tethered.' With the third blow, the top half of the lid splintered and broke open. 'Come on then, don't just stand there like a useless article, give me a hand.'

Thomas slammed back the lid and studied the interior silk lining. It was criss-crossed with bloody scratches and pieces of rotten fingernail. Miranda threw her hand across her mouth at the stench.

'You see, Miranda? He was alive! He might still be saved…'

'Can you not smell? That's putrifaction! How could he still be alive?' Miranda leaned forward and peered inside, but it was hard to see in the gloom of the guard's van. 'Pass me a lantern.' She pointed to the oil lamp in the corner. 'Do you have a Lucifer?'

'Why would I have a match? You know I don't indulge in tobacco.'

'Thomas, this is no time for your lies. I know you creep into the garden for a pipe. Light the lantern.'

Thomas did as he was bidden and brought the lantern over. Miranda craned forward.

'Well, is he wearing his ceremonial gold? Is that his royal seal?'

Thomas looked down at the body for the first time, raising the lamp and turning up the flame. He found himself standing before the open coffin, frozen, dumbfounded. His mouth dropped open.

CHAPTER SEVENTEEN
THE FOG

THE *ARKANGEL* INCHED along tracks rusted with disuse. The thick grey fog crept between the pines to the cut and tried each window of each carriage, like a swamp miasma seeking to infect all who passed. The Conductor solemnly walked ahead of the train, along the centre of the track, as if at the head of a funeral cortège. He raised a red flag before him, allowing the engine driver to set a pace. The carriages shone with a murky brilliance. There was hardly any sound now. Even the sodden birds had fallen silent.

Nicholas awoke and found Isabella alert, watching from the window.

'How long was I asleep?'

'I have only just awoken. I had the most terrible dream. I dreamed that someone jumped from the train and fell into the valley, to be torn apart by wolves.'

'These are just anxieties that enter your slumber. You mustn't worry so much.' He stretched and looked about the carriage. 'I'm cold and thirsty, and I have no luggage, no razor, no clothes to change into.' He had always prided himself on his smart appearance. 'I'll have to buy supplies at the next stop.' Then he remembered the sign warning passengers. 'Except that we are not supposed to alight at the stations before our destination.'

'The vendors come to the windows of the train. We used to have them at Chelmsk. Most of them were blind or maimed. Accidents were always happening in the foundry.' Isabella watched the train's slow progress from the window. 'So thick and grey out there, as if the world has been wiped clean away.'

Nicholas checked his pocket map once more. 'There's no way of telling where we are,' he muttered, 'no way of knowing where we might be going.'

'The fog is like a shroud. It frightens me.' Isabella sat back, nervously chewing a nail, silenced by her anxiety. Nicholas knew it was important to keep her engaged, to stop her succumbing to flights of fancy. She was, after all, a peasant girl, and he knew they were prone to superstition.

'The Conductor is walking in front of the engine,' he said. 'Did you get a good look at the soldiers who boarded at Snerinska?'

'Yes, but I think they're English.'

'We won't cross the border until after Zoribskia, but the last stop is obscured. All the maps have the same defect. A printing error, perhaps.'

'No. Something is not right. They don't want us to know where we are going.'

'Why do you say that?'

'Because if we knew, we would leave the train by any means possible. We would throw ourselves from it if we could.'

'I don't understand. What is happening? Isabella, if you know anything more than what you have told me...'

'You would not believe me if I did tell you. We are peasants who start at shadows and trust in fairytales. We make sacrifices to the spring and watch for omens in the fields. And you are a fine London gentleman.'

'Stop that. Just tell me.'

'It is in our legends, our stories, our nursery rhymes. Our elders spoke of a train that passed the town at midnight on the eighth full moon of each year. No-one ever saw it. We were not allowed to look. We just heard the whistle.'

Just then, as if it had been called upon to do so, the *Arkangel*'s mournful whistle sounded. Isabella glanced out of the window into the thickening fog. 'Those who board the train must risk their souls. Each will find himself alone, and none can help any other through his ordeal.'

'Isabella—'

'We cannot get off, and we cannot stay on.'

'My love, you are not making sense! Listen to yourself! What does any of this mean? You have never travelled before—'

Isabella would not be interrupted. 'It's just as the stories foretold. My father, my grandfather, all the men told of it. The women were never meant to know, and so we were shielded, but there are images in my head, if only I could order them.'

What unnerved Nicholas most was that Isabella seemed calm and rational. Instead of denying her fears, he tried to reason with her. 'But why us, Isabella? We've done nothing wrong.'

'It's not you, Nicholas.' She turned to look in his eyes, shame blanching her face. 'It's because of me.'

'You? But what could you have done?'

'I left the town of my birth.'

'Do you not see that this is precisely what they tell you to keep you from leaving? Your elders need young breeding stock. Without you the town would grow old and die. So they invent these fables to frighten you and keep you prisoner.'

'No, Nicholas,' she said gravely. 'There is something more. The further we travel, the more I remember. I think I first learned it from the game. My mother kept it hidden in the attic behind a locked door, but I knew where she kept the key. I played it, and I know what is in store.'

'From a children's game? You might as well play cards and believe that by turning over the Queen of Spades you are soon to die.'

'The game was created by the foundry elders to pass the time while they waited for their metals to anneal. I remember the train now, growing as big as our house. The noise, the smoke.

I remember how terrified I was. What I tell you is not fanciful, Nicholas, it is based on the truth.'

'Please, Isabella, I believe you're suffering from shock, after our flight from the town.'

'I think you're right. My poor Josef.'

'I wish to God there had been no need to hurt your Josef, but it was him or me. You need to rest now. The journey will not be easy.' He pressed a hand against her forehead. 'Lie back and try to sleep some more.'

'You'll wake me before we reach the next station?' She looked at him with pleading eyes.

'Of course. We'll leave at Schlopelo if you like and make our way across country. There must be a way that we can avoid the troops.'

The train whispered on through the deadening fog as if passing through limbo on its way to purgatory.

CHAPTER EIGHTEEN
THE BITER

IN THE WAVERING light of the oil lamp, Thomas saw.

The corpse was covered in a stained white silk shroud, its folds held together by a gold chain, at the centre of which was a spiked oval seal marked with a red enamel letter H. Set within the seal, pearls and opals alternated with sapphires. The Crown Prince's chain of royal office. The precious stones shone darkly.

'I'm sorry I ever doubted you, Thomas,' said Miranda. 'If he has been scratching at the lid, then of course we must open the shroud at once.' Unsqueamish about such matters, she reached in and carefully removed the seal from around the shrouded corpse's neck. She had to push behind its rancid head to do so, and was forced to bring her face close to the Prince's cracked yellow lips while opening the clasp.

The two halves of the seal came apart. She raised the chain and swung it in the light of the lamp, the gems illuminating her face. When she examined the back she found herself looking at the largest emeralds and rubies of all. Her heart beating faster, she carefully lowered it into the pocket of her tunic.

'Miranda, what on earth do you think you're doing?'

'It's worth a fortune,' she snapped back. 'I know a collector in London who will pay us handsomely.'

'You know a man? What man? How can you know such people?'

'I had a life before you, you know.'

'So I am coming to understand. Open the shroud and let me see.'

'That, I think, is man's work.' Miranda stepped back to allow him access. Thomas swallowed hard and came to the coffin side. Gingerly he reached in and unfolded the shroud's opening. He stared at the jaundiced creature lying exposed before him.

Although he could not see its lower half, the corpse seemed to be immensely tall, longer by far than the coffin into which it had been folded. Patches of green mold and rank outcrops of mildew covered the exposed areas of its head and throat. This was not the body of a young man killed in his prime. Atop its yellowed oval skull, clumps of dry brown hair thrust up like pond-reeds. Its pustular eyes were sunk deep back in their sockets, its jaw clamped shut as if to keep a secret. Something was moving within its right ear. A maggot stuck its head out and twisted blindly in the air.

Indeed, it was hard to imagine that this had ever been a normal man. Beneath the shroud it wore the royal military tunic of its house, emblazoned with crests and golden chains, but the jacket was only slightly better worn than its occupant. Parts of the fabric around the sleeves had rotted away. Upon the bare sections of its arms, lengths of yellow bone could be seen through broken, pustulent skin. The creature was barely of this world or the next.

Miranda was not watching. She peered into her pocket and ogled the seal, captivated by its glittering gems. 'This is the source of his power,' she whispered, 'I can feel it.'

'What are you talking about?'

'The royals have different blood. They draw their strength in other ways.'

'Whoever told you such nonsense?'

'You heard Mr Scheffen yourself. Besides, it is a well-known fact that the purity of their bloodline sustains them.'

When she looked back, the Prince appeared to have shifted somehow. He was leaning more to the left side of the casket. The carriage had emerged from the fog and was picking up speed, passing over points to round a curve.

'Miranda, I really think you should put the seal back in place. I feel something harmful may come of this.'

'Who is there to see? Who will know?' She dangled the chain before him. 'We can remove those of Mr Scheffen's papers that bear a mention of the seal. We can refix the lid and seal the wax with a taper. Stain the damaged woodwork with some of your boot polish.'

'Miranda, it is a sin.'

'Oh, *sins*.' She continued to flaunt the twisting gold rope at him. 'It is a sin to be poor as church mice. Is it so very wrong to wish for a comfortable life?'

'Actually, yes—the Bible says the humble shall be rewarded.'

'The Bible, always the Bible.'

'Miranda, you married a vicar.'

'You were in line for a better diocese then.'

'Miranda!'

'For Heaven's sake, Thomas!' And at that moment she realized he was not castigating her, but pointing behind. And she slowly turned, with a sense of mounting dread.

Something behind her was moving.

It was rising from the casket. Freed from the binding seal, it sat up. It was not at all happy about being re-awoken. Now it rose and rose.

Its eyes had now shifted to the front of their sockets and were burning red. It gave a terrible skull-grin—the widest mouth Thomas had ever seen. Its teeth were brown needles, its gums rotted away. It towered immensely above Thomas in its reeking shroud and mouldering tunic, its eyes fixed upon its releasers.

It was impossibly tall.

Thomas searched for an escape route. The door to the guard's van was on the far side of the coffin, and closed. Miranda, turning, could only stare in mute shock. The ghoul had a mouth like a mirthless laugh, a gaping grin that split its bony skull. Its head seemed to almost touch the ceiling.

Thomas was transfixed, and found himself stepping toward it in awe. A bad move, as it happened, for the Crown Prince of Carpathia bent sharply from the middle of its spine with a gunshot crack and seized him in its needle teeth, biting hard. Shaking Thomas like a dog, it nipped a chunk of cloth and flesh from his shoulder.

Thomas screamed and fought back, trying to avoid the creature's clutching talons. But the flailing, ridiculous fight did not go his way—the ghoul was far too powerful. That great mouth might grin and snap at anything that took its fancy.

They crashed across the compartment. The creature's strength was now borne of little more than leverage, but it was driven by powerful urges that sent energy to its flailing limbs.

Miranda had stared in shock at the fight unfolding before her eyes, but with Thomas's pained shriek, she awoke as if from an enchantment. She tried to pull the skeletal monster away from him, but it thrust a bony elbow at the side of her head, sending her reeling to the floor.

Turning back to Thomas, it grabbed at him again like a dog worrying a rat, until it spotted the slender onyx crucifix at his throat. Snarling, it bodily raised him in the air and slammed him to the wood floor of the van, hoping to dislodge the cross. Miranda slipped the great seal inside her jacket and backed away. Then she called to the creature and taunted it. This, it must be said, was a wifely show of support rather than an indication of any real feeling she had for Thomas.

The Carpathian ghoul stared back at her for a second or two, then returned its attention to the little vicar, picking him up almost playfully once more, digging its talons into his flesh, jabbing at his chest, wrapping long fingers around his

shoulders. Finally, it stuffed him into the gaping coffin and slammed both sections of the lid down hard. Bored now, it looked for something new to play with.

The guard's van fell suddenly silent. There was just the closed coffin, with the creature on one side of it and the vicar's wife on the other. It watched her, assessing, cocking its head as if receiving messages from the beyond. It looked about itself, understanding its surroundings. Its brain had not functioned fully in life, and was operating far less effectively now. It seemed to have trouble keeping its balance.

Miranda backed up to the guard's van door and opened it a crack. She slipped through as the creature reached the side of the carriage in a single stride, seizing hold of the door. It looked into the dark gap between the carriages, and down at the racing tracks below. Then it cracked its neck and looked down at its shroud, failing to find its dimly remembered seal in place. It frowned in disappointment, then in fury.

And it strode after Miranda.

In the third class carriage beyond the guard's van, peasants lay their heads upon one another's shoulders, in the depths of sleep. A pig roamed the floor, looking for tidbits. A snoring old woman sat nursing a fireplace grate that had been badly wrapped in newspaper. Disturbed by the noise, the oldest and filthiest of the peasants rose to his feet and wearily drew out a butcher's knife, expecting trouble.

The ghoul stuck its long-necked head into the corridor. Its height was extraordinary. It bent to pass through the door and stepped into the swaying passageway, its mouth widening even further, as if yawning. The old peasant looked up. To Miranda's mind he seemed rather unsurprised by the appearance of an Englishwoman being chased by a dead member of the Carpathian royal family. The ghoul reached past Miranda and bit off the top half of peasant's head, spitting out his skull as you would the top of an egg.

When it bit, it took out crescent chunks, leaving teeth marks

in its victims' flesh like pie crusts. Blood sprayed in an arterial fountain. It bit again and again until the peasant was finally able to fall. He landed on the floor in chewed pieces, unrecognisable as a human.

The ghoul was free and growing in strength, a supernatural force rejoicing in its power, yet also seeking its own return to dust. It needed the seal, but Miranda had taken advantage of its bloodlust to run ahead. It darted angrily forward, jumping and snapping and biting chunks out of the wood, the iron, the train itself. It lived to bite and feed.

Then it swept along the corridor, heading for the fat little commoner who could only run and scream, the one who had pocketed its most important possession.

Miranda slammed the door between the two third class carriages and fled into the one beyond. Glancing back through the window in terror, she was suddenly unsure what to do. Pressing her hands against her eyes, she tried to think, but the obvious answer—to give up the seal—simply did not occur to her. She thought briefly of hiding it, magpie-like, to return to her treasure later, but even this parting felt painful. The seal was casting its spell on her, as it had on so many others.

The great wide-mouthed ghoul watched her go for a moment. It knew there was nowhere for her to hide, so it strode back into the guard's van—perhaps to check its coffin, but who knew what it was thinking?—and stood listening intently to the hammering within.

Thomas's worst nightmare had come about. He was sealed inside the reeking casket, gasping for breath. He reached around at the padded walls and felt the coffin slide about as he fought to free himself.

Then he felt it sharply tilt, his feet rising up before him, the top of his pate slamming against the coffin head.

The creature had slid open the guard's van door. It swayed for a moment, framed in the rushing darkness, then kicked the coffin out.

Inside, Thomas deafened himself with his own screams.

The coffin lurched and dropped but got stuck halfway—it now hung from the side of the racing train, entangled in the loading chains that swung between the wheels. The ghoul looked over the side, but his rheumy eyes could not focus clearly on the hanging coffin. Even in life, the Crown Prince had not been renowned for his courtly wit and military decisiveness. He was glad to be rid of his imprisoning home, but now he tried to recall the most important thing, and remembered that his royal seal of office had been snatched by a commoner. It was always the same. In life they had tried to touch the hem of his ceremonial robes with their filthy fingers, begged him to bless their disgustingly meagre belongings.

With a weary sigh, he set off along the carriages once more.

ALL THOUGHTS OF her husband gone, Miranda sought only to save her own life. *We cannot be far from the next station*, she thought. *I could leave there. Opportunity is everything, and I must make the most of it. But I must keep that thing away from me until we reach a stop. It needs to take another victim in my place.*

In her flight through the train, she stumbled from compartment to compartment, slapping the windows to attract the attentions of uncomprehending farmers and their dough-faced wives. It seemed that no-one else on board the *Arkangel* was prepared to come to her aid. What was wrong with them all? She was a gentlewoman—surely they would feel privileged to help her? She would beg and fall upon their mercy, and then feed them to the beast. Perhaps it would go to sleep once it had eaten its fill.

She could hear the thing coming down the corridor.

As she looked into another compartment full of dead-eyed peasants, Miranda started to have a bad feeling. There was something very wrong with them, that they would ignore the distress of an English lady. They showed no reaction to her predicament.

'Somebody help me! Please!' she called hopefully, trying to summon some tears, but they stared in mute incomprehension, clutching their ugly children and even their livestock tightly as if to protect them from an enemy.

Kicking a brood of squawking chickens from her path, she jumped between the carriages, making her way along the length of the train. Finally she reached the compartment where she had left Isabella and Nicholas.

Isabella saw her scrabbling at the lock, and went to help. She tried the door, but it refused to open from either side. 'Nicholas,' she called, 'I can't get it undone. Help me.'

Nicholas shoved down the window to pull Miranda into the compartment. It was an undignified sight, the vicar's wife half-wedged through the window, and as they were struggling, the ghoul burst into the corridor and seized her legs, dragging her back out.

Nicholas and Isabella pulled hard, but the battle was already lost. The creature dug in its claws and hauled the screaming Miranda away through the carriage. It turned and looked back at them, baring its teeth like an angry, emaciated wolf, daring them to advance.

Nicholas kicked at the lock on the compartment door and now it sprang open, as if the train had decided it was safe to release them. 'What in Hell's name was that thing?' he asked. 'Where is it going?'

'We should find the Conductor,' said Isabella. 'Perhaps he will know what to do.' Grabbing his hand, she pulled him back the way Miranda had come.

'No, we must go to her aid. That foul creature had her in its claws.'

'We can do nothing by ourselves,' warned Isabella. 'We need to get help.'

The Conductor was at his habitual post in his alcove. He seemed annoyed at the disturbance, but surely he must have heard the screaming fight that had taken place just out in the corridor?

He peered around at them, unhappy about being disturbed. An inky quill stained one hand. Nicholas could see that there was a little wooden office with a lamp on a narrow desk, and a brewing stove beneath it. 'What do you want?' the Conductor asked impatiently. 'I'm logging my journey report.'

'Did you not hear?' asked Nicholas, filled with incredulity. 'Some vile creature in a white shroud has attacked and kidnapped a passenger.'

'Your English friend whose passage I arranged?' The Conductor gave a small, helpless shrug. 'She must have opened the coffin, despite all warnings to do no such thing.'

'That fiend has her! We must do something.'

'There is nothing to be done,' said the Conductor. 'And that fiend is a royal, sir, that carries a rare bloodline, as even your own royal family does.'

'He wasn't a victim of the war?'

'No, that he was not. He succumbed to his affliction a long time ago. But he had to be removed before the army found him and broke open his vault in their search for treasures. We thought he would be safe in the company of an honest English lady. An erroneous belief, it turns out. There is nothing you can do to save her.'

'But what is he?'

'In life, a man who could only survive by dining on the flesh of his subjects. In death, a Biter, an unthinking ghoul that dies and is born again to feed once more on hot human flesh.'

'There is no such thing.'

'Is that so? And yet I think you saw it for yourself. Then I cannot help you.' He began to close the door on them, but Isabella stopped him.

'How can such a creature be defeated?'

'It cannot.'

'Please. I know you. I have seen you before.'

'Indeed you have, young lady,' the Conductor conceded. 'And on the course of this journey, perhaps you will remember

when and where. I daresay we shall speak of this again. Now, I think you should return to your compartment and concern yourself with your own welfare. It is time for the vicar's wife to face her demons, and either she will prove herself or she will be taken. There is nothing you or I can do.'

'But surely we can aid her in some way?'

'There are people dying needlessly all over this great land. Would you help all of them too? You Westerners, how you love to interfere in matters you do not understand. Have you ever thought that perhaps the rest of the world does not welcome your intervention?'

With that, he was gone.

'Nicholas, we must go after her,' said Isabella, grabbing him. 'We can't just leave her to her fate.'

'He's right, Isabella. What can we do?' he asked. 'This is not our land. We are meddlers here, nothing more.' In truth he did not wish to fight something so ungodly. If it had come to take Miranda, she must have done something to anger it. 'Let's do as the Conductor says. Who knows what fate might befall us if we fail to follow his instructions? And how do we know that this is not all some nightmarish delusion?'

Isabella had no choice but to obey. There was nothing she could do alone. Reluctantly, she stepped over the smears and blots of blood, following Nicholas back to the safety of their compartment.

CHAPTER NINETEEN
THE DECISION

MIRANDA LOOKED BACK and saw that the Biter was having trouble seeing clearly. There seemed to be something wrong with its eyes—once they must have witnessed the rise and fall of kingdoms, but now they could barely find the way ahead. A caul had formed on the corneas, hardened in sickness and death. It wanted its seal back, obviously. She had torn her way out of her brocade jacket and freed herself from its grasp, but how could she make her escape when there was nowhere to run to?

And why had Nicholas not tried harder to save a compatriot? He and Isabella had headed in the opposite direction, and her husband was trapped inside the creature's casket. The other passengers would not help her distract the creature. She was alone.

The Biter appeared to be in no rush. It moved in an extraordinary fashion, as if in terrible pain, or fighting against a strong wind, its bones old and cracked. Every step was an effort, but it sucked at the bloody strands of peasant flesh in its teeth and gained strength. Perhaps it had been incarcerated for too long, and needed to eat more.

It crossed Miranda's mind that she might be safe if she returned the seal. But why should she? In times of war, the

spoils belonged to the victor. She had reached the end of the carriage. She tried the door, but the lock was stiff and would not give. She turned to see the Biter coming closer. Suddenly it left the floor and sidled up the sides of the corridor, stretching its limbs across them like a pale spider. It seemed as if it could gain purchase on the walls and run along them more easily than dealing with the rocking floor.

Then, as it neared her, it opened its mouth to reveal row upon row of its gleaming, bloody needle-teeth. It was still chewing on a piece of farmer, but it was ready to bite again.

The train shunted sharply, dislodging it from its perch in the corridor. Miranda staggered back and fell hard. Rising to her feet, she punched at the door and now it gave, allowing her to leave the end of the carriage. She seemed to have become turned around, and could no longer tell what direction she was facing. The train was playing games with her, twisting back on itself, as non-orientable as a Mobius strip. More sure of herself when it came to diamonds and emeralds, she pressed hand to her breast and felt the gold chain with the royal seal coiled snugly inside her shirt.

But the Biter followed. With renewed strength it scuttled along the ceiling above her head, defying gravity.

At the next junction between the carriages all was a chaos of rushing wind, steam and smoke and fog. Miranda attempted to see through the mist of her own fear and keep moving. *Be rational,* she told herself. *The creature is clearly not feeling in the peak of health.* Sometimes when the carriage juddered, it nearly fell. She could keep ahead of it.

The Biter lunged and seized her from behind. As it opened its stinking mouth, its tongue uncoiled, split down the middle and wrapped itself around Miranda's neck.

It started to drag her back inside, but Miranda held tight to the handle of the carriage housing the observation car. It was strong enough to take victims by surprise, but not much more than that, and she was surely the equal of a sickly dead

royal. The thought that it was holding her by its tongue was disgusting enough.

But then the Biter pressed its fingers into her throat.

THOMAS WAS TRAPPED inside the coffin as securely as if he had been sealed in it after his own death. The great casket shifted above the racing rails as the train coasted a bend on raised track. He felt the floor drop again, and sensed he was inches from oblivion.

He tried to shift his weight back and forth, to swing the casket onto a safe perch, but without the benefit of sight he could not tell if he was placing himself at greater risk. He would have to fight down his fears and wait for someone to release him.

But the crawling darkness planted fresh horrors in his brain and he felt the walls close in over him. He kicked and hammered at the coffin lid, but now the box was being so violently buffeted that he found it impossible to keep up the pressure. If he stopped for a moment, he knew that his terror of the suffocating dark would overwhelm his senses, spiralling him into hysteria.

The wind hit the wall of the train in a broadside. As the casket swung and slammed against the guard's van, the wax cracked and a glimmer of light entered.

With a scream of triumph he kicked out, and the hinged top half burst open. Thomas found himself hanging at a steep angle over the rushing tracks. He tried to sit up, but was buffeted by rushing air. Grabbing the edge of the doorway, he attempted to pull the coffin back toward the van, but the weight of the wood worked against him, and he fell further toward the rails.

'Damn you, Miranda!' he yelled, 'this is all your doing!' He saw now that he had made the mistake of marrying a greedy, vain, selfish social climber. And it had taken this monstrous journey to realise the error of his ways. Snatching at the chains ensnaring the coffin, he pulled upon them with all his strength.

* * *

MIRANDA WAS LOSING consciousness. Black sparks danced before her eyes like cinders. Dimly remembering the seal, she pulled it from within her shirt and thrust one of its spiked ornamentations into the Biter's bifurcated tongue. It gave a scream and she felt the sticky meat retract into its jaw.

The hellish creature had the advantage of height and a dangerous mouth, but she had her wits. She made a dash for it, heading back to jump over the coupling. To reach her, the Biter had to straddle itself between the carriages, but its reach was long, and it had her again, stretching forward as fast as a darting cobra. It settled on her to feed, taking a tentative bite out of her left shoulder.

Miranda shrieked and kicked out with the heel of her boot, catching the Biter's rotted shin and knocking it off-balance. The hock of her arm seared as if it was being cauterised in a smithy's fire. The ghoul rolled to its feet, shook itself down and slunk back to watch her, trying to understand why she showed so little fear.

Miranda was a force to be reckoned with. From her earliest days, as one of six children at her family home in Leigh-on-Sea, she had been required to hold her own against five bullying brothers. She had married a man who would give her security, knowing that he would not be able to exert control over her. All her life she had waited to seize some grand opportunity and be tested on her own mettle, and now her moment had come.

She would not surrender easily. The ghoul was eyeing her from its corner, like a whipped dog watching its master eat.

With a grunt of pain, she tore the embroidered trim from the sleeve of her shirt and wrapped it around the bite as tightly as she could bear, praying that it was not infected. She transferred the precious seal to the pocket of her skirt.

She had damned well earned the right to keep it. She would remove some of the precious jewels from their settings and sell them anywhere, to anyone. Then she would take the rest to London and auction it to the highest bidder. Even if she was

only paid a fraction of its true worth, she would be free to start her life anew, away from her whining husband with his roving eyes, his wet little hands, his snide asides, his pathetically low aspirations. She was glad to be rid of him. How typical that she had been forced to undergo this ordeal alone. She had always known that Thomas would never be of any use in a crisis. He had always been afraid of his own shadow. He had always hidden behind his Saviour. How would he react if she told him she no longer believed in God, that her parents had only wanted her to marry him for status?

It had taken the train to make her realise who she was. It had given her this chance. She offered silent thanks to the *Arkangel*. And then she slumped down on the floor and cried.

CHAPTER TWENTY
THE HALT

SHE CRIED FOR her worthless waste of a marriage. She sat crying and bleeding, alone and helpless, pushed up against the wall of the car. The Biter was creeping closer and closer, like a jackal scenting death. It had unfurled itself beside her and was opening its jaws an inch at a time, preparing to attack once more. It bit down tentatively—almost tenderly—on her shoulder again, in exactly the same place as before.

This time she was ready for it. Throwing up her arms, she fought to dig its jaws apart. The needle-teeth pierced the heels of her palms but she would not allow them to close over each other, any more than she would permit herself to release the seal and return it.

Beneath them, the wheels hit a set of points and the carriage sharply shook. The Biter fought to steady itself, but its feet started slipping. In another moment it would be forced to release her.

The pain in her shoulder prevented Miranda from thinking clearly, but she knew she could not stay on the train for another second. Knowing that she was no longer strong enough to keep the creature at bay, her only hope was to reach up and pull the brass chain of the communication cord above her head.

The Biter pushed down as Miranda shoved herself from the wall. Grabbing for the chain, she yanked hard.

The *Arkangel*'s whistle shrieked. Its wheels locked as if the engine had suffered a heart attack and seized up. It began to slide to a halt. The centre of gravity shifted. Bags fell from luggage racks, and passengers on their feet in the other carriages were pitched forward. Caught off-balance on its raw, spindly legs, the Biter lost the last of its grip on Miranda and slithered away along the corridor.

AT THE OTHER end of the train, the sudden stop swung the coffin violently back through the open door of the guard's van. Unfortunately, as it did so the top lid caught the wall and slammed shut once more, trapping Thomas back inside. He screamed himself hoarse, but there was no-one to hear him in the chaos of the sudden halt.

IT WAS THE Conductor who found Miranda and helped her to her feet. He offered no other aid or condolence, but clicked open a carriage door and allowed it to swing wide, revealing the stars and treetops. An escape route.

The fresh night air from the open door helped bring her to her senses. She checked her arm, and found it had stopped bleeding, but it felt infected. Leaning out, she saw a row of glowing oil lamps in the distance. The *Arkangel* had drawn to a stop just before the next station, Schlopelo, at the start of the platform. Without thinking twice, she tumbled from the carriage and hobbled across the tracks.

The station looked forlorn and derelict. There were no passengers waiting to board here. She ran up onto the slope to the deserted concourse. Whispy trails of mist hung beneath the station canopy like spiderwebs. Passing beyond the circles of dim light cast by the hanging lamps, she trod carefully in the

gloom and called, 'Is anybody there?'

There had to be someone. Why else would the lamps be lit? She glanced back and saw the great train idling, panting steam, catching its breath, as if waiting for her to decide what to do. It felt as if the *Arkangel* and its stations were colluding against her, deliberately unleashing this disgusting creature upon her to draw out her basest instincts.

The thought was absurd, but surely no more impossible than the pale reeking monster that had stalked her. The Conductor would probably be checking the compartments now to find out why the cord had been pulled. Thomas was useless, gone, caring for nothing but himself. She would find a way out of her predicament unaided. Some cold part of her heart had always expected that she would be required to do so.

Miranda peered into the shadows and saw what appeared to be stacks of luggage piled against the walls, so somebody must have been here. On closer examination she saw that the bags were covered in dust and cobwebs. At least there was a waiting room, even if it looked as if it had not been used in fifty years. She would sleep there if she had to, and set off for the nearest town in the morning.

She searched back along the platform, hearing a shuffling behind the rusted equipment that lay stacked against the station walls. Rats were watching her, but there was no sign of the ghoul. Perhaps it was unable to entirely leave the train. Who could begin to understand the arcane rules under which it survived?

As she walked, she saw that the station windows were crusted with grime and cracked from one corner to the next. The building appeared to have been long abandoned. But according to the map it was on one of very few rail routes through the country.

Pulling her jacket about her, she assessed her situation. She needed warmth, sustenance, medical help for her bitten shoulder, and it didn't seem that she would find it here. But she couldn't go back to the train, not so long as that thing was on board. Damn Scheffen—he must have known what

could happen. That was why he'd been so willing to part with company cash—he hadn't wanted to undertake the job himself. He had danced her about like a string puppet. And her husband had met the fate he most feared.

Something scampered across the platform, vanishing into the fog. She tried to see what it was, but dismissed it as a fox or cat. She was a country girl, not easily disturbed by creatures whose appetites she could understand.

She entered the wooden ticket hall, pushing apart cobwebs. Finding a dust-caked window, she peered inside. The room showed no sign of habitation, and yet something was moving about within.

She peered closer, startling a great red-eyed rat.

Stepping back, she let it pass, watching as its pink tail trailed across the floor, longing to beat it with a broom.

It was too cold to stay here, and too dangerous to return to the train. She had no jacket, no bags, and her shoulder hurt like Hades.

As much as she had at first felt safer at the station, she now also sensed something terribly wrong. An odd bitter smell of earth and animals and death, growing heavier by the second, and a faint sound, like a cow breathing. It was coming from above.

Slowly she looked up.

The Biter was hanging upside down from the ceiling. Its claws dug into the plasterwork, which sifted down onto her. Its shroud was folded about it like a great blanched bat.

There was no more screaming now. Miranda ran. The Biter dropped in near-silence and scuttled after her, enjoying the chase. Back out on the platform, she reached the edge of the tracks, dropped down and set off over cinders and gravel. *I can be too easily found on the station,* she thought. *It will be safer away from the lights. Royal family! Hunting its prey like vermin, so much for the dignity of fine breeding.*

It was not following. That was good. No—not good. Enshrouded by the mist, she had not seen that she was entering

the station's siding, leading to a dead end.

Her hunter was in no hurry. It knew that she was trapped, and could close in for the kill at its leisure.

She realised what was bothering her. It had been here before. It knew the station's layout. But how was that possible?

With the idling train still at its back, the Biter followed her at an ambling pace, raising its head to sniff the air, coming closer through the parting fog, waiting for the moment to strike. As it bore down on her, she looked up and saw it in magnificent triumph, stalking her with great patience, immensely tall and rotted, wreathed in scraps of glistening night air. There was an air of decayed nobility about it, as if even in life it had enjoyed preying on its subjects.

Miranda had reached the end of the siding, where coal was stacked for the tenders. She saw with a sinking heart that there was no possible way out. Climbing the fence and the embankment would take too long.

The etiolated creature was through with playing. It wanted to feed. It cartwheeled toward her, settling upon her like a vast bat, parting its needle teeth to take out her throat. It fidgeted to find the best position.

As the ghoul prepared to feast on her blood, Miranda knew that these were the last moments of her life, lost in the darkness of a strange land, far from the country she loved, abandoned even by her cowardly husband, the man she had been foolish enough to marry. All she felt now was the disappointment of not having appreciated the rules of the game.

Reaching down, the Carpathian buried one clawed hand into her wounded shoulder, causing her to yelp in pain while it snatched back the royal seal with the other. She saw its mouth, smeared with her blood. Its eyes were growing brighter.

THE RAILWAY SIGNAL changed its position with a clang. Back on the train, Nicholas heard a terrible inhuman cry out in the

night and ran to the window. 'God, what is that?' he asked Isabella. Unclipping a torch from the carriage rack, he shone it into the dark.

There, in the siding, something white was hunched over, feeding.

'Hey, driver,' he shouted, leaning from the window, 'more light!'

The driver heard his call and raised the train's fierce main beam. It caught the signal and the scene beyond it. The Biter reared up above Miranda, baring its bloody teeth, lost in sensual gluttony.

Nicholas saw the raised light from the train hit the siding signal. It threw a huge crucifix of shadow over the ghoul, transfixing it. Miranda seized the unexpected moment, shoving the unholy creature back into the centre of the cross.

The Biter flinched in pain and looked up to find itself trapped within the negative cruciform. Much to its surprise it burst into flame, as Miranda screamed with delight.

The Biter's body scarred in bloody segments as it shifted about, trying to free itself. The crucifix of shadow seared its skin. Miranda seized the moment to snatch back the seal. As the train curved towards her, she scrambled to her feet and ran.

The *Arkangel*'s wheels turned more quickly as it began to pick up speed and leave the station. Miranda was losing blood, losing consciousness, but she had regained her booty, and now there was only one thought in her head—*Get back on board before the chance is lost*. In its death throes, the burning ghoul managed to roll free of its trap. Summoning the remains of its dying strength, it soared up and strode behind her.

Hunter and pursued were caught in the glare of the train. As the *Arkangel* rolled forward, its headlight grew more intense. Miranda looked up in time to see the Biter's flaming form come at her, its screaming mouth agape. It was in agony, and nothing would stop its attack.

Isabella had seen the ghoul catch fire from her window. Now Miranda was running toward her, bloodied, wailing, the

creature closing in behind her. Opening the door, she leaned out as far as she dared and outstretched her arm, calling to her.

Miranda knew that if she could reach help she might still leave the Biter behind. But even now, when she had a slender chance to save herself, she fought to retain the monarch's golden seal, gripping it tightly to her breast. It was all she had left.

'Damn you!' she yelled in the creature's startled face as it appeared beside her, 'Don't you think I earned this? You're dead, what do you need it for?' But of course the ghoul had more need of it than she, for without it there could be no true rest.

Miranda had managed to hang onto the seal, but its spikes were searing her palm. Still she would not relinquish it.

She had almost reached the carriage.

Isabella's fingers touched Miranda's—she had hold of her, but Miranda had the gold seal in her other hand, and the demon was reaching for it, its hands opening and closing in a grasping gesture, then seizing and dragging at the chain, determined now to remain attached.

Miranda pulled at the golden rope but it would not come free. Pressing its advantage, the Biter used the chain to pull itself forward. The creature's spindly legs kept pace beside the train. The righteous flames that tormented its skin had burned out, and it was starting to revive.

Miranda tried to pull the chain toward her, but the Biter would not let go. Her greed had locked them both in place, conjoining their fates. The train was rapidly approaching the signal, which reared up before them like a great standing cross.

The Biter swung in to avoid it, but there was another smaller signal behind. She saw it happen moment by moment. The second signal's metal arm went through the Biter's rotten flesh, slicing it open at the hand and the shoulder, severing its limbs and freeing its yellow head, which bounced and tumbled away from the train as its body collapsed. It was an undignified end for a man who had once been a crowned prince of Europe. She wanted to laugh in the face that rolled over and over, still eyeing the seal.

Suddenly released, Miranda fell back, covered in the Biter's gore—she was free, still holding the burning chain as the train passed her. But why was it growing hotter? The seal was still in the control of its owner, it was as if it had a mind of its own. Looking down, she saw the Biter's lopped-off hand, still tightly gripping the chain.

She was free, and had managed to pace beside the train. Its doors and windows were tauntingly close.

Miranda felt the chain move, and looked down as the end with the clasp snaked out into darkness and under the rolling carriage, lost from sight. She tried to stop in time to pull it free, but it was too late.

It felt as if it was wrapping itself around the axle of the train's wheels, and although she tried to let go her flesh was stuck to it now. The seal was holding her back. Suddenly the chain went taut, then pulled hard.

It dragged her underneath the hurtling cars, slamming her body over the sleepers. The vicar's little wife was quickly torn to bloody scraps of flesh and bone, until there was nothing recognizably human about her.

And the Biter—

—the biter—

—the bite—

—bite—

CHAPTER TWENTY-ONE
THE STUDIO

'BITE.'

'What?'

'A bite. Look, just here. You brute.'

Emma twisted about before the mirror and examined the small blue bruise on the back of her neck. The hotel bedroom was unbearably hot, but they had not been able to turn off the radiator.

'Show me,' said Shane. 'Good God, did I do that? And on your arm. I didn't mean to. I get carried away sometimes.'

'Sometimes?' Emma arched an eyebrow at him. She was wearing the most extraordinary brassiere, like ribbed white armour plating. He had given up trying to get it off. Perhaps all Englishwomen wore them. Emma was a different species to the kind of women he met in California: paler and calmer, with a confusing sense of privacy that stopped him from knowing which subjects were off-limits. Surprisingly free-minded in bed, though.

She rose and went to the window, sliding it open a little while he lit a cigarette. The wood was damp and stuck in the frame. She could smell the trees, the river, the night. She picked up a dogeared paperback from the table and examined it. 'Getting ideas from this?'

'What, the Austro-Hungarian Empire and the history of the First World War? Sort of. It all goes into my head and comes out into the typewriter. No idea appears by itself.'

'Interesting. I'll never really understand how writers work. I suppose this is a holiday fling for you. Five days to write a script. End of day one. What an awful lot you've achieved.' He had let her read the pages, and couldn't tell if she was making fun of him.

'If the screenplay flies, I'll stay,' he said. 'I have no reason to go rushing back to Hollywood.'

'I'm not sure that's such a good idea. I think you'd find it all a bit small here. And you'd probably end up hating me. I just don't want you to feel trapped.' She turned to him, radiant and resigned. 'What I mean is, it's fine as it is. I'll be fine.'

'I'm sure you would be.'

She tried to frame her words a little more exactly. 'I mean, your reputation precedes you. I knew what I was getting into.'

Shane had been romantically linked with one of Corman's leading ladies. He was surprised she had heard about it. 'I guess word travels fast. Well, don't believe everything you hear. And don't forget we'll be working together.'

'I'm not sure the place is quite your style. If you only knew how the company worked.'

'How does it work?'

'Like God, in mysterious ways. Michael has a brilliant business head, like his father. But how anything gets done—well, that's the question. We've always rather muddled along. Nobody saw the horror thing coming. It was the X certificate that made us, you know. We were making crime thrillers, potboilers, terribly tame stuff. Jimmy Sangster's scripts were always good, but it was adding the big X into our title treatments that got the kids in. *X The Unknown, The Quatermass Xperiment,* such a simple idea. It made them feel they were seeing something their parents wouldn't approve of, something forbidden.'

'But reinventing Dracula and Frankenstein, that was clever—'

'Those films were only around a sixth of our output. We

didn't know they'd work until the censor started complaining. And then the newspapers—well, now you can't imagine the uproar but at the time you'd have thought we were inciting teenagers to commit murder. After that it was a red rag to a bull, and I suppose we baited poor old John Trevelyan a bit. You know, put a bit of extra gore into the scripts for him to remove. And all in glorious Technicolor. The vicars of Britain and their county wives were up in arms.'

'And now?'

'Michael's more worried about the Americans than he lets on. They're taking bigger chunks of the profit, taking more creative control. Every picture has more lawyers working on it than the last. And the box office admissions aren't what they were. We can't go on forever. It upsets Michael that we've never been able to crack American television. We tried a series in 1958—'

'*Tales of Frankenstein*. What went wrong?'

'Oh, the usual. The networks got nervous. Problems with the subject matter. The Americans remain rather a mystery to us. No manners, our producers reckon, all in it for the money. They hold the purse strings. The rising empire always lords it over the fading one. Michael doesn't think they'll have the upper hand forever, though. He thinks the East will eventually make the West look like paupers. Hong Kong has a very robust film industry. He's already looking for an output deal with them. You could help to turn our fortunes around, Shane. We need new blood.' She laughed. 'Rather appropriately.'

'Well, I think I've nailed the first part of the script. If I can get the rest right and deliver by Friday, maybe we'll make a hit and save the company.'

'Things aren't quite that desperate yet, but one can see which way the wind is blowing. They don't know where to go next, you see. I think our films need a bit more oomph. We don't have much success with our young male leads. Some of them have the right look, but they never really seem to come alive, if you know what I mean.'

'Did you go to film school?'

'I did a course at the LFS, but I think I got the job because I could type and I have good legs. Women don't think of coming into a business like this. They haven't got the confidence.'

'Would you help me?' Shane rose from the bed and looked around for his shirt. 'Read a few pages back, make sure I'm following the house style.'

'What's in it for me?' A smile touched her lips.

'If I get the job, I get to stay.'

She pushed at his bare chest, shoving him back onto the bed. 'Let's not get ahead of ourselves.'

'We have all night.'

'You need your sleep. Besides, I know the landlord here and I don't want him to get the wrong idea. He puts a lot of our talent up. I have my reputation to think of. Not that I make a habit of this. I'm a nice girl.' She rose and dressed, pushing her hair back in place. 'I'll pick you up at around eight thirty and bring you to the studio. I want you fresh and full of ideas by tomorrow.'

After she had gone, he closed the window to trap her scent in the bedroom, unscrewed the cap from a bottle of Haig whisky and removed the dust cover from the typewriter.

Then he climbed back on board the train.

CHAPTER TWENTY-TWO
THE CONDUCTOR

THEY WERE ON THE MOVE AGAIN. Isabella ran back along the corridor, looking for Thomas. He and Miranda had started off toward the guard's van shortly after their journey had begun, to undertake a mysterious mission that would pay their passage. Only Miranda had re-emerged, chased by some kind of bone-yellow hell-demon, and now she was dead.

Isabella rubbed her forehead, wondering if she was suffering from hallucinations. And yet even as the thought struck her, she felt sure that what she had witnessed was true. The train—they had accepted its invitation to board, and now there was no way off, and no way back.

She reached the door of the guard's van and opened it. Inside stood a battered, magnificent coffin wrapped in chains, but there was no sign of the little vicar.

There were signs of a fight, though—something violent had happened here; splinters of wood, drag marks to the guard's van door, which stood wide open. She slid it shut. The creature that had pursued Miranda must have emerged from this.

But if it had come from the coffin, why was the lid now closed, and what was that noise coming from inside? She knelt down beside the casket, placed the flat of her hand on the wood, and

listened. It must be Thomas who lay inside. Exhausted by his efforts to escape, he had fallen still, but she could hear him panting for breath. There couldn't be much air within.

Isabella felt a sting in her hand and looked down to see blood on her palm. A gold crucifix was sticking out of the crack in the lid. She wiped her palm and watched as it moved back and forth. In one last desperate attempt at freedom, Thomas had torn his cross from his neck and had jammed it into the seal of the lid.

Rising, she frantically searched the van for something to use, and spotted the shovel. She raised it high and slammed it into the crack between the two halves of the lid. The shovel blade slid in easily and sank deep, stopping when it encountered flesh. There was a pained yell from inside. Isabella twisted the blade with all her might and felt the wood crack.

Gasping and retching, Thomas burst from the splintered coffin. He clutched at his throat, trying to speak. He was sweating violently and white-faced, his terrified eyes starting from his head.

'Isabella—the creature—'

'Calm yourself. There is nothing to be done.'

'My wife—I saw it all, like some terrible feverish nightmare! I fear I have gone quite mad—the minions of the Devil, stalking the earth, and only a servant of God is privileged to see them!'

'No, I saw the creature too. Stay here,' she told him. 'Get back your breath. I must find Nicholas.' She could not bear to tell him what had happened.

'I need to...' He reached out to her in thanks.

'No time now. You must rest and restore your strength. Please, I'll come back shortly. I must go.'

She ran back along the corridor, to where she had last seen Nicholas. She found him slumped in a compartment, holding his head.

'You saw what was happening to Miranda,' said Isabella. 'Why could you not save her? Why could neither of us—'

Nicholas shook his head in puzzlement. 'I saw it and yet I didn't, not truly. Did you?'

'Yes, but it was as if it was somehow happening in a dream—and yet it was all so clear to me. And the other passengers, they all appeared to be in the same state. What is happening to us, Nicholas? The Conductor—he holds the key to this.' Isabella grabbed his hand and pulled him from his seat.

'What do you mean?' Nicholas demanded to know, even as he allowed himself to be pulled along by her.

'The *Arkangel* is not just a train.' She peered in at the compartments as they passed. Passengers stared into space or dozed, oblivious to the horrific events that had unfolded outside. 'Look at them all, you'd think they were dead. They are not of this earthly existence.' She pointed ahead. 'Don't you feel it? We are different to them. We live and breathe, and feel. Look there. I see him at the end of the carriage.'

The lights flickered as the *Arkangel* shook over badly joined rails. Isabella and Nicholas were thrown against the corridor wall, but the Conductor never lost his balance. His straight back was turned to them, his pale hands knotted behind him. He seemed utterly unperturbed by the events of the last few minutes. A terrible thought occurred to her. Perhaps what was taking place now happened on every trip, over and over, and once started, it could not be stopped.

'We have to speak further with you,' Isabella demanded. 'You must tell us what is occurring.'

'You are just passengers on your journey, as others have been before you, and others will be after.' The Conductor turned and gave a graveyard stare.

'Ask him specific questions or all you will get is absurd riddles,' Nicholas warned.

'We want to know about the train,' said Isabella. 'What is the *Arkangel*?'

'You have not yet earned the right to that knowledge,' said the Conductor.

'You make it sound like some kind of a game. Well, what if we don't want to play? We can just get off at the next station.'

'If you do, the game is over and you are lost.'

'What do you mean we're lost?'

'By boarding the *Arkangel* you entered into a contract. If you leave before you are tested, you forfeit your soul. If you fail your test, you are damned for all eternity.'

'Oh this is madness!' cried Nicholas. 'This is the twentieth century, man. Your peasant beliefs hold no more credence. The war has brought about the end of superstition. Men are killed by the machines they have built to destroy one another, not some—'

'What would happen if we found a way to win?' asked Isabella.

'Well, that would change everything.' The Conductor made it sound as if the idea was unthinkable.

'You mean that nobody has ever won.'

'Of course not. How could they?'

'We're wasting our time with him,' Nicholas told her. 'Come on.'

'What do we do now?'

'We'll simply get off,' he said, watching the dark countryside flashing past the window.

'How would that be possible?' Isabella dropped into the nearest seat, overwhelmed. 'You heard his terms. If we alight the train before its final destination, we forfeit our souls. We will be damned for all eternity.'

'Only if you believe in such claptrap.'

'I do, Nicholas. It is how I was raised.'

'And for those who have no faith? What happens to them?'

'Everyone has faith of one kind or another.'

'In your small world, perhaps. Not in mine. Not with what I've seen of man's ways. In London a man may be damned and have a whale of a time. And you believe all this credulous claptrap.'

'Tonight you saw a woman pursued by a supernatural being and torn to pieces beneath this train,' she cried. 'What more would it take to convince you?'

But even as she spoke, she knew the answer. If Nicholas was to be tested, it would certainly make a believer of him.

CHAPTER TWENTY-THREE
THE MAJOR

BEHOLD THE *ARKANGEL*.

A diabolical machine, thundering through the turbulent night, pistons pumping, steam building pressure, lights a-flicker. The flashing squares capture so many separate tableaux, their silhouetted inhabitants framed and frozen, each telling its own story, of loves and betrayals, lingering hatreds, hard lives and violent deaths. For a moment the carriages are swallowed by dark trees, then they appear again, rocking and racing through the war-torn world.

The train was moving fast once more on its pre-ordained journey. Nicholas continued to watch from the window, annoyed that Isabella should believe he was no longer the master of his own fate.

'Miranda failed,' said Isabella miserably. 'Thomas is in the guard's van. He nearly died too.' Nicholas tried to comfort her but was unable to do anything useful. 'There are just two more stations before we reach the terminus. Which one of us must confront the Devil now? Who will be next?'

Nicholas had had enough. Jumping to his feet, he backed out of the compartment into the corridor. He needed air and rationality.

'This is the most appalling superstitious nonsense,' he told her. 'Nobody is going to be 'next'!

Suddenly two British soldiers sprang as if from nowhere, knocked him over the head with their pistol butts and dragged him away.

Isabella screamed. The Conductor appeared in the doorway, blocking her exit.'You cannot help him,' he said. 'You of all people should know that he must do this alone.' He closed her compartment door, and she found herself unable to open it. She hammered on the window, but the inside blind dropped down as if it possessed a will of its own, as if the train itself was once more choosing to act against her.

NICHOLAS SLOWLY CAME round. The train was moving through the night, swaying softly in a dark lullaby. Everything seemed calm and orderly once more. The back of his head hurt. The horror of Miranda's death… had that really just been a fever dream? If so, where had she gone?

He looked about. Opposite him slumped a portly, balding man with a fat, weak chin and a clipped moustache, sleeping with his mouth open.

Nicholas rubbed his sore head. The man was wearing the drab olive uniform of a British army officer. He checked his epaulette; the fellow was wearing crowns. A Major.

Something was wrong. He felt constrained. The soldiers who had jumped him had chained his left hand to the door handle. Regulation army handcuffs, cheaply finished but strong and unbreakable. The officer opposite grunted, shifted and snored. The carriage rocked. He awoke with a start and looked about.

'What the deuce—oh, it's you.' The Major's blue eyes flared at him for a moment, then lost interest.

'Hey,' said Nicholas, 'Why am I like this?'

'I don't know,' said the Major. 'What did you do with your uniform?'

'What uniform? What happened?' Nicholas rattled the handcuff.

'The war may be over for you, Lieutenant, but you'll address me as Major Carstairs, damn you.' He tapped Nicholas' left wrist with his swagger stick, a gesture intended to remind him why he was handcuffed to the handle of the door. 'You won't get away this time. We usually shoot men like you. Thought you'd slip back home in civvy clothes, and instead you managed to get the whole town chasing after you. Not too bright, was it?'

'I don't know what you're talking about.'

'It may surprise you to learn that you're still in the British army,' said Carstairs. 'You don't get away from us that easily.'

Tethered to the door, Nicholas fell back in his seat, dumbfounded.

IN THE NEXT compartment, Isabella pulled at the lock, but it remained stuck fast. Then, entirely by itself, it slid slowly open, an invitation from the *Arkangel*.

As much in confusion as relief, she ran out into the corridor and checked the next compartment. She slid back the door. 'Nicholas, are you all right? What on earth has happened—'

The Major tipped at his forehead. 'I'm sorry, Mamselle, there's no talking to the prisoner.'

'Isabella, he's mistaken me for someone else.'

'Ah,' it dawned on the Major, 'you didn't tell her.'

'Tell me what?'

'Your fancy man is a deserter, young lady.'

'I don't understand.'

'Apparently the British Army wasn't to his liking, Ma'am. He left just as things were getting interesting. By a stroke of luck some of us appear to have found the same train home.'

Behind Isabella, two privates appeared. The Major waved his stick at them. 'Get this young lady back to her compartment.'

Nicholas gave Isabella an imploring look as she was bundled

away protesting, one soldier holding either arm. 'No!' she called, 'Nicholas! This is your test! Be careful!' She was pushed into an empty compartment further along the carriage.

'You won't be seeing your boyfriend again, love,' said one of the two soldiers, smirking at her. 'If you get lonely, just knock on the wall and we'll come and see you all right.'

They closed the door, laughing, and locked it. She didn't understand; all the doors seemed to work differently at different times. The *Arkangel* could turn upon itself like a funfair maze. She had no choice but to leave Nicholas to his fate.

IN HIS SEAT opposite the Major, Nicholas strained at his handcuffs.

'You know, you might have made Captain if you hadn't made such absurd accusations against our Brigadier,' said Major Carstairs. 'You should plead insanity at the trial.'

Nicholas barely found the voice to speak. 'I don't know what you're talking about.'

'Don't remember your own reasons for desertion?'

'No. Tell me.'

'You accused your commanding officer of being a lunatic. Said you saw him cut a private's throat with a straight razor. But you didn't. You turned coward under fire and imagined it. It was your own fear of dying turning on you. It wasn't because we had a madman in our midst. We're the army, nobody's mad here.'

Nicholas tired to think. The Major's story seemed not entirely true, nor yet completely false. His head throbbed. He struggled to understand what was happening. 'I don't remember... only pieces.'

The Major leaned forward, speaking confidentially. 'Look, we've all seen the most frightful tragedies at the front that appear barely possible when you look back on them. It's been a tough war on all of us, and it's far from over yet. I must say, I

had high hopes for you. You were well-liked by your men. But I'll see you get a fair hearing.'

There was a rap at the door. A senior officer stuck his head into the compartment. Blue-chinned and long of face, his small dark eyes were set under a heavy forehead. 'Ah, Carstairs. We've found some brandy. We're in the forward car. Care to join us?'

'Oh, jolly good, Brigadier,' said the Major. 'I'll be along presently.'

Nicholas stared at the Brigadier as a bloody image flashed into his head. He saw the officer hunched and armed at the base of a flooded trench, cutting a young soldier's throat with an army-issue razor.

'Good Lord, that's him!' he said, 'he's insane.'

'He's not insane, he's a British officer. Now look here, lad, you must try to get control of yourself.'

'I saw him a moment ago with a razor in his hand. Drinking the blood of his own men.'

'No,' said the Major patiently. 'You saw him in the doorway here.'

'I mean in my mind's eye. I remember now. We were in the Piccadilly trench.' The unit had named all of the earthen passageways after London streets, so that new recruits could find their way about. Trouble was, half of them were from the country and didn't know Oxford Street from a hole in the ground. Everyone got lost from time to time. And on one of those occasions, Nicholas had blundered upon a scene that he had tried very hard to erase from his mind. An officer taking the life of one of his own men. But now he was remembering more with each passing moment.

'You know where you went wrong?' said the Major. 'Your mistake was to panic. The only crime in the British Army is failure to obey.'

Nicholas had some vague recollection that he was to be tested, and tried to think fast. His head was full of an obscuring mist. He needed to adapt to what he knew.

'Could I have a cigarette?'

'You've got a nerve, asking for favours. All right, just this once. I'll see what I can do.'

The Major heaved himself up and left the compartment, glad of a chance to stretch his legs. Nicholas studied the handcuff attaching him to the door. He gave it a few experimental kicks with his boot. It was too strong to break, and there was no way of removing it from the handle.

What the hell have I got myself into? he thought, and then; *Perhaps this is the life that might have been, had I stayed in the war and not fled back to England. How I behave will determine if I keep my soul or lose it.*

If she hadn't boarded the *Arkangel*, Miranda might have spent decades as a vicar's wife in Henley-Upon-Thames or wherever Thomas had agreed to take the diocese, running sewing circles and complaining bitterly about her lot in life. Instead she had experienced another version of her destiny, one in which she fought back from her husband and paid the price for her greed. He thought of the track ahead diverging in a hundred different directions, like all the paths of life. The *Arkangel* had switched him onto a different track in order to test his mettle.

I must not let my most base flaws destroy me, thought Nicholas. *The train is searching out my weaknesses. It must not find them.*

CHAPTER TWENTY-FOUR
THE BRIGADIER

MAJOR CARSTAIRS PASSED what he thought was the Brigadier's compartment, but oddly, the blind was down.

He tried to peer around the edge of the blind. The Brigadier's bloodshot eye suddenly appeared in the gap, making him jump. He returned the Major's gaze, warning him away. Carstairs stepped back, startled, and bumped into a young private. 'Robertson,' he snapped, 'what the bloody hell do you think you're doing?'

'Sorry, sir,' Robertson apologised. 'Looking for the Brigadier. Been summoned.'

The Major pointed to the compartment door. 'Well he's in there, but I don't think he wants to be—'

'Thank you, sir.'

Just then the Brigadier yanked his compartment door open a few inches. 'I'll take care of this, Major,' he said, dragging Robertson inside and slamming the door shut in the Major's face. The blind on the window shot up for a moment and was hastily pulled back down.

Major Carstairs attempted to peer in under the blind. He moved his face close to the glass. Suddenly, there was a gasp and a dreadful, familiar gurgle. A single spurt of scarlet spattered the blind.

'Everything all right in there?' called the Major.

'Fine, thank you,' said the Brigadier. A violent kick. More gurgling and thuds. Then silence.

'Oh, well then—right-ho.' The Major walked away, confused.

He returned to his compartment and handed Nicholas one of his own cigarettes. They were of a better quality than the straw-filled coffin nails he filched from privates, but he decided to spare one. He seated himself opposite his prisoner. 'The oddest thing,' he began, then shook his head, glancing back into the corridor, rattled.

'What is it?' Nicholas asked. 'What did you see?'

The Major frowned. 'Nothing. I'm tired. That's what comes of listening to your infernal nonsense.'

'I once met an officer on his third tour of duty who told me he had begun to enjoy the taste of his own men's blood,' Nicholas said. 'It was the only way he could survive the madness.'

'I thought I saw blood,' said the Major thoughtfully, continuing to look outside.

'I knew it.' Nicholas was elated. 'I'm right.'

The Major reached a decision. 'No. It's you. You have to be kept away from the others.'

'Sir?'

'You're quarantined. We can't have you infecting any more impressionable lads with these paranoid delusions. What if they all started thinking like you? Where would the British Army be if people started believing their leaders were mad?'

'But others could be in danger.'

The Major's nerves were jangled. It had been a hellish tour of duty, ending in a rout. He had tramped more European streets than a Latvian whore. 'Let it go, old chap. For my sake. We're all exhausted.'

Nicholas slumped back in the seat, watching the Major. *Survive the test,* he thought. *You have to think this through yourself. You need a plan. You need—*

'I need the toilet.'

The Major sighed. He would get no rest on this journey. 'I can see you're going to be a nuisance all night. Come along.' Digging about in his fatigues, he produced a key and unlocked the handcuff.

ISABELLA WAITED UNTIL the soldiers had sauntered off, and tried the door. Once again, it opened by itself. The train was like a mechanical trickster, opening and closing passageways at will, manipulating all those held within its grip. She and Nicholas had become a part of Miranda's challenge. Could she now become a part of Nicholas's?

Checking to see that the coast was clear, she stepped out into the swaying corridor. It was empty now. She could hear soldiers laughing further along the carriage. Making her way back along the train, she reached the guard's van and tried the door, but it was shut.

'Thomas,' she begged, 'open the door, it's me.'

Thomas released the catch and sat down beside the shattered coffin, closing his eyes. He looked terrible.

'Thomas? How are you feeling?'

'I really don't know. Quite odd, if you must know. Everything's a terrible mix-up. Where's Miranda? Why isn't she here?'

Isabella hardly knew where to start. 'You don't remember?'

Thomas unsurely pulled himself to his feet. 'What happened to my wife?'

'Thomas, I am so sorry—'

'My God, it's all coming back to me. That ghastly thing in the casket; the fight.'

'Miranda is dead. And Nicholas is now in danger.'

'Dead. She shut me in—no, the creature did.' He tried to piece together what had happened.

'Your wife was dragged beneath the train. She had a golden chain in her hand—'

'That's horrible. She was determined to steal it. Wouldn't

take any instruction from me. She never did.'

'At least her end was quick.' It wasn't entirely true, but the occasion called for a small lie.

'Mind you, she hadn't been happy since I married her.'

'She was kind to me.'

'Kind? Let's be honest. She was a greedy bitch and she made my life a misery.' He slapped himself awake. 'Right, let's get out of here.'

Miranda went to the door, but now found it had somehow locked itself. 'It's the train,' she explained. 'It's keeping us apart.'

'What are you talking about? The corpse in the coffin was still alive. Epilepsy. It had nothing to do with the train.'

'How can you say that? It was not of this world, Thomas! You saw what happened!'

'Mass hallucinations. Hysteria. It happens all the time in the church. You should see some of my parishioners after hymn practice. You'd think the Angel Gabriel himself had come down and made advances to them.' Pushing her aside, he grunted at the lock. 'Let me have a go. It's just jammed.' He picked up the shovel and started to smash at the hasp. 'Stand back, we'll be out of here in no time.'

THE MAJOR LED Nicholas to the toilet at the end of the corridor and let him inside. A ceramic bowl, a basin, no towels, a narrow window. Nicholas looked around for a means of escape. He tried to force the window, but it proved impossible to open.

One of the young privates who had escorted Isabella away came running up. 'Sir, the Brigadier wants a word with you. Wants to know our destination. Some kind of problem.'

The Major glanced back at the shut toilet door, weighing up the odds. 'All right. Stay by this door. Don't allow him out of your sight. Wait here with him until I get back.'

Nicholas heard the Major's response. He waited, listening for the boy on the other side of the door. The private had shifted

closer, also listening. Nicholas gripped the handle and opened the door hard, slamming the private in the face. Swinging himself around the door, he grabbed the young soldier and rammed his head into the wall twice, three times, until he was knocked out.

Nicholas moved up through the train, searching the compartments one by one. When he reached the Brigadier's compartment, he saw the white blind spotted with crimson. He slowed down, filled with apprehension.

He rested his hand on the door handle. He was sure that if he opened it he would find himself face to face with his worst nightmare.

Your test waits inside.

Twisting the handle, he looked in.

The Brigadier was standing in the swaying compartment, hunched over the boy. The soldier's boots were beating against the floor, as if he was having a fit. What was going on?

When the Brigadier heard the door open he slowly rose and turned around, the sconced wall lights casting an eerie glow on his face. His chin was bearded with crimson blood. His right hand contained an open straight razor. His eyes glittered with madness. Nicholas looked down to the floor. There was a deep hole in the prone boy's throat. The floor was slick with dark blood.

'Come in,' said the Brigadier, clearing his throat in an effort to speak without the thickness of passion. 'It's good to see you again, Lieutenant. I remember you well from the Piccadilly trench.'

ISABELLA AND THOMAS took turns to hack at the guard van's door, but it was no good. Thomas was panting from the exertion. 'I don't understand,' he said. 'It wasn't locked.'

'I told you, the train needs to keep us all apart.'

'But why?'

'So that we can't unite against it.'

Thomas continued to hammer at the lock with the shovel.

Finally, a piece broke off. Then, incredibly, the lock mechanism rebuilt itself, folding back wood and metal, fusing into a solid piece once more. Thomas stood back, aghast. He thought for a moment. 'Um, perhaps I was wrong. I suppose we could be in the realm of the supernatural. In that case, how can we save ourselves?'

'Right now I'm more concerned about saving Nicholas,' said Isabella.

NICHOLAS STOOD IN the compartment doorway, facing the bloody Brigadier and his prostrate victim. The boy soldier had tried to rise but had fallen across the seat, a second bloody mouth gaping at his throat. The Brigadier took another swipe with the razor, spraying blood. He dipped his hand in the wound and sucked his fingers as if finishing a plate of buttered asparagus.

'Brigadier...' Nicholas began.

The soldier fell back to the floor and released a terrible, agonised gurgle. Turning his attention to Nicholas, the Brigadier advanced stealthily, a wily old panther stalking a deer. Nicholas knew enough to start backing up. The Brigadier seemed suddenly to realize that he was covered in blood, and wiped his chin.

'I got a taste for it in the trenches,' he explained.

'What you're doing is against God.'

'The world has grown too dark for gods. You've never killed before.'

'No.'

'Then you don't know what you're missing.'

Amazingly, the boy on the floor was not quite dead. He tried to sit up, but a startling spill of crimson fell from his slashed throat. The Brigadier grinned, thick blood leaking between his teeth. He came toward Nicholas.

Nicholas turned and ran, heading off down the corridor with the Brigadier in pursuit.

'Deserting the fight again?' called the Brigadier. 'Show some spirit, lad.'

The Brigadier was almost upon him when Nicholas crashed into Major Carstairs coming the other way.

'What on earth are you doing unescorted?' said Carstairs. 'Where's my boy? I can't leave you alone for a minute, can I? Get back in there, man.'

The Major shoved him back into their compartment and swiftly locked his wrist to the door handle once more, pocketing the key and stranding him back where he started.

'He's struck again,' said Nicholas. 'If you don't believe me, go and look in the next carriage. The man has become completely psychotic.'

'Are we to have this nonsense again? I really think it has gone far enough. Get some sleep. Give your nerves a rest.'

Nicholas couldn't rest. He peered anxiously out at the corridor, expecting to see the Brigadier at any moment. Pinned once more within the carriage, there was nothing he could do but wait for the attack.

CHAPTER TWENTY-FIVE
THE LOOP

THE BRIGADIER STUCK his head from another compartment doorway and checked to see if the coast was clear. His eyes were as wild as the night. The blood he'd consumed had only made him thirsty for more. It burned in his throat, swelled his chest and gave him an erection. He had passed two years of active combat in some of the worst spots in Europe, and it had changed him. Something about the ease with which innocent life was taken had altered the way he viewed the world. Killing the young private had appalled him, but had also made him realise how easy it was. He had fought down the impulse to do so again, and the urge had remained buried until he had boarded this train.

Suddenly, shockingly, it seemed that his purpose had crystallised, and he could do as he pleased. The train would sanctify his behaviour because he could actually do good, preventing these poor lads from the horrors of having to return to the frontline. He would take their lives here on board, swiftly and easily, letting no-one else know.

Except that damned lieutenant, Castleford. He would have to take care of him. He watched the trees and mountains rushing at his back, thinking.

* * *

THE MAJOR HAD started to doze again. Nicholas waited until his head nodded to his chest, then reached over and very carefully unthreaded the handcuff key from his chain. He had one advantage; the men on board were dog-tired.

He unlocked the cuff as quietly as he could and pocketed the key. Then he quietly let himself out into the corridor.

The Conductor was watching him.

Neither of them moved. *Is it his job to stop me?* thought Nicholas, *or must my actions be taken alone?*

As the train trundled over points, the lights in the corridor flickered and went out. Nicholas knew he was in grave danger. He tried to understand the rules that would govern his own survival. He was being tried, just as Miranda had been tried, and would forfeit his soul if he failed. The train was a soul-catcher, racing around the countryside, scooping up the most vulnerable and putting them to the test. Carpathia was in turmoil as never before—virtually everyone's soul was up for grabs. The deck was stacked on the *Arkangel*'s side. He had to show he was up to the task.

Returning to the compartment where he had last seen the Brigadier, he now found it empty. Where had his nemesis gone?

He opened and closed each compartment door in turn, looking in until he had reached the end of the carriage. Closing the last, he found the Brigadier standing right behind it, grinning at him through a beard of cracked dry blood. In his raised right hand was the gleaming blade of the bone-handled cut-throat razor.

The Brigadier took a wild swipe, slashing Nicholas' cheek. Excited by the smell of fresh blood, he attacked again. Nicholas ran, but the Brigadier was faster. He punched Nicholas in the face, flooring him. Honing the blade on the line of his trousers, he leant over to slash Nicholas's wide, tanned throat.

A private came out of the compartment behind him just as the blade descended.

'Sorry, sir,' he began, then 'Oh, Lor!' as he saw what was going on. The Brigadier spun smartly on his heel, the blade slicing the air. The private's face was gashed wide, soaking Nicholas on the floor. He watched in horror as the Brigadier sucked noisily at the soldier's wound.

His instinct was to flee. Struggling to his feet, Nicholas prepared to go to the next carriage, then stopped, realizing that he had fallen into a trap. It was what had been expected of him. He would run and the Brigadier would pursue, placing those who remained behind in danger, just as Miranda had done with Thomas. It was time to stop running away.

End this now, he thought, closing his eyes, turning and opening them—only to find that the Brigadier had somehow vanished. Standing astride the corridor at the end of the carriage, he looked back along the mist-filled passage.

The private's bloody corpse was being dragged away; he saw its feet disappearing around a corner. A moment later he heard a door bang back, and the body vanished, kicked out into the rushing night. The Brigadier was cleaning up as he went.

So that's how it's to be, he thought. *No-one else will see his carnage except for me.*

Reaching a decision, he set off in that direction. *Head toward your fear, not away from it. The thing must be tackled and beaten, face to face.* He was almost at the spot where he had seen the body shift when the Major stuck his head out of his compartment and made a grab for him.

'Seems I can't trust you to behave like a gentleman,' said Carstairs. 'Give me back the key. Come on.'

Nicholas was horrified to see the Brigadier appear, approaching from the Major's back.

'No,' he said, 'he's behind—'

'Don't make this any worse than it already is.'

'—behind you.'

'I didn't come down with the last shower. Give me your wrist.'

'He's right behind you!'

'It's not panto season. I know most people think I'm soft—'

Nicholas could only point. But it was too late. The Brigadier's razor came straight through the Major's throat from the back of his neck, opening it in a spray of arterial blood. The amount he drank merely fed his lust. The Brigadier wiped his mouth and grinned. 'Enough men,' he said, 'I need something more full-bodied.'

Nicholas had not had time to formulate a plan. There was no way of grabbing a straight-razor from a man who knew how to wield it. He could only turn and flee. The silent, desperate chase continued down the corridor.

A peasant couple appeared in a doorway, struggling with their bags. The man was carrying a live cockerel. The Brigadier grabbed Nicholas by the throat and held him close until they passed.

'I am your commanding officer,' he hissed. 'Find me a woman.' He dug the razor into Nicholas's throat and nicked him. *No, it's blood-lust,* thought Nicholas, *if he sees my blood flowing it will set him off again.* He tried to twist away but was held in place.

A pair of soldiers came into the corridor with heavy kit-bags and had to squeeze by them. The Brigadier slipped the razor away but retained his grip. Killer and victim waited for them to leave.

That's it, he thought, *the nature of my test. For some reason, the Brigadier can't take action without giving himself away, and I can't accuse him in public without being recaptured. It's a stalemate. We could go on like this for all eternity.*

BACK IN THE guard's van, Isabella and Thomas stared incredulously at the rebuilt lock.

'This is ungodly,' said Thomas. 'Bloody clever trick, though.'

'Your crucifix. It worked on the coffin, and on the creature that attacked your wife. We have to get out, for Nicholas' sake.'

Isabella searched the floor where it fell, found the gold cross and pressed it into the lock. The metal hissed and recoiled. 'If the train is from Hell, it needs to be fought with the opposite,' she said.

She kicked out at the lock, shattering it easily. Together they fled into the corridor.

As SOON AS the soldiers had passed them, Nicholas brought his elbow back into the Brigadier's solar plexus and fought his way clear of the flailing officer. This was no mindless monster, like the thing that had attacked Miranda. There was something different about this peculiar turn of events. He needed a moment to think, but there was no time.

As he watched to see what his foe would do, he was horrified to see Isabella coming toward him with Thomas. He called out to her, but was too late. The Brigadier had stepped out in front of her.

'Isabella, no! Stay out of my test!' he protested.

But the officer had been presented with a dilemma. He was in the middle of the passage between two potential victims. He wanted the girl—those eyes, that body!—but he needed to silence his opponent. Whirling, he shoved Nicholas into the Major's old compartment and snapped the dangling handcuffs shut with practiced ease.

'It's been too long,' he hissed. 'A man can go strange without a woman. I'll be back for you in a minute.'

He glanced back at Isabella. 'Make that fifteen minutes.'

Nicholas looked down, appalled, at the handcuffs he could never seem to escape. *It's a loop*, he thought, *it will go on forever unless I can find a way to break it.*

CHAPTER TWENTY-SIX
THE HANDCUFFS

THE BRIGADIER CLOSED in on Isabella. Her innocent flesh seemed to glow in the corridor lamplight. In the trenches he had been surrounded by bone and wasted skin. Village girls were plump and tanned and ripe.

'Please,' said Isabella, 'There's been a mistake. Nicholas is not who you think he is.'

The Brigadier was not interested in discussing the matter. 'My dear, you shouldn't concern yourself with him. His mind has turned. He's seen terrible things.'

'What has he seen?

'I can show you.' The Brigadier smiled at her; blood was leaking between his teeth. Slamming Isabella against the carriage wall, he clapped a hand over her mouth and tore at her blouse. As she tried to fight him off he licked at her breast, leaving behind a wide crimson smear on her skin. 'I hope you taste as good on the inside,' he said, offering her a bloody leer.

NICHOLAS TRIED TO squirm his way from the handcuffs, but the ratchets were too tight and cut into his wrist. 'Thomas!' he called, twisting about, 'Christ, man, where the hell are you

when I need you? Get me out of these damned things!'

He kicked against the door handle, each blow burning and digging into his flesh. Straining as much as he dared, he smashed at the handle with his boot heel and threw his body weight against the door. The handle came free, but a great spear of wood tore away with it. He had no choice but to drag the fragment of door with him.

Heading out into the corridor, he found the Brigadier sucking at Isabella's bared breast. She had fainted, and lay draped across his arm.

'Let her go, you filthy brute.'

Nicholas swung the chunk of door, slamming it around the Brigadier's head. The blow barely affected him, but at least it caused him to stop feeding for a moment. With a cough of blood, he flung Isabella aside.

Nicholas saw Thomas appear at the end of the carriage, but knew there was nothing the little vicar could do. The Brigadier grabbed Nicholas once more and hurled him along the corridor, but Nicholas swung back, charging the Brigadier with his makeshift spear.

The splinter caught at the officer's neck, snagging his skin and eliciting a scream of pain. The Brigadier pulled the splinter free, but was unable to resist the smell of his own blood. Nicholas watched in horror as he thrust his bony fingers into the wound and sucked them. 'I told you, you soon get a taste for it,' he explained with the apologetic air of an addict. Then he came after Nicholas once more.

They burst from the end of the carriage, into the rushing gap between the cars. Blood-fed, the Brigadier was faster and stronger. He quickly closed the distance, then tackled Nicholas, slamming his head against the door of the next carriage.

Nicholas tried to keep his balance, but the train was lurching. He fell backwards into the space between the doors, and for a moment felt sure he would be crushed beneath the thundering wheels. He managed to clamber up, but became stuck between

the two carriages. His arms were not strong enough to lift him further. The Brigadier towered above him, triumphant.

'You're insane,' Nicholas shouted.

'All the greatest leaders are insane.' The Brigadier stepped down onto the carriage truck and raised his boot, pushing on Nicholas's chest. Beneath him, the sleepers raced past in a blur.

'I'm leaving the *Arkangel* at the next stop,' said the Brigadier. 'My work in the world is just beginning.'

'If you leave me alive, I'll hunt you down.'

'All of us?' The Brigadier gave a hoarse laugh. 'In times of war, men like me multiply. But this, old chap, this is where you divide.' Reaching down, he yanked open the release lever between the two carriages, and the coupling began to part. Nicholas felt himself slipping. He would fall to his death any second now. Nicholas sank lower as the coupling separated. *I must have a fighting chance,* he thought. *The train would never have allowed me to break the door if it only wanted me to lose.*

He swung his fist, still attached to the fragment of door, but missed. His arm fell back, the wooden spear trailing and fracturing against the tracks. The Brigadier heard the noise and leaned forward to see if his quarry had lost an arm. Mustering all his strength, Nicholas swung again and this time lodged the door-sliver deep into the Brigadier's chest, staking him.

Nicholas grabbed the Brigadier's boots, pulling himself up, and used the momentum to kick in the stake, then again until it burst out of the Brigadier's back.

As the train started to brake, he grabbed the collapsing Brigadier by his ears and shoved his head between the closing coupling, keeping his foot on it. The carriages slammed back together, shattering the Brigadier's pate with a sound like someone shooting a melon with an elephant gun. There was a shower of brains and skull-shell, and the wrecked body slumped.

As Nicholas rose to his feet and climbed back inside the carriage, he was immediately seized by his fellow soldiers.

'That's the one,' said the first, dragging him to another compartment and handcuffing his right hand to a fresh door-handle. 'Deserted his own men,' the private told his comrade. 'Left them to die. Couldn't take the war. I've heard about men going mad at the Front. Look at him, fairly covered in the stuff.' He relocked the handcuffs firmly around Nicholas's wrist. 'Don't worry, pal. You won't get away this time.'

Nicholas looked down at his gore-spattered body, then at the handcuffs. He started to giggle, and the giggle became a laugh, and he found he could not stop. Behind him lay the bodies of the Major and the headless Brigadier. Isabella was crying, held back by Thomas.

Behind them, the Conductor stood watching on impassively.

Nicholas realised how it must have looked, but he also knew it was time to admit something else. 'It's true, Isabella,' he called hoarsely to her from his prison, resigned to honesty. 'I told you I was an adventurer, but before that I was a soldier. Three weeks of shelling, day and night, I couldn't take it anymore. Our senior officers were all dead. The last few men left alive were looking to me to get them out. Instead, I ran and left my men to die. I'm a deserter.'

'But you saved these men by slaying a madman,' said Isabella. 'You've done a good thing. This isn't your life, it's just the train trying you. Remember who you really are.'

'I think I had already failed my test before I boarded the train.' He gave a weary shrug. 'The *Arkangel* found my flaw and exposed it, just as it did with the vicar's wife.' He turned to the arresting soldiers. Neither of them was a day over nineteen. 'Listen lads, a court marshal is one thing, but a murder charge will drag you both away from the war. You'll be required as witnesses. Let me loose and I'll take the right way out, I promise you. I'm still a man of honour. You saw what happened. You must judge for yourselves.'

'No, Nicholas.' Isabella cried out. 'Please.'

The soldiers discussed the matter, then fell to arguing, before

finally reaching a decision. One of them came forward and opened the handcuffs.

Nicholas rubbed his bleeding wrist. 'I'm so sorry, Isabella. Don't you see? I failed because I failed you.' He walked to the carriage door and opened it, preparing to leap into the rushing night.

And suddenly the Conductor was calling from the end of the corridor. 'The next stop is Blankenberg. Blankenberg, next stop.'

The privates realized what was happening and went to grab Nicholas, but were too slow. As the train started to brake and the station hove into sight, he threw the door wide and was gone, wheeling away into the darkness.

Isabella tried to see where he had fallen, but had no way of telling if he had survived. When the train finally heaved to a stop in Blankenberg station there was no sign of him. She could only pray that he had made his escape.

It seemed unlikely that she would ever see him again. Had Nicholas failed his test or passed it, though? Had he lost his soul or survived? He had surely won the challenge, but what if leaving the train had cancelled out his victory? She wished she understood more clearly how the train ruled his fate, for she felt certain it must change everything in her own life.

CHAPTER TWENTY-SEVEN
THE STUDIO

SHANE TURNED THE handcuffs over, feeling their weight. Emma told him that they had come from the set of *Frankenstein Created Woman*. A scene in which the female lead, the stunningly beautiful Susan Denberg, was to chain a lover to the end of her bed, had been cut in the anticipation of censorship problems.

'The British Board of Film Censors have quite a bee in their bonnet about the linking of sex and horror,' said Emma. 'But in such an obscurely defined way that nobody is quite sure how to deal with it. You should see some of the letters that go back and forth, two seconds of heaving breast traded for a one-second splash of blood. Blood on breasts, their biggest bugbear—quite ridiculous in my opinion. We all know the supernatural's not real. The stories are fables.'

'But they explore real states of morality,' said Shane. 'They have the logic of dreams.'

'Dream logic—yes, I like that.' Emma was showing him around the stage set, an Eastern European tavern with a bar, a fireplace and part of a staircase. It had been cleared of furniture and was due to be struck the following morning. The tavern windows looked out onto a village and a forest respectively, both beautifully painted cycloramas. 'The carpenters are due

to move in tomorrow and rebuild this as part of the set for *The Mummy's Shroud*,' she explained. 'Bavaria will be transformed into Cairo. Or was it Mayfair? I think we're still undecided.'

'I've always loved being on an empty film set,' said Shane. 'There's something magical about walking across it after the crew's packed up and gone home, knowing a drama has unfolded just a short while before. I guess at close quarters the fakeness kind of takes on its own reality.'

He was looking for inspiration. Emma had to go home tonight and get fresh clothes. She lived in Henley, and her sister was visiting, passing through on her way to Bristol University, so he resolved to return to the pub later and keep working at the script. But it was Tuesday evening and Carreras had thrown him by asking—very politely—if it was at all possible for him to have the script early on Friday morning, so that he could talk to the others about it. 'The others' apparently included Peter Cushing, Christopher Lee, Andre Morell and a number of possible Hammer Glamour girls who could be relied upon to spice up any screenplay with ample displays of cleavage and the requisite amount of screaming.

Shane was convinced that his script would need a strong female lead. Hammer had relegated their women to shriek-and-faint roles for too long and, after all, this was 1966, not the 1950s. He knew he would need a few of Hammer's traditional 'creature-carrying-girl-in-nightdress' poses to sell the picture, but he wanted his leading ladies to be as indelible as the men.

Seating himself in a chair before the artificial fireplace, he tried to imagine himself in rural Eastern Europe in the late summer of 1916. He would probably end up using a fictitious country in the script. Carpathia was the popular choice, but if there was a real-life equivalent it would have been Romania.

'I want to get the setting right,' he told Emma. 'Imagine the fear that must have infected the entire nation during the war in Europe. The uncertainly, the inability to trust anyone. Romania's careful neutrality lasted for the first couple of years,

then ended in mass slaughter. Its population tried to flee the onslaught of soldiers from Hungary, Turkey and Bulgaria.'

'It's not a history lesson, it's a horror film,' Emma reminded him. 'The audience doesn't care if it's Transylvania or Siberia. Hammer films are really about England and the English, anyway. Not the jolly old England you've probably been brought up with in America, but something I daresay you'll find a lot stranger.'

'What do you mean?'

'Our films are about human weakness, cruelty, sex and death. All the sort of subjects we find amusing.'

'You're right, that's pretty strange.

'What you don't understand,' she said, seating herself on the edge of the bar and swinging her long legs, 'is that in this society horror movies get to the heart of a particularly cruel type of English personality. I think our films succeed because they're made in a morally hypocritical country. The supernatural is turned into something unwholesome and sensual, and that's linked to the growing freedom of our times. It's a subject that's guaranteed to make the Old Guard start yelling about the nation's social fabric being undermined, and that's always a good thing; it gets the column inches. We hit on a formula that surprised everyone, most of all ourselves. It's a paradox, isn't it?'

'Explain.'

'Well, the grand sets, the classical theatre acting, real performances from Peter and Christopher, and yet all that graphic gore, you'd think it wouldn't fit together. But it does, perfectly. This country is still riven by class problems. We capture the callous attitude of the English upper classes in a way that no-one else has ever managed to. It's just a subtext, but it's always there. But of course if you try to talk to Michael about any of this, he'll act like he doesn't understand.'

'Does he?'

'Understand how we hit on the magical formula? I think so. But I'm not so sure he knows why our fortunes are falling.'

'One more horror film isn't going to change that.'

'I know, darling. If you ask me, the cycle's just coming to a natural end. Nobody gets to ride the crest of the wave forever.'

'So I arrived here at the wrong time. Story of my life.'

'One last big hurrah, though. Wouldn't that be nice?' She smiled at the thought. 'You and your script could take us out on a B-movie high.'

'There's a thought.'

'You could combine the portmanteau approach with a traditional script, and add a wraparound framework, set in the present day. You know, get all the major audience types in. The marketing boys never really think about things like that.'

'You could be right. You know, I can't help thinking you're a bit too smart for this job. And there's a correlation between the present-day and the script. Imagine, during the Great War everything was so uncertain—people had no idea what tracks their lives would follow. And now we're in the sixties and the old guard is ending, and the future is just as unknown.' Pulling out a hipflask and filling his cup with malt whisky, he toasted her.

'I'm sure you'll do us all proud,' said Emma, taking the cup from him.

Later, settled once more in his cosy, over-floral room at the top of the Red Lion, he sat back in his chair, closed his eyes, and returned to the thundering decks of the *Arkangel*.

CHAPTER TWENTY-EIGHT
THE DEAD

IN THE SCORCHING heat of the engine room, the stoker paused before the open doors of the boiler, listening for the soul of Nicholas as it crackled and popped in the flames. But he heard nothing. He frowned at the Conductor, who shrugged.

'Not my fault,' said the Conductor. 'It wasn't his time.'

'What do you mean, it wasn't his time?'

'Passenger Castleford had the misfortune to bump into some of his old regiment,' the Conductor explained. 'Everything that happened to him was their doing, not the train's. It had nothing to do with me.'

'Then what the hell were the soldiers doing on board?'

'They must have died nearby. I try to keep an eye on everyone who boards, but some slip through the net.'

'But Castleford left the *Arkangel*—he forfeits.'

'Only if he fled the train as an escape from his test. He clearly did not do so. I don't make the rules. I'm afraid we lost one.'

The Conductor strode back through the carriages, checking his silver pocket watch. 'Train now arriving at Blankenberg,' he called as the *Arkangel* came to a halt.

* * *

COUGHING AND STAGGERING to her feet from where she had been flung by the Brigadier, Isabella steadied herself. She wondered how much of what she had seen was truth, and how much was fantasy. She was hurt that Nicholas had left without her, but could also see that he'd had no choice in the matter. She suddenly wanted to be home in Chelmsk, nestled with Josef in her father's inn, but she knew it was no longer possible. The soldiers would have overrun the town by now. The foundry would have been requisitioned for the manufacture of weapons. Sides would have been chosen, troops garrisoned in the tavern, women endangered, the townsfolk made prisoners in their own homes. The world had been turned upside down and given a thorough shaking. Nothing could go back to being as it had once been.

But what if she survived her journey on the *Arkangel* and went on to beat the Devil himself? The game she had played as a child had offered her a choice between Hades and Paradise. If she won, could she reset everything?

She had no choice but to try. She was alone on the train with no destination, and only the Devil for company.

No, there was Thomas, too. He had just appeared by her side and seized her arm now, calling her back. In his left hand he held his valise. 'You feel it as much as I, don't you?' he was saying. 'The lines between what's real and what's unreal are blurring the further we travel. I am determined to leave this train, and you must come with me.'

'We daren't leave,' she told him, resisting. 'You know what will happen if we do. You remember being shut in the coffin, and I saw what happened to Nicholas. We are all a part of this now. We must help each other survive, and see it through.'

'I'd rather take my chances out there in the dark. If we stay on board we'll surely die.'

'No, only if we fail the tests. This way we have a fighting chance.'

'I am not as strong as you, Isabella. I know I have weaknesses, and I fear the train will chance upon them.'

'But if you leave, you won't even have that chance.'

She had a point: the station was forbidding, empty, mist-shrouded. Thomas had been prepared to disembark without her, but perhaps she was right.

'Nicholas said he failed not because of what he did when confronted by the Brigadier, but because he abandoned his men. But that was only his opinion of himself. He felt himself a failure. I think the train knows the nature of its passengers. It sensed your wife's selfish heart, God rest her soul. Perhaps it saw a cowardice that had once existed inside Nicholas, or perhaps he happened upon the soldiers by chance. I am only sure of one thing. If we can overcome our weaknesses, we can survive.'

Thomas did not look comfortable with the idea. He guided Isabella back to her compartment and seated himself beside her. 'But surely all of us have flaws within our natures? If the Devil wishes to test us, how can we ever hope to win?'

'We have to fight for what is right. That is human nature.'

'But I am only human, as are you, and I must tell you that I have the capacity to sin.'

'In what manner, Thomas?'

'My feelings toward women—' He looked down at his hands, uncomfortable. 'They are my burden and my weakness. It is difficult for me to explain.'

'Then you must find a way to control yourself. I, too, am aware of my faults. I have Pandora's curse of curiosity. Ever since I was a little girl, it has got me into terrible trouble. No matter how I try, there seems little I can do to control it.'

Thomas fretfully knotted his hands. 'It is so vexing. I feel as if evil is pressing down on us, trying to invade the very marrow of our bones. I have never felt such a force before. At home in my little parish I preach every Sunday about the Devil. I talk about him all the time from my pulpit without ever really imagining him to be real. But now I see his power all around me, in the faces of the poor passengers whose souls he has snatched. For the first time in my life I am coming to an understanding of how he works.'

He looked down and found that his sleeve was being tugged, as if by invisible hands. 'What the—?' He was pushed backwards and out of the compartment. The door slid shut on its own, locking him in the corridor, and the blinds rolled down over the windows.

'Isabella! I can't open the door,' he shouted.

'Thomas! You must be strong. It's you, you're next!' called Isabella. 'You mustn't weaken!'

With a great blast of steam, the *Arkangel* lurched and left the station of Blankenberg. Thomas was pushed along the carriage to whatever fate the train had prepared for him. The Conductor peered at him impassively from his alcove, then turned away.

Thomas was pushed relentlessly back through the carriage. A sudden squall of rain lashed the train, spattering through the partially open windows. The glass rattled with thunder. In the other compartments, the passengers stared straight ahead, refusing to catch his eye as he passed them.

'You!' he called to the nearest, a red-faced peasant nursing a piglet in her lap. 'Please, help me. If you know where we're going and what will happen to me, I beg you to tell me!'

The old woman stared at him as if placing a curse. In the next compartment, the two soldiers who had arrested Nicholas drank in sullen silence. As Thomas was forced on through the carriage, he became ever more disturbed. The blank faces watched as he passed, turning their heads in a single movement. But the more he called to them, the more they ignored him.

The realization hit him like a blow to the stomach. Why had he not seen it before? Everyone else who had boarded the train was dead. Their souls had been taken. The soldiers, the farmers, the townsfolk—he and Isabella alone were intact. The *Arkangel* was ridden by all those who had gone to Hell. The four of them had embarked on a voyage of the damned—Miranda had already been lost, and who knew what fate might have befallen Nicholas?

The force that had been dragging at his clothes fell away like dying wind. Thomas righted himself and looked from the rain-

spattered window, trying to see out. The raindrops were going backwards up the windowpane, as if time itself was reversing. In the light of passing signals they looked like drops of blood.

The world seemed to be slowing down. He felt calmer now. He took a deep breath. Perhaps his fears had simply overwhelmed him. *For all I know,* he thought, *I'm still asleep in my comfortable first class compartment, dreaming. Perhaps all four of us are.*

He found he had reached the compartment where the Red Countess sat playing cards with a young peasant girl, a pretty little thing in a black velvet dirndl, with blue ribbons knotted through her blonde hair.

The Countess glanced up at him through the glass. Her black eyes glittered beneath her crimson veil. She indicated that the girl should turn over her card.

It was the Queen of Spades.

The Red Countess reached forward and closed her hand over the girl's. She spoke softly to her, then rose and briskly took her leave. The girl was indeed lovely, in an unspoiled country way. Thomas stopped to look at the Countess as she swept past him in a rustle of silk, her chin raised high, her attention focused elsewhere.

A sudden noise brought him back to the girl with the card. She had slumped against the window, her head hitting the glass with a thump. Thomas stepped across the threshold of the compartment and bent down to check on her. He caught a sudden terrible stench of decay. Brushing her hair away from her cheek, he saw with a shock that she had aged years within seconds. Her skin was yellow and papery, as wizened and old as dried leaves. There were crimson pustules around her mouth, and her gums had dried out like old brown apples. She was growing sicker as he watched.

'What is happening to you?' he whispered, 'What is wrong?'

Her hoarse reply, in a Carpathian dialect, meant nothing to him. 'I don't understand,' he told her.

Carefully trying not to touch her, he loosened her collar and turned to open the window, but while he was trying to get her to some fresh air, she started to choke.

She fell silent for a moment. He took her pulse, but could not think what else to do. As she turned to look at him, her eyes lost their light and sank back into her head. There came a sound from deep inside her, a bubbling haemorrhage of tearing tissue. She clutched at his arm, screaming, spitting, spraying blood, clutching at his shirt. He tried to push her back down, but the old woman—for she now looked to be eighty, not eighteen—clawed at his eyes, sending him reeling backwards.

Thomas locked her inside the compartment, but she threw herself at the glass with a bloodcurdling scream, breaking her nails, smashing her nose. He held onto the door and shut his eyes tight, waiting for the dreadful noise to stop. The woman expired gruesomely, her bloody hand leaving a print on the glass.

CHAPTER TWENTY-NINE
THE SHOWMAN

ISABELLA COULD NOT stay where she was for another minute. She was sure she had somehow altered Nicholas's destiny, allowing him to escape the train while his fate was in the process of being decided. What if she could do the same for Thomas? She did not particularly like the little English vicar but that was beside the point. She might save a life.

Just a few hours ago her world had been static and immutable, unchanged since her childhood. A single rash decision had ended all that. Now her actions had consequences. She was starting to wonder if she might be responsible for changing the destinies of everyone on board.

She could not unlock the door, so, padding her skirt over her fist, she punched at the window. After the third try it cracked enough to allow her to open the handle from the outside. Bloodied but determined, she set off to find Thomas. She found him in the next corridor in a state of panic.

'Isabella, thank God you're all right,' he said, seizing her. 'You must help me. A young girl has died—what I saw was real, back there…'

'You are being tested,' she told him firmly. 'We'll soon be at Zoribskia. You must hold out until then.'

'No. This is no hallucination—it's happening throughout the train. There's a sickness on board. It may be cholera. I've seen the signs before. In one of the towns through which Miranda and I travelled, there was a quarantine in place. The priests had locked the infected in their houses and left them to die. The disease is initially caused by drinking infected water, but there are those who act as carriers. Look.' He led the way and showed her the dead girl in the compartment. 'She aged and withered beneath the touch of the Red Countess. We have to get off before she infects us all.'

'Some kind of illusion,' said Isabella. 'The only way to guarantee our chances of survival is to stay on the train. You know that now.'

'This is no fancy, Isabella. Look at her ravaged face! We cannot spread contagion to Zoribskia.'

'If it's real and there is plague, then the Red Countess must be a carrier, even though she is unmarked by it herself.'

'I saw her leaving the compartment. She touched the girl. Suppose it can be spread by her touch?'

Further along the carriage, they found another victim. The passengers were gathered around an ancient man lying across a compartment floor in a state of liquefaction, his body fluids seeping from his eyes, ears and mouth. Suddenly unable to catch his breath, he turned red in the face, thrashing about, the tendons of his throat corded like whips. The crowd looked down impassively.

'Look at this poor wretch,' said Thomas. 'What can we possibly do to help him?'

The victim's boots were drumming on the floor of the carriage, his muscles knotting and twisting in agony. He fell back with a final gasp, dead.

'The train is a trickster,' warned Isabella. She looked around at the dead-eyed passengers, mute and moving together with the sway of the train. Being near them made her skin crawl. 'We cannot trust our senses. We must remember that we still

live and breathe, armed with the power of rational thought. We must do what we feel is right, and remain true to ourselves. It is the only way to stay untainted by all of... this.'

'How do you know, Isabella?' Thomas was sweating with fear. 'What happened to Nicholas, was that real or his imagination? He was a deserter—that's a fact. He jumped from the train. How can we tell what's genuine or false?'

'But that's how the Devil works, he makes you doubt yourself. He makes you disbelieve the things you see with your own eyes.'

'I was a student of medicine before I was a man of God. I can't let innocents suffer.' Thomas knelt and picked up a red lace glove from the floor. The Countess had left behind evidence, daring him to follow.

'Was she here?' he asked the crowd as he rose. 'Was the Red Countess just here?' They stared back in silence.

'They're damned souls, Thomas, they have no interest in answering or helping you. This dying man has died before and will die again. You must feel no sympathy for him.'

'I cannot allow myself to believe in these superstitions, Isabella.'

'If you believe in God, you must surely believe in the Devil.'

'Yes, but this cannot be how he goes about his business, damning the dead to trick the living! This train will soon arrive in a real station, carrying the disease. I must prevent it from being spread.' Thomas took the victim's identity papers from his jacket and examined them. He showed them to Isabella.

'It says here that this... *thing* is twenty-six! That's impossible. No disease can age a man eighty years in a matter of seconds. This is her work. You're right, you can't help me, and if this is to be my test I must rise to the challenge. Perhaps the Devil is at work, or perhaps it is contagion. Until I can discover the truth, I must face her alone.'

Thomas pushed away from the gathering and moved on through the train. Ahead, he caught sight of a stately crimson train brushing the floor as the Red Countess retreated to the

carriage beyond. As he approached, she paused before another compartment and reached in to touch a sleeping passenger, stroking her face gently.

The passenger, a city woman in late middle age, convulsed and withered in her sleep. Within moments her skin had dried up, and she had started to bleed. Her eyes rolled back and fell into her head. Her lips thinned, breasts dried, arms turned to little more than winter branches. She was ageing years in seconds. Thomas followed in helpless horror, clutching the glove, an unwilling observer—and yet he was caught in the Red Countess's wake, repelled but fascinated.

She reached into another compartment to touch a sleeping child, a little girl with her hair in braids and a rag doll nestled in her arms.

'No!' he cried, running forward. What if the girl was an innocent who had boarded the train as they had? What if she still possessed her soul?

The girl awoke and looked up. The Red Countess stayed her ungloved right hand.

'Wait, I beg you. Please.'

The hand hovered above the little girl's face, before it pressed down onto her forehead, spreading black rot. The girl began to convulse, but the Red Countess had already grown uninterested and was moving on.

'I have to know who you are,' said Thomas. 'Why are you doing this?'

She turned to study him imperiously.

'Who are you to speak to me? You, a commoner who will not even play cards with a lonely old woman?' She flipped the train of her gown away and departed to the next carriage.

This is a problem, thought Thomas. *How can I defeat a nemesis who will not even deign to speak honestly to someone she considers beneath her station?*

The *Arkangel* was slowing down. Thomas could see the station sign, Zoribskia, the last stop before their unnamed

destination. He glanced back and saw the Conductor balancing on the step between the carriages, sparks flying around him as the train applied its brakes.

'What am I supposed to do?' Thomas asked the Conductor.

'You cannot change what must be,' he replied, noting Thomas's anguish and feeding on it.

'We'll see about that,' Thomas replied, his resolve strengthening.

AS THE TRAIN pulled into Zoribskia station, Isabella ran to the window. She longed to disembark, but knew it would be fatal to do so. Perhaps there was another way. A boy was standing nearby on the platform. She called to him.

'I'll give you these coins if you fetch the stationmaster and ask him to order the passengers from the train.'

The boy turned away from her. Leaning as far as she dared from the window, she reached out her hand to touch his shoulder. 'Please, you must help us, take the money!'

The boy turned back to reveal dark dry holes where his eyes and mouth should have been. Isabella recoiled in horror. She saw now that the station was crowded with the dead, passengers boarding and disembarking, every one of them a damned soul.

It was all too obvious what their final destination was to be. Had there ever really been any doubt? No wonder it had been torn from every map and erased from every sign. But were there any others like them, passengers who had boarded with their lives and souls intact? Perhaps if they could be identified, their help could be enlisted.

Or perhaps Isabella and Thomas were alone.

As the *Arkangel* built up steam, getting ready to pull out, Isabella called to an alighting passenger, a farmer carrying newspaper parcels.

'Please sir, can you help us?'

The farmer turned to look at her, but his eyes were blank white balls, as hard and dry as marbles. His mouth opened

and the dry stump of his tongue waggled inside it. 'Get thee to Hell,' he rasped with some difficulty. It seemed that the train had the power to preserve the dead in a fit state only while they were on board.

Isabella's cries were lost in the sound of the carriage doors slamming and the station whistle shrieking as the *Arkangel* pulled out of the Zoribskia.

She decided to search the compartments. If there was just one more passenger on board who was still in possession of his soul, she would find him.

In the second class carriage she spotted a tall box with the yellow painted flag that read: 'Professor Io's Marvellous Nightingale.' It was propped up against a seat like a coffin. The man sitting next to it with the mutton-chop whiskers looked up from his newspaper and smiled, touching the rim of his silk top hat.

'Good day to you, Ma'am.' His formal politeness marked him as an American. 'Are you looking for a place to sit? I believe these seats aren't taken.'

Isabella was suspicious. She remembered seeing him come aboard at Snerinska. How had he not been touched by the commotion taking place up and down the length of the train? She pushed back the door and gingerly stepped inside.

'I'm afraid you'll have to speak up a little,' he all but shouted. 'I'm as deaf as a coot. I used to work with Barnum and Bailey's Human Cannonball and the gunpowder did for my eardrums. They could be firing guns out there and I wouldn't hear a darned thing. Professor Io's the name. After Phineas Barnum died I travelled the world with my marvels, amazing the populace. At least I used to, before the war robbed me of my audiences.' He gave her hand a vigorous shake. 'I'm a showman. Part illusionist, part huckster, I'll admit, but I always give 'em a darned good show. We Americans are the best showmen in the world.'

'Professor Io,' said Isabella, unsure where to start, 'this may seem an odd question, but do you remember where you boarded the train?'

The Professor thought for a moment, stroking his right sideburn. 'You know, I'm dashed if I can recall now. It's on the tip of my tongue. It began with an S but that's about all—'

'Snerinska.'

'That's the one, little lady. I had to cut short my tour. The troops were moving in and they weren't too interested in my little entertainment, I can tell you. I barely got out with my life.'

'Your entertainment—is that it in the box?'

The professor dug out a cheroot and lit it. 'In part, yes. I had to leave my performing dogs behind. Would you like to see?'

Yes, do anything that will show me which side of the divide you exist on, she thought. 'Please,' she said aloud, and he rose and unclipped the door of the crate, swinging it aside. Reaching in, he pulled something from its protective wrapping of straw.

'She's my Swedish songbird,' said the Professor, stepping back to reveal a girl apparently made of porcelain. She was dressed in a gossamer gown of silver thread that stopped high on her thighs, and had long gold hair in braids over her white breasts. Her blue eyes were set in a smooth, featureless china face.

'Allow me to demonstrate.' He turned the figure around and wound a large tin key in the small of her back. Then he set her facing front once more, steadying her with difficulty against the rocking of the train. A music box began to play a Strauss waltz, and the doll raised its arms in a ballerina pose. Then she opened her tiny mouth and began to sing. The sound that came from her lips was astonishing, as high and pure as mountain air.

'She's beautiful,' said Isabella, fascinated, stepping closer.

'Isn't she though? She sings more than twenty melodies. She is my fame and my fortune.'

Isabella could not help but smile. It was the first pleasing sound she had heard in the last few hours. The song wound down and came to an end.

'Where are you heading?' asked Isabella.

'To the terminus,' said the Professor, puffing on his cigar.

'See, I've done this journey before. Would you like to hear another song?'

'Thank you, I must—'

'Aw, come on, just one more.' He rewound the key, pleased with her reaction. 'It's good to have an appreciative audience again, I can tell you. The nightingale once sang for all the children on the train,'

'There were children?'

'Sure, a seaside outing. The maiden voyage. But that was long ago.'

'What do you mean?'

'Why, you must know about the *Arkangel*'s first trip.'

'I seem to remember something,' she began. 'Something people said in the town. But I was young, I wasn't supposed to hear. My mother always said little girls—'

'—should be seen and not heard. Oh, boy, I've heard that a few times.'

'But I think my uncle was there.'

'Indeed he was.' But before he could continue, the nightingale began to sing again, an aria from Gounod's *Faust*. The china girl raised her arms straight out and spread them wide as her voice rose in scale. The sound was different now, slightly harsher. 'There's a bit of a pitch problem there,' the Professor admitted. 'Nothing that can't be fixed with a little elbow grease.'

She felt his hand in the small of her back, urging her to take a closer look. A warning signal sounded in her brain. He was pushing her harder now, his fingers pressing against her spine, and the doll's voice was rising, becoming more shrill. Her nightingale song had turned into the startled shriek of a child in pain.

'Wait,' said Isabella, 'stop.'

The doll's face was a pink china heart, but her eyes looked tormented. Isabella tried to take a step back, but the nightingale's arms slid forward and locked themselves around her, gripping ever tighter.

She had realised her mistake too late. She tried to move, but found herself pinned. The doll's arms were pushing together, starting to crush her. Its mouth opened and shut, opened and shut, and she caught glimpses of glistening red inside like the innards of an animal. Isabella yelped in fear.

'That's it, little lady, you just cry out now,' said the Professor, laughing. 'Isn't going to do you no good, 'cause everybody on this train is dead except you and your friend the vicar, and he ain't going to be around for much longer neither. Oh, and there's someone on board you won't get to meet. He's in charge of the whole shebang. We're just his slaves. Yessir, you'd better pray you never meet him, 'cause there's fates much worse than death, if you know what I mean. So you just yell out now, and all it's going do is make the other passengers excited.'

Isabella twisted and turned as the doll screamed in her face and its grip grew tighter.

CHAPTER THIRTY
THE ESCAPE

NICHOLAS HAD CARTWHEELED into the long grass at the edge of the station platform at Blankenberg, and lay on the wet soil, panting. He tried to assess whether any limbs were damaged. His right leg hurt at the knee, and he had landed badly on his left wrist, but nothing appeared to be broken. With a grimace, he pulled himself upright. Below, the track twisted back on itself in a broad loop, like a railway line on a board game. The *Arkangel* was pulling into Zoribskia station. It was hard to see from where he sat, but the waiting passengers looked as dishevelled and strange as the rest of the travellers he had seen on board.

Climbing to his feet, he found himself still smeared with the Brigadier's blood, but his mind felt different, unclouded and clearer. Now that he was away from the train, he seemed to be free of its baleful influence.

He thought back to the events that had led him to jump from the *Arkangel*. He had vanquished his nemesis, but more importantly he had admitted the truth about his desertion. Moments later, he had leaped into the unknown.

Miranda was dead, the victim of her own greed, and Thomas could not be trusted. Nicholas had seen the lascivious look in his eye, and felt sure it would be the path to his undoing. Each

uncovered flaw would lead to destruction, just as his own fear of dying had almost proven the undoing of him. The vicar's lust was his weakness, but what was Isabella's? Her innocence? Was that a mark of human frailty? Her curiosity? Either way, she would be no match for the wiles of the train.

But what did he care? He dusted himself down, testing his leg. Isabella was just another girl in a long line of bored and boring village beauties whose heads could be turned by any man with a mellifluous voice and no stains upon his shirt. He had found girls like her wherever he travelled. He owed her no loyalty. If he had left her in Chelmsk, one of two fates would have awaited her; she would have been raped by the arriving soldiers, or protected by Josef until they had gone. But Josef had been left far behind, and he had abandoned her to her fate.

But if he didn't care, why the hell couldn't he get her out of his head?

Isabella was different from the rest. She was more than merely innocent. She was the very spring of life.

Sharper-witted now, Nicholas realised he had been a fool. She had found a way under his skin, and perhaps—against all the odds—he had finally met a girl who could tame him. Yet he had abandoned her at the moment of her greatest need.

Now he was seized with the need to make amends. He had to board the train once more. It was the only way to know for sure. She was probably frightened, hating him for leaving the way he did, but what else could he have done? He had known the station was approaching, and they had not. It had been the only way out.

He could not leave her to fight on alone.

Nicholas limped down the hill toward the distant platform. The *Arkangel* stood in the station, almost as if it was waiting for him, daring him to try and board. He dropped lower through the grass, and found the going easier. The stations were really no distance from one another; the track had been forced into its circuitous path by a succession of rocky outcrops.

In another few minutes he was no more than a dozen yards from the rear carriage. The engine's pistons pumped and it breathed steam, preparing to leave once again.

Ignoring the pain in his leg, he ran harder. The platform was in darkness. He could see no guard or stationmaster, only passengers who had been refused the right to board. The carriages were pulling out and the engine quickly gathered speed, but he was pacing beside the train. He looked in through the windows and saw bright, empty compartments, just as he and Isabella had seen when they first ran for the train—an illusion provided to lure the innocent. For all he knew, all Hell was breaking loose in there again.

He was beside one of the door handles now, ready to board and take his chances with Isabella. He reached out to open it, but his weak right leg folded beneath him and he fell sprawling, almost slipping from the platform under the thundering wheels. Gripping his leg in pain and rolling over, he watched as the *Arkangel* thundered past, too fast to board.

I've failed her, he thought. *There's nothing I can do now.*

Hobbling back to the ticket office, he watched as a pair of Bulgarian soldiers dismounted from their motorcycles and strode onto the platform. They headed to the ticket office and began a drunken argument with the collector over some perceived transgression.

Nicholas backed out, and ran to one of the bikes as quickly as he was able. Its engine was still warm, and the ignition was operated by a single switch.

He had ridden a motorcycle before, but had trouble turning on the headlamp. The train was building speed, leaving the station behind. He set off after it.

The road ahead was filled with potholes and poorly lit, but it appeared to follow the tracks. There was no other traffic. Accelerating as much as he dared, Nicholas followed in the wake of the speeding locomotive.

Zoribskia had been the last station marked on the *Arkangel*'s

route. Unless it made an unscheduled stop further down the line, he would have to try and board it from the speeding bike. That meant drawing alongside the open observation platform and jumping in, but to do so he would have to leave the road and somehow cross the gravel track. He knew it was an almost impossible feat at the speed he was travelling. He could be killed in the attempt, but there was no other choice open to him.

I finally get the freedom I craved and now I risk everything for a girl I barely know, he thought. *What an idiot.* He had almost drawn level with the train. He needed to wait until the bed along which the track had been laid was the same height as the road. His headlamp picked up the line of bushes, broken fences, scrub and rocks that separated him from the railway. He had to get closer.

The red tail-light of the train swung back and forth in his beam, taunting him. The *Arkangel* appeared as deserted as the *Flying Dutchman*. His front wheel was almost level with the rear buffer. He twisted the throttle and the bike surged forward.

Ahead he could see a point where the road crossed the track—the railway line dropped down to lie flush with the stones. As he approached, he gripped the handlebars with his right hand and reached out with his left, but the bike quickly became skittish and unstable.

He looked up and caught sight of a dark figure standing at the rear of the train. The Conductor was at the rail, watching him. The crossing-point was approaching fast. Pushing forward harder still, he drew alongside the train and rose in his seat, disengaging his right leg.

Then he leapt.

CHAPTER THIRTY-ONE
THE DOLL

ISABELLA COULD NOT catch her breath.

The porcelain arms tightened their grip still further. How could something so graceful and delicate be so strong? She was being crushed against the doll and found it difficult to draw in any air at all now. Her hair was caught in its joints. She felt herself slipping against the rocking floor, and the doll sang on, more harshly than ever.

'Please,' she gasped, 'make it stop, I can't—'

The singing was growing more shrill with every passing second. The noise was unbearable. The Professor seemed not to notice. He smiled to himself and tapped his foot along with the music.

'Isn't that a pretty tune?' he said, ignoring her pain. 'I could hear Gounod over and over, and never grow tired of it. Just as well, 'cause I don't get much choice about that.'

She felt herself starting to lose consciousness. Her arms were bruising, the joints cracking. It felt as if the very marrow from her bones was being forced out. Seams of fire shot up her spine. She could hear the clockwork ticking now, the grinding of gears, the hiss of tiny pistons. The eyes in the porcelain face seemed to belong to a live girl, and were filled with pain.

Isabella's sight and hearing began to fade.

Suddenly the train lurched as it ran over a set of points, and the doll rocked and threatened to tip over. Isabella used the momentum to push as hard as she could with the tips of her toes. Secured to the doll, she felt her weight pull the pair of them over.

The Professor was in the process of tapping the ash from his cheroot, and was too late to stop them from falling. Isabella and the doll crashed to the floor, and the china arms split open. Tearing herself free, she kicked out at the doll's face as the Professor came for her, crying out.

She looked back at the nightingale and saw the truth; there *was* a girl inside it. The face was raw and bloody, the teeth and jawbone exposed, the skin of the arms split apart to reveal the meat and bone beneath. The Professor gave a cry of anguish. 'My precious darling,' he called out, 'my little songbird, my poor daughter.'

At that moment, Isabella knew that the Professor had failed his own test on the train many years before. 'How could you have done that to your own child?' she asked, revolted.

'I had no choice,' he moaned, clutching at her broken, bleeding head. A row of china teeth had fallen out. A dead tongue lolled inside her china lips. 'She was dying of a rare anaemia, and I was offered the chance to save her life.'

He pulled the plates of porcelain from her face to reveal the diseased and rotted flesh beneath. Isabella saw the clockwork mechanism that had been inserted into her body to make her sing and dance, the cogs and wires and bloodied pistons that had been woven through her ravaged form.

'The men who built the *Arkangel* said they could rebuild anything in the world. They saved her.'

'But at what cost?' asked Isabella, aghast.

'You would give up your soul if it would save a loved one,' said the Professor, cradling his shattered doll. 'Anyone would. That's what real love means. My poor, poor baby. Run now, little girl, run before I tear your head from your shoulders.'

Isabella rose and fled.

CHAPTER THIRTY-TWO
THE SIGNALMAN

NICHOLAS KNEW AT once that his leg had not cleared the motorcycle. Driverless, it twisted and fell beneath him, catching his left boot, turning his body.

He was not going to make it.

Throwing up his hands to protect his head and bringing up his legs, he fell short, landed and rolled, slamming into a thick clump of bushes. Their stems were soft, though, and covered in springy leaves that cushioned his fall.

He raised his head in time to see the train's crimson lamp swinging away from him. The whistle gave a mournful double hoot.

At least no limbs were broken. Standing, he looked about; dark hills to the North, low forest to the South, no street-lamps or towns. Rain fell softly on his face. Ahead, a single square of light shone from a cabin. He had no choice but to head in its direction.

The narrow, brown wooden hut looked like a signal box, and as he approached he could see a bearded bear of a man moving about inside. When he got close, the man came out with a shotgun held at his chest.

'Easy, friend,' said Nicholas, raising his hands, 'I'm not here to hurt you.'

'English,' said the signalman in surprise, lowering his weapon. 'Well, you've chosen a bad time to visit us. What are you doing out here?'

'I was on the train that just passed through.' Nicholas pointed along the track. 'I jumped from it.'

'Wait, you were on board the *Arkangel*?' He raised the gun again.

'Yes, but I escaped before harm could befall me.'

'You're lying. No-one escapes that train. I've worked on this line for two decades and I see it pass at this time each year, when the August moon is full. I know what it is, and what it does to people.'

'Then you know that every passenger must undertake a wager with the Devil, and the outcome decides his fate.'

'I come from Chelmsk,' said the signalman. 'Of course I know.'

'That is why you speak English.'

'Yes, we had a teacher from England but—'

'He was shot, I know. I'm Nicholas.' He held out his hand.

'And I am Dimitri.'

'I need to get back on board that train.'

'What? Are you insane, man? If you really escaped as you say you did, then you know by now that your very soul was at stake.'

'There is a girl on board. She has not yet been tested, but she will be, and I fear she will fail. I need information.'

'There are things about the *Arkangel* it is best not to know, Nicholas. Not if you value your sanity.'

'Have you ever been on board?'

Dimitri gave a hoarse mirthless laugh. 'I was raised to be afraid of that accursed engine. I have stayed out of its path ever since.'

'Tell me, where does its journey start, and where does it finish?'

'Now, that's an interesting question. It emerges from the line beyond the foundry in Chelmsk, but I know not from which station, or if one even exists. And the journey ends...' He raised his hands and moved them apart. *In thin air.*

'The maps on board are all obscured. What happens?'

'After it passes Zoribskia it goes further down the line beyond this point. The tracks past here branch in several directions, inland and to the coast, and another that passes over a viaduct, but the *Arkangel* takes none of them. One minute it is on the line, and the next it is not. There is something you must understand about the train. It was built in this world but belongs to the next. What you see from outside, and what you see from inside—they do not match.'

'How do you know this?'

'My son was taken, and just before the train disappeared, he too, jumped. But he was not so lucky as you. He spoke to me of the sights he saw, and how his soul would remain on board no matter what happened to his physical body. Moments later, he died in my arms. I buried him beside my signal box, where he had loved to play as a child.'

'I'm sorry.'

'There are many of us who lost children to that monster,' said Dimitri, his voice sharp with bitterness. 'There is no way of fighting it, any more than there is of fighting the Devil himself. Believe me, if there was a way I would have thought of it.'

'Still, I have to try,' Nicholas replied. 'I cannot let Isabella face her fate alone. How far is it before the train vanishes?'

Dimitri pointed behind him. 'Not so many kilometres from here.'

'Then I am lost.'

'The distance is not great, it's true. But the train must slow down as it heads into the forest. It passes this way but once a year, and until it heads off into the netherworld it is subject to our laws of nature. The *Arkangel* is taller than all other trains that pass, and the forest grows thick and deep, so that the topmost branches of the trees catch its carriages. When it reaches the wood it reduces speed, and the stoker must cut away the obstructions.'

'Could I board it there?'

Dimitri glanced at the clock on his wall. 'You would have to be fast. Even now, it approaches the forest.'

'Do you have a vehicle?' Nicholas asked.

'No,' said the signalman, 'but I have a horse.'

'Then I must try.'

'Friend, I do not doubt you but I would not allow a man I have just met to take my horse, even if I was related to him. However, I will take you.' He closed the door and ran down to a tumbledown stable. 'We must go right now if you are to succeed in your mission.'

There was no time to saddle the enormous black stallion that Dimitri released from its stall. He swung his bulk onto the animal's bare back and reached down, pulling Nicholas up as if he was weightless. 'Hold on tight,' he warned. 'Every second we lose bears the train farther from us.'

They set off, reaching a crossroads and cutting over the meadowland that led to the forest.

The stallion galloped hard, but Dimitri thrashed his steed until it cried out in anger. Nicholas clung tightly to the signalman's immense back. 'I can see it through the trees,' he called over his shoulder. 'You must be ready to climb aboard when I shout.'

They cut down into the forest, the branches whipping their faces, the horse's hooves skipping on loose shale. Several times it threatened to unseat Nicholas as it vaulted fallen pine branches and ploughed on through narrow paths cut into the woods. Here, away from the hazy glow of the moon, all they had to guide them was the light of the passing train.

Nicholas could hear the familiar *clackety-clack* sound growing closer now, slowing down like the tick of an unwound clock. For a brief moment, moonlight shone a quicksilver outline around the carriages. 'There is an open deck at the rear of the train where I can board,' called Nicholas. 'If you can get me close, I'll try to jump on.'

'If you make it, I want you to promise me something. You'll

kill the bastard who murdered my son,' shouted Dimitri. 'He's they one they call the Conductor.'

'If I make it, I'll bring you his head,' Nicholas shouted back.

Dimitri kicked his bootheels into the stallion until its sides bled. 'Come on, then.'

CHAPTER THIRTY-THREE
THE SEDUCTION

THOMAS RAN ON through the rocking train, witnessing the trail of sickness and death that lay in the wake of the Red Countess.

So many passengers were dying of the virulent plague, which aged their bones and rotted their skin. They lay collapsed in their own blood, their eyes vanished. The very air grew miasmic and foul, the nightmarish scene sweetly reeking of contagion. It seemed obvious to him now that everyone on the train was dead except for himself and Isabella. There was nothing that could be done to save the others, but he wasn't meant to; perhaps he was seeing them as they really were—how they would be after the train's arrival at its final destination. How they were for every night apart from this one.

Thomas pushed on along the corridors, searching for the woman he needed to confront. *All those years in England, talking to families about facing up to evil and overcoming it,* he thought, *all those empty words when this—this is what I should have been doing, fighting real harm—pestilence, war, corruption, degradation, societies rotting from within, and in my safe little world I could not see the truth, for I was blinded*

from it. I am glad to be tested. If I fail, at least I can say that I faced my demons and found a form of redemption.

He was approaching the private section of the first class carriage. He knew he would find her here. There was a set of four suites, artfully arranged and bedecked with tasseled velvet curtains and banks of cushions, reserved for the most moneyed of travellers. And here, the Red Countess had sunk onto a grand filigreed chaise, distractedly turning her cards on the table set before her, in time with the rocking of the carriage. Joss-sticks burned in the corners, removing the bitter tang of death, filling the compartment with a nauseating sweetness. The light from the sconces flickered across her veiled face.

'You are the cause of this,' Thomas accused, standing in the doorway. 'You cannot deny it.'

The Countess looked up, regarding him through her veil. 'Did I address you? In my world, the Countess speaks first.'

'But you are not in your world.'

'Oh, come in,' she beckoned. 'I don't usually talk to commoners, but I suppose as a man of the cloth you are at least partially exempt from human experience.'

'You cannot frighten me,' he said, 'but you must be stopped.'

'Please sit down and spare yourself any further embarrassment. I can see you quaking in your shoes. Look, your hands are all a-tremble. There's no need to be afraid. I knew you would return. Men always return.'

'There are terrible things happening, a great evil at work, and I know you are the cause.'

'In this world sickness is terrible but unavoidable. Do you think me evil too, or just the disease?'

'I... don't know.'

'You can't help the sick. You're a man of God and cannot forget the world, but you must also know that you cannot change it. Sit for a moment and take a glass of tokay with me.'

The Red Countess was casting a spell on him, confusing him. A card, the Queen of Spades, lay beside her glass. She took a

sip of the amber wine from her crystal cup and poured a second glass, sliding it toward him. Was it tainted with contagion? Thomas stared at it.

'Go ahead. Take a sip.'

Thomas felt himself falling under her compelling influence. Despite the sickly horrors aboard the train, the atmosphere in the salon was mysterious and intoxicating, unlike anything in his life, and like everything dark from his dreams.

His hand moved toward the glass. She raised her own to her lips once more.

'Let's drink to passion, and leave the terrors of disease outside, safe within our own boundaries. Be honest. Isn't that why you joined the church?'

'I joined to do good, but somehow I got lost.' He watched as her ruby lips touched the rim of the glass, branding it.

'No more faith, then? Drink with me. It is so much easier just to drink.'

He knew that this was a part of his wager, and was determined to be unafraid. Raising the glass to his lips, he took a sip. The liquor was no ordinary tokay. It was stronger than wine, with the sweet scent of Manzanilla but the bite of Eau De Vie. It filled his throat with fire.

'That's better. Now come closer, sit beside me.' She patted the seat as if encouraging a dog. Drawn to her, Thomas came to her side. She was more intoxicating than the drink, and knew it.

'Closer.' She leaned toward him. He glimpsed her kohl-rimmed eyes glinting behind the veil and reached out to her. It was suddenly very important to discover who she really was. To get to the heart of her secret. Everyone on board had one.

His fingers touched the hem of the veil, slowly lifting it. He tried to prepare himself for what he might discover underneath.

'Closer still,' she whispered. He could feel the coolness of her body next to his. She actually seemed to be lowering the temperature in the cabin, annealing the lividity of illness, spreading a deathly calm.

His fingers raised the veil. He tried not to flinch. Age, plague, a soul in torment—he was prepared for all—but not for what he found.

A stunningly beautiful woman in her early twenties. Long dark lashes, pale high cheeks, seashell lips, perfection in stasis.

'But… you're beautiful.'

Her eyes were downcast now, and sad. 'Once I fled my country aboard this very train…'

He closed his eyes and allowed her words to enter his head.

We are all being told stories tonight, he thought, *a veritable cascade of them, but which of the tales are real, and which are intended to lead us into betrayals?*

He closed his eyes and listened to her sugared words. As she spoke, the images appeared in his head. He saw a sumptuous Russian *fin de siècle* ballroom swathed in French red velvet, a scuffed parquet floor, an orchestra in evening dress, couples dancing, sputtering candelabras, falling snow outside. An onion-domed building finished in white wood and topped with gilt, a graceful *dacha* far removed from the peasant rabble in the city streets.

He saw the Countess surrounded by handsome young men in starched white shirts and tail-coats. One, waiting at the back behind her suitors, was a plain country priest, not unlike himself, sunburned, wrongly dressed, out of place. Two of the other men were secretly mocking him.

'A man of God. So young, so desperately in love with me. Why, he might have once been you.' The Red Countess sighed. 'So many suitors. I thought it sport to make them want me. My compatriots were dying in the revolution and I cared only for my pleasures. The arrogance of wealth and youth and beauty. I still ask myself why I chose the little priest.'

Thomas watched as the eager young man rushed forward to kiss her hand. He failed to see that his fellow suitors were making mock of him.

'I suppose I made love to him for the novelty. The others were

all of my social class, all so readily available, all so filled with a sense of entitlement. To the priest, my mere presence was a privilege. I liked that. So would any woman. But of course, I was no ordinary woman.'

He saw her bedroom in the *dacha*, the Red Countess stretched out, pale and naked and languorous in her boudoir as the priest made fervent, clumsy love to her. He heard the apologies, saw the fluttering hands, the awkward thrusting, the fading novelty, the familiar returning *ennui*.

He heard the Countess sigh as she drew her robes about her voluptuous breasts and rose from her bed, drifting from the bedchamber without a single glance back.

He saw the priest's carefully crafted missives returned, ignored, left unanswered, the pages torn, the ink rainwashed in the gutters of St Petersburg.

'To those who are spurned,' said the Red Countess, 'love is as serious as death.'

It was an absurd sight—the little Bolshevik priest, returning to the court, waiting in cold anterooms before supercilious servants, lurking outside her summerhouse. Those whom the Red Countess rejected were never able to forgive her, but those she had taken and then discarded were never able to forgive themselves.

At first it was sport to make him wait, but she grew tired of his persistence. Displays of emotion were vulgar and commonplace. He sent bunches of garish flowers and bottles of mediocre wine he could ill afford. When he burst into a dancehall where her admirers were toasting her with pyramids of champagne glasses, the young men fought him and the glasses smashed, and he was thrown out into the snow.

Anxious to ensure that the priest would make no further scenes, she had a letter hand-delivered. Her words were carefully chosen to be cruel, and were not kindly received. In despair, the priest threw her farewell note onto the floor and stamped it black. Thomas caught words as they fluttered past his vision.

Caprice—foolishness—embarrass—forbid.

The priest returned to his tiny town apartment and climbed onto a chair with a length of rope in his hand. He painstakingly looped it around a large iron pipe set in the ceiling.

He said a prayer, one of the shortest he had committed to memory, and kicked the chair away.

But the pipe could not hold him. As the rope tore into his throat and his body began to thrash in death, it bent and broke beneath his shifting weight.

Thomas followed the pipe down in his mind's eye. It was connected from the toilets above to the drains below, but now it was fractured. Filthy sewage flooded out over the priest's convulsing body.

In his mind's eye, Thomas followed the spill of effluent. He watched as it poured down through the floor to the drains and the tanks and the fountains below, into the city's drinking supply. He saw the Countess's fine suitors in their town apartments, watched as they drank deep and sickened, the disease spreading out across St Petersburg like a water-stain.

The bloody sewage overflowed from the fountains, flooding off into the run-offs and the canals, flooding down toward the station, to the platform, dripping into the gutters.

He saw the train filling its water supply from the polluted tank. The murky poison burst into clean water like a storm-devil, tainting with its touch. The water dripped from the tank to the pipe to the open window of the carriage, where a single germ-filled drop, carried by a sudden gust, fell into the Countess's luncheon glass.

Flirtatiously smiling at her new beau, an army corporal with cold eyes and luxuriant moustaches, the Red Countess raised her glass and drank from it. As she collapsed, her crimson silks swirled about her like mist.

'But you lived,' said Thomas. *Perhaps*, he thought, *something of the doomed priest's spirit entered you. Perhaps that alone was enough to save you.*

'Would I look like this if I had died? See how I am.' The Red Countess lay back, her crimson robes unfolding to reveal her flawless bare body. Thomas had never seen flesh so alabaster. His glass slid from his hand and cracked on the floor.

She reached forward and pressed her lips on his, unfurled her hot tongue into his mouth. His hands cupped her breasts. She loosened his shirt. Her crimson nails cut his chest, his back. His breeches came open, her thighs parted. The Red Countess released a tiny sigh of pleasure as her robes rode up about them both.

The train roared and rocked. The candles guttered. The joss-sticks wreathed them in dusky scent. Thomas was in the throes of an exquisite passion. It went without saying that this was quite unlike anything he had ever experienced with his wife in Henley-upon-Thames. As he climaxed, he saw that the Red Countess had shut her eyes in ecstatic satisfaction. It thrilled him to know that he had pleased her.

Spent, he pushed back and looked down at her body.

He had been penetrating an ancient, skeletal woman with rancid skin, straggly grey hair, veined grey dugs and claw-like liver-spotted hands. Her grip was not borne of amour but rigor. Opening her snaggle-toothed mouth, she sucked at his tongue and bit.

Thomas screamed in horror and tried to pull away.

Her nails tore bloody strips from his back. Disgusted, he broke free and tumbled into a corner, trying to cover his shrivelled manhood, to wipe the reek of rot from his mouth. Shaking violently, one thought reverberated in his brain. *I've lost, I've lost, I've lost.*

CHAPTER THIRTY-FOUR
THE SIREN

But we must look elsewhere aboard the *Arkangel*, for at this moment another drama was unfolding.

Isabella had located the Conductor at the entrance to the last carriage, staring in the direction of the open deck. Following his gaze, she was amazed to see Nicholas climbing from the back of a galloping black horse to the platform. A huge bearded man was pushing him from behind, making sure that he could grip the guard-rail before taking off.

She ran forward and grabbed him, pulling until he had safely fallen to the deck. 'You came back,' she cried, embracing him so tightly that he could not breathe.

The Conductor watched in amazement. No-one had ever tried to come back on board the *Arkangel* before. For a moment all sense of protocol left him.

'Are you all right?' Nicholas asked Isabella.

'I am alive. And you?'

'I still have my soul. Where is Thomas?'

'He is with the Red Countess, and I fear he may have succumbed.'

'Then let's find him. Perhaps it is not too late to save him.'

'Wait.' The Conductor stood in their way. 'This time, I cannot

let you come to the vicar's aid as you did before, freeing him from the coffin.'

'Why not?'

'I let you help because it was not his time, but his wife's. Now he must face his demons alone, as you must eventually.'

'Please,' she pleaded, 'he's done nothing wrong. I was the one who fled the town. Thomas and his wife were innocents.'

'He boarded the *Arkangel* of his own volition,' the Conductor reminded her. 'He could have stood his grounds and faced the soldiers at the station.'

'But he is a man of God, he would not have fought—'

'That is no concern of mine. We must see if he has the mettle to survive. Wait and watch. And remember, I'm saving you for last. As for you, deserter.' He turned to Nicholas with a sour face. 'You are either very brave or even more stupid than I had imagined. You had your chance to escape, and here you are, returned.'

'Whatever befalls Isabella must be my fate, also,' he said, taking her hand. Seeing her again had cemented his feelings. They would not be parted so easily next time.

'I see you do not understand,' said the Conductor. 'You have boarded the train. You know the rules. You must undergo a trial. Every living soul who boards the train must take the test.'

'But I passed—'

'That was not the train's doing. It was caused by your own circumstances. The challenges are set by the *Arkangel*, not by its passengers. Your platoon died in the trenches after you left them, but some of them boarded the *Arkangel* by chance.'

'Then you are not infallible. There are forces at work here which are beyond your control.'

'The *Arkangel* was designed to remove human imperfections from the war between good and evil,' said the Conductor indignantly. 'Any errors that occur are always caused by outside forces. The behaviour of the passengers is not so easily predicted.'

'You think evil will triumph by removing humanity's interference?'

'I am no fool. Perhaps this war will never be decisively won, for each side is required to act in fairness to the other. But we can make sure that the pious and the doubtful are never able to destroy our empire.'

Reaching out his tapered pale hands, he pushed the lovers apart. 'Enough now. You,' he pointed to Isabella, 'go forward. And you.' He pushed Nicholas down into a seat. 'You must stay here and prepare yourself. Your time is close.'

In the Red Countess's suite Thomas pushed himself back against the wall as his seducer's raddled face loomed closer.

'So you see,' said the Red Countess, 'I died aboard the train, and so I was reborn in living death. Doomed to travel on the *Arkangel* for all time, carrying disease in my touch.'

She had edged very close to Thomas. The Red Countess was like a scorpion, unable to prevent herself from striking. 'When beauty is tainted with cruelty it becomes a curse,' she explained. 'I was very beautiful, and very cruel.'

They were almost touching now. Thomas was mesmerized and horrified. He looked down at the backs of his hands, expecting to see the skin break out in pustules.

'I don't understand. I am untouched.'

'But you lost.' The Red Countess smiled sadly.

'What does that mean?'

'You know the cost already. You are dead and damned. You will join us on the train. I will keep you young and make love to you each night. Until I tire of you. My demon lover.'

'Never—I'd rather...'

'What? Kill yourself?' The Red Countess's girlish laughter turned into the wheezing cackle of an old woman. 'And how will you do that, exactly?'

'Damn you.' Fighting his way out of the suite, Thomas staggered into the corridor.

The Red Countess rose and followed. She seemed to move

without walking. As she came for him, she stopped before a compartment that held a sleeping farmhand and reached in, sucking the youth and vitality from him for the fun of it, strengthening herself. The absorption of such innocence restored her so that she became more beautiful with each passing second. Youth and sensuality was returned. She seemed to glow within the gloom of the corridor, lighting it with her presence.

Thomas had reached a deserted section in the first of the second class carriages. Leaning against the wall he stopped to look back, but his eternal suitor was suddenly nowhere in sight.

He was disgusted with himself. He had felt ashamed after visiting the whores of Rotterdam on an ecumenical trip, but this was far worse. Tearing off his shirt, he went to a window and pushed it down, allowing the cleansing rain to splash in on his chest. He watched the storm-lashed forest hurtling by. The train was stifling, unholy, claustrophobic. Every passenger had their own grotesque tale of failure and demise to tell, and each one seemed to lead to another ghastly cascade of events. He leaned out of the carriage to feel the raindrops on his face.

As he raised his eyes, he sensed the Red Countess hovering overhead, on the roof of the carriage, her scarlet silks billowing. She roared down toward him, an avenging scarlet siren. She was outside the train, looking in at him, not subject to the laws of gravity.

'I am not finished with you yet,' she yelled. 'You are not permitted to decide the outcome of your test.'

'This is witchcraft!' he screamed. 'How did I ever stand a chance against you?'

'You men of the cloth have such vanity,' she hissed in his ear. Reaching in, she seized him by his shoulders and pulled him upwards, clean out of the carriage and up onto the rain-slick roof.

'Get away from me, you godless whore!'

'Oh, it's always God when it suits you, isn't it? I'll show you what I really am.'

As the storm-wind hammered at them and the branches of

trees slashed past, her wizened face began to blacken and rot away, strips of her flesh flying off into the night, melting to putrescence until her teeth and her skull shone in the darkness like ivory.

She came at him in all her wild anger, thrusting her rotting hands around his throat, but Thomas was determined not to go down without a fight. His foot found purchase on the train's steel trim and he fought himself upright as she bore down on him, slicing at his face, knocking him back.

He kicked out at her. He had never hurt a woman physically, but the Countess had not been a woman for a very long time. He crawled along the juddering roof as she clawed her way toward him, her nails shrieking on the metal.

The Red Countess stalked Thomas. Even in her half-flayed form, she remained a regal spectre. She stood tall and magnificent, her red silks flashing about her in the maelstrom of rain and steam.

Coiling, she sprung upon her victim.

As the *Arkangel* raced downhill toward its final destination, the pair fought on the roof of the rushing train, the Red Countess trying to force Thomas over the edge. The rocky slopes flashed by in scalding steam-filled blasts.

Thomas grabbed at her face only to find that the remains came away in his hands like a fleshy dish-cloth, oozing between his fingers, leaving behind a rotten shell.

The Red Countess elegantly stepped out of her silks and her skin as though disrobing before a lover, and became a ragged skeleton, leaving her mortal flesh behind. Her bony arm extended to seize Thomas by the throat. Her leathery tongue thrashed lasciviously about in her skull—reaching forward, she thrust it into Thomas's mouth, to remind him of his eternal nightly duty.

Just let me die, anything other than this, thought Thomas. The Red Countess had her eyes closed in ecstasy.

She had not seen that the train was approaching a tunnel.

She embraced her new lover, crushing the life from him, and he held her tight to prevent her from seeing. *Wait,* he told himself, *wait.*

At the last possible moment, Thomas shoved her away as the wall of the tunnel approached.

She hit the brick surround and was smashed to smithereens like tinder sticks thrown at a wall, to be dispatched beneath the thundering wheels of the *Arkangel* like so much ghostly offal. Only the train could take her life again.

Exhausted, Thomas dropped hard to the roof and slid, lowering himself back through the window, crashing onto the floor of the carriage. A tumbling card—the Queen of Spades—settled on him, all that remained of the Red Countess.

He felt the floor beneath his body rocking him back and forth. In retrospect, he supposed, the test had been too easy.

After a few minutes, he climbed to his feet and made his way back to try and find Isabella. He found her heading towards him along the corridor.

'I won!' he cried excitedly, not entirely believing it himself. 'I thought I had failed but I defeated her!'

Isabella ran to him and held him tight, grateful to see that he had made it through the ordeal alive. And yet he looked wrong somehow.

'Are you well?' she asked, pulling away to study his face, trying to avoid the reek that emanated from him.

Thomas glared back, shaking his soaked head. 'I am well, but that woman... like all of her kind,' he spat. 'How they deceive us.'

'Thomas, Nicholas is back on board and must undergo an ordeal set by the train. We are approaching the last stop. There must be something we can do. If only we could halt the engine.'

He stared strangely at her. There was a feral glint in his eye. 'Why should I trust you? Miranda dead, then Nicholas disappears. How do I know you're not lying? And as for that bitch...'

'Thomas, you know she was sent to test you.'

He ignored her. 'Bitches. How I hate them. I've always hated

them. They're all the same. It's always the women. Behind every despot, every tyrant, every politician, every embezzler, every censor, there's a woman pushing and pushing and pushing. And *you*. It all began with you. This is all your fault.'

'No, I had to leave the town, Nicholas said he could take me away—'

To her horror, she could see his true character. *The woman hater. The seducer. The cheat. And if I can see it, so can the Arkangel...*

When he came at her she thought she would be ready to fight him off, but he was stronger than she imagined. Gripping her tightly by the shoulder, Thomas's free hand closed around her throat.

Her fingernails caught his lip and tore it clean off his jaw, like ancient meat. Before her horrified eyes, the flesh rippled with putrefaction and fell away from his face, riddled with fat white maggots. His nose fell off. One of his eyes dropped onto his bony cheek. He did not seem to understand what was happening. His ears slid down his head. His skull gleamed through rank flesh like a caramel apple. Still he would not let go.

Screaming, she tried to push herself free of his arms, but they stayed locked around her, even though they no longer seemed to be attached to his body. Thomas's remaining eye rolled in and he dropped, crumbling into stinking carrion.

Isabella found herself holding the only part of him that had remained intact—his beating, bloody heart.

CHAPTER THIRTY-FIVE
THE CAST

SHANE CARTER TURNED the card over in his pocket. The Queen of Spades. A good luck charm for the Hammer meeting.

The rain battered the leadlight windows of Bray's oak-panelled dining hall. He heard creaking trees, the pop and hiss of radiators, someone laughing softly in the hall. He could smell luncheon cooking, the comforting aroma of puddings and pies.

He'd thought it would feel like being summoned to court, but he had been the first to arrive, and instead it felt as if he had called them. If he had been English, he would have been embarrassed about that, but he had an excuse; he was a foreign interloper. Last night after finishing his pages he had tried watching English 'telly.' He had found himself faced with two channels that largely consisted of windmills, puppets and pottery wheels, interspersed with elderly men smoking pipes while they discussed Harold Macmillan in Old Etonian accents. It was a world apart, and made very little sense to outsiders.

Floral teacups had been laid out for half a dozen, chairs assigned, as if this was a daily ritual. There were footsteps in the corridor.

First through the door was Michael—impossible to think of him now as Mr Carreras—shadowed by Emma, who was

looking more radiant with each passing day. A conceited part of him thought that her wellbeing might have something to do with his own sexual prowess.

Then there were two familiar faces, though for once not painted with light upon a giant screen; Thorley Walters, taller than expected, rotund and merry-faced, Santa in autumn. And Frances Matthews, slender, debonair, in a silky grey suit and cufflinks, every bit the monochrome hero, friendly and sensible.

Freddie Francis had come along, relaxed, chatty, hands in pockets. Technically speaking, he was still working with Amicus, having scored a hit for them with *Dr Terror*, but there seemed to be no bad blood between the two studios. Shane had heard that he still preferred the atmosphere at Hammer. Although the Amicus head, Milton Subotsky, shared the same cinematic ideals of mood and atmosphere that fascinated Francis, Subotsky was famously antagonistic and hard to work with. Amicus was a production house, not a studio, although it poached stars from Hammer and liked to think of itself as equal. But everyone knew that Amicus was the pretender, making lofty artistic promises before always returning to the bottom line of the budget sheet.

Shane rose and shook hands with everyone, feeling increasingly nervous as the group was joined by two more figures who arrived together, an ill-matched duo lost in quiet conversation. Peter Cushing was in his fifties, gaunt and small-boned, but the litheness of his movements suggested surprising youth and fitness. Christopher Lee seemed even taller and grander than he had expected. It was rumoured that Lee was the son of an Italian Countess, that he had aristocratic passions that included fencing and languages, but on screen he often seemed cold and aloof. Did he ever smile with his eyes?

Perhaps that was the secret of his friendship with Cushing. Everybody loved Peter; his warmth and authority lifted the dullest scripts. It made Shane wonder how successful Hammer would have been without the pair of them.

Christopher Lee gravely shook his hand. Peter Cushing smiled at him with great, watery blue eyes. He felt embarrassed by their deference, and nervously fingered the script pages on the table. Emma had sat with him typing until 2:00am, but the last section was still unfinished.

'Have some tea,' said Carreras. 'It's single estate, high-grown Ceylon. Thought we might break out the good stuff for a change.'

Tea was poured. Cake appeared. Everyone relaxed into their chairs. He realized that Carreras was waiting for him to begin. Shane cleared his throat.

'I'm aware that Mr Cushing told the press he always wanted to make a film set on a train. And when—Michael—suggested I should write something with the same location, it chimed with my own ideas to develop such a project. I've always felt there was a theme at work in the Dracula films, the eternal battle to keep the Devil held at bay. I'm proposing we explore that idea in more detail. I see the train as a great repository of fates and fables, like Chinese boxes. That sounds kind of grand, I know. Let me see if I can simplify it.'

His confidence grew as he outlined the script. The assembly remained silent, only interrupting to concur or add a comment. He couldn't imagine such a meeting happening like this in Hollywood. The executives would have been making power plays by now, cutting each other's hearts out.

Lee steepled his long fingers, listening gravely and intently. When Cushing wanted to speak he merely sat forward slightly, and everyone turned to him. 'I wondered—have you any preference about the roles you'd like us to play?' He elegantly rolled his Rs. His language was clearer than glass, so that he never needed to raise his voice.

'Well, I hadn't really—'

'Only I rather think I'm a little long in the tooth to play your vicar, although I'm sure Christopher could manage the deserter, Nicholas. Would I not be better suited to play the Brigadier?'

'I daresay he has me earmarked for the Conductor,' said Lee,

'an agent of evil.' He gave a deep mirthless laugh. Everyone else laughed, just in case they were turned to stone.

'Certainly that was what I had in mind,' said Shane.

'Veronica Carlson would be good for Isabella,' said Freddie Francis. 'And Barbara Shelley for Miranda?'

Was this really how films got made in this country? It seemed an extraordinary way to hold a script session. They were already talking about casting without having read a word he'd written. Surely there was a point where the politeness ended?

'It occurs to me that you could have some doubling up,' said Carreras. 'Roy Ashton's brilliant at changing people's appearances, and it might stretch the team a bit to have them playing more than one role.'

'Interesting metaphysical idea,' said Francis, 'as if the tests were being played over and over with the same protagonists.'

'Does that mean we get paid twice over?' asked Thorley Walters. Everybody laughed. *No.*

'WELL, I THOUGHT that went rather well,' said Emma, hanging back after the others had left the lounge.

'I still can't believe it,' said Shane. 'I'm pouring sweat. My hands were shaking.'

'I don't know why. They seemed to think your ideas were very sound. We have some lovely young writers in here sometimes, very earnest, utterly clueless. Michael listens to all of them. He still wants the finished script tomorrow morning, you know. They're all heading off before lunchtime.'

'Then I have to write another role for Peter Cushing,' said Shane. 'This is too great an opportunity to miss. Are you free later?'

'I'm typing up scripts until around seven. More rewrites on *The Mummy's Shroud,* not that I imagine they'll save it. I could meet you back at the pub.'

'It's a deal. It's cold in my room, though, and I keep finding dead beetles around the bed.'

'It's the time of year. Perhaps we could set up in the snug and work there.'

'Emma...'

'Yes?'

'If this doesn't fly, if they turn it down, I'll have no reason to stay. I don't know where that leaves us.'

She smiled back at him. 'Look, there's a window of opportunity. We have a cast. We need a script. If it doesn't work out, don't worry. It just means that I'll never see you again.'

He watched her swing her handbag onto her shoulder and head for the door. She didn't seem to have a care on the world. This was her home. She fitted in perfectly, like Isabella in her family's town. If he failed to deliver, or was turned down, she'd no doubt express disappointment or even regret, but he knew she wouldn't wait around for him. Writers were ten a penny. Despite the warm welcome he had been given, he felt sure that someone else could be brought here on Monday to deliver another script, and the same process would begin all over again. The smiles. The tea. The kindly persuasion. The endless politeness.

There were no more chances left for him. LA was a bust. He had burned his bridges there, and there was no other work on the horizon.

It was tomorrow or nothing.

He had an advantage. He was a storyteller. He could do that anywhere, write about pretty much anything if he had the research to hand, and if he gave this his best shot, who knew what the future might hold? Because the next piece of work was always the one that held the key to his fate. And the British seemed more honest. In LA he'd felt more like the victim in one of his own horror films, bled dry by sinister creatures who were only after his life force.

He returned to the inn and set to work once more.

CHAPTER THIRTY-SIX
THE SPECIMEN

ISABELLA LOOKED DOWN again, but now there was no beating heart in her hands.

Has she been hallucinating? She thought back, trying to understand what was real and what was false, sifting the events out from each other.

When Miranda had been tested, Thomas had been locked in the coffin. She had seen Nicholas face his demons, but those had turned out to be real. The soldiers who arrested him were still sitting further along the carriage. All of them had seen the Red Countess board the train, and the dying victims had been played by damned passengers. The *Arkangel* was enlisting its performers as they were needed from the stations through which it passed. All of them were puppets commanded to appear, being called into service to allow the Devil his day. That was why the Conductor had performed a rigorous selection process at each of the stops.

It meant that the dice were loaded against any of the living surviving their tests.

'If Nicholas fails, I will be the only one left alive,' she said aloud as the full horror of the thought hit her. *The only one left on a train filled with the soulless dead.*

Exhausted and fearful, she entered the nearest compartment and dropped heavily into a seat, to find that she was not alone. Sitting opposite her was an elderly man in cream-coloured tropical clothes. His myopic, watery blue eyes peered out from a kindly face at her, eager to engage. She had seen him boarding the train at Snerinska. Above him on the luggage rack were a set of leather suitcases, a butterfly net and a steel box with straps.

He looked harmless enough, but she knew better now than to trust anyone.

'Dear me,' said the old gentleman, 'are you quite all right?'

'I'm sorry—it's just, well, it has been an eventful journey.' She made an attempt to tidy her hair while covertly studying him. He had looked like any other passenger when he boarded, but then so had the murderous Professor Io. Had he been a part of her test? Real or imagined? Dead or alive? *How could you tell?*

Perhaps the damned weren't all under the control of the Conductor. She felt that Professor Io had acted out of grief, and, being a wily showman, could not easily be kept in his place. Besides, if he had been her test, what flaw of her nature had he been trying to expose? She had to be on her guard. She could still be in danger.

'Can you tell me, what is the name of the next stop?'

'I'm afraid I don't know,' said Isabella.

'I've been on so many trains in the last few days, I'm really feeling rather too exhausted to care. But I imagine it goes to the border. What is our final destination?'

'It's been removed from all the maps.'

'Ah, the war, I suppose. They're being careful about security.' He reached forward and offered his hand. 'Dr. Arthur Freely. I'm not supposed to be on this train.'

'No, none of us are.'

'And whom do I have the pleasure of addressing?' His kind eyes twinkled at her.

'I am Isabella.'

'Well, Isabella, what is a nice young lady like you doing by

yourself on a train in the dead of night, not knowing where she goes?'

'I was travelling with an Englishman, but he fell from the train.'

'Good lord! Do you suppose he's all right? Are *you* all right?'

'I don't know. Everything has been...' She stopped herself, wary of giving out too much information. He looked like an elderly angel, but for all she knew, he might be a lizard, a vampire or the Devil himself.

'Forgive my questions, you must think I'm terribly rude. An unchaperoned young lady travelling alone, please allow me to set your mind at ease. I'm on my way back from the Far East,' he explained. 'Burma, actually. I missed my connection. The war, everything's upside down. A dreadful crossing, missed trains, and then this one appearing out of the blue. It's not on any schedule, did you know that? The porter was unable to give me any information. Rather a rude fellow, I thought.'

'It is all very mysterious,' Isabella cautiously agreed.

'But that's the war for you. I was lucky to get this far, really.' Above him, the steel box shook suddenly and its straps rattled. Dr Freely looked up in concern. 'I've been collecting specimens for the Royal Gardens in London. They sent me to Burma in search of entomological anomalies. Made quite a find up there. But I don't think it's very happy being taken from its home territory and jostled around.' He pointed to the luggage rack.

Isabella was amazed to be having such an absurdly sensible conversation. She was still thinking of Thomas's bloody heart in her hands. 'I'm sorry,' she said, 'what do you mean?'

He pointed to the box. It was buzzing violently. 'It will make my reputation. An entirely unknown species, smuggled out of the densest part of the jungle.'

The train seemed to be speeding up. Isabella looked at the darkened windows. 'I think our destination...' she began. 'We really have to find a way off the train.'

'I agree. There was a terrible commotion in the corridors

earlier. Some rowdy soldiers, a lot of shouting. I heard some awful singing that sounded like shrieking cats. Then it sounded like someone was running along the roof. What was going on out there?'

'Evil, sir,' she replied. 'A powerful evil.'

'Then perhaps we're safer staying in here. It is the way of the world at the moment. Everything is in upheaval, and I'm afraid it will only serve to make us mistrustful of our fellow men.'

She looked at him uncertainly. He seemed to divine her thoughts. 'But of course, how thoughtless of me once again. A stranger on a train, whatever must you think. I left my spouse behind in Mandalay. Here. A pretty little thing.' He showed Isabella a cracked sepia photograph of his wife. *Pretty* was hardly the first adjective that jumped into Isabella's mind. Dr Freely's wife had a face that could send a dog under a table. 'I must get back to England. I don't know how long I can keep it alive, you see.'

'I don't understand.'

'My specimen. *Coleoptera Freely*. Well, I haven't sorted out the proper Latin name for it yet, so I have taken the liberty of appending it myself.' Above them, the box shook and threatened to fall. 'I wonder if it's unhappy about being kept in the dark? Would you like to see?'

'I don't—'

Before she could protest further, Mr Freely rose and took down the box. He hesitated to open the lid. 'A word of warning. Don't get too close. It seems to get over-excited by females of the species.'

He carefully loosened the leather straps and opened the lid of the box. Inside was a wooden cage, which he gingerly raised. Hardly daring to look, Isabella peered between the bars.

Inside was a fist-sized, boring-looking green and black beetle clutching the end of a twig. Relieved and glad of the distraction, she turned her attention to the insect and moved closer for a better look.

The insect suddenly split its carapace, revealing large iridescent emerald wings. Then it opened its mouth—a mess of whirling, spinning thorn-like claws. It made a rapid clicking noise like fingers being fed into a rotary fan. Isabella jumped back.

'And it's hungry all the time,' said Mr Freely.

'What is it?' Isabella asked.

'Do you know, I haven't the faintest idea. It was living in a Fever Tree. *Acacia Xanthophloea*. I made the cage from its bark. Apparently that's the only thing that will hold it.' He put the cage back in its box. 'I say, you really don't look at all well. Can I get you something?'

Isabella felt faint. Every time she closed her eyes, she saw blood. The compartment was overheated, and the events of the evening had exhausted her. It was almost midnight. 'Thank you. Some water, perhaps.'

Mr Freely rose and left the compartment, happy to help.

The insect was still buzzing in its cage. Isabella eyed the box with suspicion. The insect could scent her. It was hammering at the tree-bark cage, trying to get a grip on the bars with its mandibles.

She felt her curiosity gaining a foothold and tried to fight it, but the beetle was making the most extraordinarily odd noises.

Isabella took a closer look. It gleamed darkly in the foliage, rather beautiful. The wings were retracted now, so that it hung by its hooked mandibles from a twig, gleaming like a Faberge egg made of black enamel.

Leaning over the lid of the cage, her crucifix dangled between the bars. When she raised her head, she found herself stuck. The cross was caught.

She tried to free it, but the crossbar of the crucifix was too wide. A wooden pin held the cage lid shut. Keeping one hand firmly on the lid, she carefully removed the pin. The beetle had dropped back into its foliage and was motionless once more. She opened the lid a crack and freed the cross.

Outside, the wheels of the train screeched, making her start.

Turning her attention back to the cage, she quickly closed the lid and sat down.

But now the cage was silent. It had stopped rattling.

What if Dr Freely's prize specimen had become over-excited and had expired?

She peered into the box, trying to see down through the lid of the cage. It was no good, she couldn't discern any movement. Lifting the handle, she raised the cage from its box and tried to see inside. Where the beetle had sat was now just a flattened patch of leafage. There was nowhere for it to hide. The cage was empty.

In the few seconds that the lid had been opened, she had let the bug out.

Surely that wasn't possible? She removed the peg once more and checked inside the cage. Could it have escaped in the brief moment that the train had braked and gained her attention?

She looked around the compartment but could not see it anywhere.

She searched in the luggage racks. She dropped to her knees and checked under the seats. Was this the test? To make sure that someone's prized specimen did not escape? Was Mr Freely even part of this, or just a harmless, confused old explorer? She peered into the darkness beneath the cushions.

The bug flew right at her. The noise it made was astonishing. The sound seemed to vibrate inside her bones. Its iridescent wings were a dark blur. They were beating a hundred times a second, propelling it with immense force. She threw herself onto the floor, out of its path. It tore the air above her head, ruffling her hair.

The insect bored straight through the seat and the wall opposite in a shower of horsehair and wood splinters. She rose and stared through the hole. It had gone through into the next carriage.

She looked up. Mr Freely was standing in the door with a glass of water in his hand, astonished.

CHAPTER THIRTY-SEVEN
THE BOY

NICHOLAS SAT IN the open carriage to await his challenge. He could not allow his eye to stay from the door. He had no idea what to expect. He was shivering and wet, but alive and close once more to the woman he was now sure he loved. He would survive for her sake.

A small, thin figure appeared in the doorway, too dark to make out, and yet there was a familiarity about it. Reaching out an arm to steady itself against the wall, it made its way toward him.

It was a boy of seven or eight years, with protruding ears and black hair fringed over his eyebrows in a pudding-basin cut. Thin, pale legs emerged from short blue flannel trousers. He wore a ragged woollen vest and a blue jacket several sizes too large. His brown sandals were torn and scuffed.

'Can I sit here?' he asked in French-tinged English, studying Nicholas with large dark eyes. He looked as if he was recovering from a serious illness, and had yet to find his sea-legs.

Nicholas moved over, eyeing the boy warily. 'Who are you?' he asked.

'My name is Jean-Guy,' the boy replied. 'Where am I?'

'You don't know?'

'No. I was sitting on the bay looking out at the ships, and

then—' He looked about, frightened.

'You were summoned,' Nicholas explained. 'I cannot tell you more.'

'When can I go home?'

'When you have fulfilled your task, I imagine.'

'I cannot stay long. Mama will be angry with me. She is at home, making *bouillabaisse* for supper. I promised to help.'

Nicholas had a sudden bad feeling about where the seemingly innocent conversation was heading. 'Where do you live, Jean-Guy?' he asked.

'In Nice with my mother.'

'Do you have no father?'

'My mother says my father died before I was born.'

'What is your mother's name?

'Marie-Helene.'

At that moment, Nicholas knew he was sitting with his son. He reached forward and hugged the boy. There was nothing of him; he was undernourished and sickly. He wondered what on earth he could say that would not hurt the child, and decided to keep his counsel. Jean-Guy had been summoned to test him. The question was how?

'Do you have anything for me?' Nicholas asked, releasing him.

Jean-Guy thought for a minute. 'Yes, I believe I do.' He felt inside his vest and pulled out an oilskin packet. He seemed surprised to find it there. Nicholas accepted the packet and carefully unfolded it. Inside was a knife with a chased silver blade. He had won the knife in a game of poker at the casino in Nice, taking it from an Arab who had accused him of cheating. Before they had fallen out, the Arab had explained that the *Kusha* was meant to be carried in a special compartment attached at the side of his belt. Its double-sided blade was heavy, downward-curving and engraved in geometrical lines, with a filigreed silver grip.

'It's very beautiful,' said the boy, reaching out to touch it.

'No,' said Nicholas, pulling the knife back. 'It's very sharp. It has killed many men.' He remembered the stories the Arab had told him about the blade. 'Why have you brought it with you?'

The boy's brow furrowed. His countenance was so melancholy that he almost moved Nicholas to tears. 'I think you have to kill me with it,' he said.

'I don't understand.'

'That's what the man said. I'm to give you a message. The message is this: you have a choice. Kill the son you abandoned, or kill yourself. That's all he said.'

So this is the nature of my test, thought Nicholas bitterly. *I'm to trade my life for the life of the son I walked away from when I was but eighteen years old. How can I choose? The lad means nothing to me. And yet—*

He looked back at the shaking boy, sitting with his thin arms wrapped around him, and drew him close. 'Don't be frightened, lad,' he said. 'I won't harm you.'

But the choice needed to be made. 'How long do I have to decide?' he asked.

'You must make your decision before we have sat together longer than five minutes, or we are both lost,' said Jean-Guy tonelessly.

There had to be a way out, but the test seemed to present an impossible paradox. If he made what he suspected was the righteous choice and saved the boy's life, he would die, stranding Isabella alone. But if he chose the selfish path, he would surely fail the test and lose his soul. The boy wiped snot from his cold nose and stared at him with huge sad eyes.

'Tell me something of your mother,' said Nicholas, anxious for clues.

'She misses my father.'

'Surely she found another father for you?'

'No, she could not.'

'Why not?'

'She loved my father very, very much and prays for his soul

221

each night before she goes to bed. She is a good Catholic. Our neighbours are mean to us because she has no husband.'

'Do you go to school?'

'No, I must help my mother make paper flowers to sell in in the *Cours Salaya*.'

Nicholas was overcome with shame. To have fathered a boy and walked away, leaving his mother in penurious circumstances when he was winning fortunes at the gambling tables, was abhorrent to him now.

He picked up the knife and felt its weight. Touching his thumb against the blade, he watched as a pearl of blood formed on his skin. He could cut his own throat and barely feel a thing.

But what of Isabella? How would she survive? Guiltily, he realised that the train was forcing him to ask questions about his own nature that he had never asked himself. 'I don't want to hurt you,' he told the child. 'But if I leave, how will you return?'

'I think I am just supposed to close my eyes, and I will awaken at home,' he said solemnly. 'I will either awaken there, or in paradise.'

Nicholas told himself that he had intended to go back and see Marie-Helene when the time was right, but he doubted that this was the truth. *How can I prevail if I can't even be honest with myself?* he thought. 'Tell me about your life,' he said.

'Each morning I arise at five and eat with my mother, and we make the flowers. Then we go into the market with them, returning home at midnight. It is a hard life for both of us. We have no-one else but each other.'

The train rattled over a set of points and began to descend a hill toward its final destination. 'You must make your choice now,' said the boy.

CHAPTER THIRTY-EIGHT
THE HUNT

ISABELLA AND THE elderly etymologist headed out into the corridor. Isabella carried the cage containing the fever tree leaves, and Mr Freely had collected his net, but if the insect could bore through a solid wooden wall, there seemed to be little chance that it would be stopped by some pieces of string on a bamboo pole. Isabella cursed herself for giving in to her curiosity, and knew that the only way she could win now was by stopping the beetle before it came for her.

'It must be in the next carriage,' said Mr Freely. 'It can't go far.'

'Why not?' Isabella asked.

'It uses up too much energy. It will need to feed.'

In the next compartment, a fat farmer's wife sat with stale cabbages piled at her feet and her eyes shut. Mr Freely and Isabella gingerly entered.

'Please, Madam, don't be alarmed,' said Mr Freely, raising his hands in a placatory gesture, 'we have a rare beetle on the loose. Have you seen it?'

The fat lady made as if to speak, but when she opened her mouth no sound emerged. Instead there was a terrible whirring noise and the bug drilled out. It must have entered from the back of her neck. She coughed blood over the shocked pair, her

eyes widening in pain and terror.

As she fell forward, the bug roared up to the ceiling, hovered motionless for a moment like a hummingbird, then dived back into her, burrowing another hole, this time through her coat and shirt and the fatty flesh of her chest, and out with a bloody explosion into the wall behind.

Mr Freely peered into the splintered hole in amazement. 'Incredible,' he exclaimed, not without a hint of admiration.

An eruption of wood and a crack of glass brought them running. As the bug smashed its way from compartment to compartment, causing havoc, they were barely able to keep pace with it.

'I said to Mrs Freely we must take it alive,' panted her husband. 'We have to recapture it. We may never get a chance like this again to study such an exotic creature.'

The insect was powering its way through to another cabin when the drone of its wings suddenly stopped. Cautiously, Isabella and Mr Freely peered in but could not spot it.

They entered slowly, searching the seats, but the compartment appeared empty. 'Wait—over here.' Mr Freely pointed to the entry hole in the wall, but no exit.

'I don't understand,' said Isabella. 'There's nowhere else for it to go.'

'We have to trap it. It's a female. It's looking for somewhere warm to lay its eggs.'

Isabella bent down, searching the seats. As she looked, she felt something moving slowly up her leg. She turned in time to see the beetle disappearing under the hem of her dress.

She watched in horror as the lump beneath her clothes continued moving upward. Carefully and quietly, with the minimum of movement, as one would when faced with a nest of hornets, she unbuttoned her outer skirt and dropped her petticoats.

'Don't kill it!' cried Mr Freely, throwing out his hands in protest. They watched as it burrowed about in the

undergarments, but before the etymologist could seize the lump it shot out, back into the corridor.

Running after it in her underwear, Isabella realized they had reached the train's observation platform at the rear, where Nicholas was sitting talking to a large-eyed child who looked remarkably like him. Neither of them appeared to notice Isabella. It was as if they inhabited a different sphere of existence.

The bug was hovering above the railing, darting and buzzing beside them.

'It won't leave the train,' said Mr Freely with assurance. 'It has a food source now.'

'I don't understand,' said Isabella, puzzled, her attention torn between the beetle and the man who had come back for her.

'I'm rather afraid that's my fault. I think I gave it the taste.'

'What do you mean?'

The bug swerved and turned, heading back toward them.

'I fed it,' said Mr Freely apologetically.

'What did you feed it?'

'I fed it my wife.'

The bug flew straight at Isabella. Mr Freely was watching in great excitement. For him it was obviously another chance to witness the creature's feeding rituals at close range. The bug dived right at Isabella's open mouth. She clapped her hands over it as it diverted towards her eyes. Its legs scratched crimson lines on her palms and wrists as she fought to hold it away from her face.

The insect's force was incredible. It remained inches from her eyes, its mandibles snapping crazily. No-one had ever grabbed it before. She fought to keep its wings from opening wide and allowing it to reach full power. The beetle hovered above her and tipped its carapace to unfurl a curved crimson stinger, bloated with poison. It whipped the stinger at her, but could not quite reach her face. She recoiled in revulsion, wondering what kind of entity could create such a creature.

Isabella flung the *Coleoptera Freely* aside as hard as she could. It hit the rear wall of the observation deck and dropped to the ground.

'No, you mustn't hurt her!' Mr Freely yelled. He dropped to his knees, looking for the bug.

It came flying back up with an angry drone and hit Mr Freely hard in his surprised face, ploughing straight through his right eye. He rose and turned to Isabella, spraying her in blood. The bug flew out and burrowed back in. Then out, and in again, stitching a bloody pattern through Mr Freely, who shook violently as he was riddled with passages. 'She wants to lay eggs!' he cried, 'I'm to be her nest!' He sounded thrilled at the prospect, then dropped onto all fours and fell on his face.

Isabella could hear the bug buzzing inside him. She bent over him with the cage held open above his head, expecting the bug to come roaring out of the top of his skull. But as she listened, the whirring died away.

Tracing the insect as it moved down through Mr Freely's body, she flinched as it came tearing out of his rear end. The bug flew straight into the cage held in Isabella's hands, but was travelling so fast that it smashed the wooden prison to smithereens.

Isabella found to her disgust that she was covered in the less savoury parts of Mr Freely. Shocked, she looked back at Mr Freely, who was still convulsing violently.

'Mr Freely?'

Suddenly the entomologist's body jerked upright as if attached to strings, and he vomited egg sacs over Isabella. A gourmet might have suggested that they looked like ravioli in oyster sauce. Covered in egg-sac slime, Isabella screamed and stamped them into the ground. The cage lay shattered on the floor. The bug was still free.

She understood instinctively that she had to kill it in order to survive, but how? She had no weapons, nothing with which to lure it except the scent of her own body.

But that, it seemed, was enough. The beetle appeared from the darkness and roared after her once more. She could only leave the deck, where Nicholas and the boy had failed to notice her plight, and run as fast as the swaying carriage permitted her. She knew that the insect would be closing in behind.

Fool! she thought as she ran, *fool! You mentioned Pandora aloud and the train presented you with a box that should not be opened! Could you not have withheld your curiosity for once in your life? Always causing upset as a child, and still you have not learned a thing!*

Diving into the nearest compartment, she slammed its door but the bug came right through it, shattering glass and scattering oak splinters in her hair. Isabella screamed, and the train's whistle magnified her terror, echoing it into the dark hillside.

The *Arkangel*'s wheels turned ever faster as the stoker shovelled coal into the boiler, readying it to receive a soul.

As Isabella hurtled through the train, pursued by the bug, she began to realise just how many passengers had died during the course of the *Arkangel*'s journeys. And then she had reached the engine, and there was nowhere else to run.

CHAPTER THIRTY-NINE
THE DECISION

'CHOOSE,' SAID JEAN-GUY. 'It is time to make your choice.' He sounded deeply regretful about having to force the matter.

'Very well,' said Nicholas, still dumbfounded. In the last few moments there seemed to have been some kind of commotion in the air of the observation carriage, but he could not see what had caused it. 'May I ask you one final question?'

'Very well,' said the boy gravely. 'But you must be quick.'

Whoever had set the tests for the *Arkangel* had done so very cleverly. They had sent a boy this time, someone without the guile to lie, so there could be no accusations of cheating. 'Tell me,' said Nicholas, 'how did your mother look when you last saw her?'

Jean-Guy thought for a minute. 'She was very sad. She was crying.'

Nicholas raised the knife and watched as the carriage lights slithered down the blade. 'And where were you?'

'I was in her arms.'

'And how did you feel?'

'I was hot, then I was cold.'

The questions were getting him nowhere. He realised now that he would have to save his son. It would mean leaving Isabella to fend for herself, but he had a feeling she could

manage well enough without him. In the last few hours, her independence had been born and was growing fast. It was time to make amends for his misdeeds, to do what was right.

There was no time for any further thought. Turning the tip of the knife toward his chest, Nicholas took a final deep breath and pushed the blade deep between his ribs, into his beating heart. There was surprisingly little blood. He felt nothing, just an icy numbness.

The boy did not appear surprised at his action. He began to jerk strangely, then was still. He fell gently and soundlessly to the deck.

As his surroundings began to fade, Nicholas realised his terrible mistake. *Hot and cold,* the boy had said. The cholera outbreak in Nice had killed his son. That was how they had been able to bring him here. The boy had to be dead to be summoned.

Nicholas fell beside Jean-Guy. He watched as the boy's body began to sparkle with errant electricity, then fizzle away into the cool rushing air, his spirit returning to the grave.

Nicholas drew his hand away from his chest in a red glove. Dying now, he left the observation deck, but not before he had shed a tear. He had failed, and had been granted a glimpse of the life he had chosen not to share, and this hurt more than losing ever could.

As HE SHOVELLED coals into the boiler, the stoker saw what was coming and wisely jumped out of the way. The bug hovered in the engine room, its shadow thrown onto the wall so that it appeared enormous. Trapped against the caboose, Isabella watched in horror as *Coleoptera Freely* prepared for the kill.

The stoker stared, mesmerised. Isabella stepped in front of the boiler and turned to him. 'Open the door.'

'But Miss, the heat—'

'Open it!'

As soon as he did so, the flames at her back ignited the laces on her corset. She knew the furnace would burn her alive if she continued to stand there, but she dared not move.

'So you want somewhere warm,' she told the creature, waving her arms at it. As the beetle dived, she dropped sharply to the floor and it roared straight into the boiler. Isabella kicked the door shut. There was a belch of flame around the door's edges as the beetle's body expanded and exploded. Isabella rolled in the coal-dust to extinguish her petticoat.

Burned, bloodied and bruised, stripped to her brassiere and knickers, she rose unsteadily and attempted to leave the engine room with the tatters of her dignity as the stoker looked on in amazement.

The *Arkangel* went faster still, approaching its final halt. Isabella turned to the stoker, who was still staring at her in surprise. 'If you stop the train and I get off, what happens?'

'The train will take you,' said the stoker. He grinned at her, blocking access to the emergency brakes.

'So the train wins.'

'The train always wins.'

'You let Nicholas escape.'

'He came back, didn't he?'

Picking up the glowing coal shovel he had just set aside, she held it before his face. 'You must know a way to get us out of here.'

'If I did, why would I tell you?' He advanced on her, taking pleasure in her growing fear.

Isabella shut her eyes and punched the burning shovel into the stoker's throat.

He looked down in some surprise, then pushed it from his seared flesh, with a grunt of vague annoyance. He grinned at her. 'You can't kill what's already dead, my lovely.'

'But I'm not dead. I am the victor. What do I get?'

'I bear you no malice. In fact, I rather admire you, but I am just the stoker, so no-one cares what I think. I'll tell you this,

though. No-one has ever got so far before. You must approach the Conductor and ask him what happens now.'

'Where will I find him?'

The stoker touched his weeping red throat, feeling for a scar. 'Why, he's where he always is.'

With no other plan left in mind, she made her way unsteadily to the Conductor. He was standing in his alcove, where he had remained for the most part of the journey, as immobile as a votive god in a Roman household, to be touched for luck in times of crisis. He seemed to be expecting her and raised an eyebrow, waiting.

'Well?' he asked.

'It is done,' she replied. 'We have each been tested in turn, and I have passed your test. We have a deal, I believe, and I demand some answers.'

'You chose to board the *Arkangel*.'

'I had no choice.'

'There is always a choice. This is not my concern. But perhaps you have earned the right to ask. We have entered unknown territory here.'

'What has happened to Nicholas? Has he survived with his soul?'

'I will answer that question in due course.' The Conductor considered how to proceed. 'First, though, I think it is time you were told the secret history of the *Arkangel*.'

CHAPTER FORTY
THE SATANIC RITUAL

THE CONDUCTOR HAD a faraway look in his eyes, as if remembering an unimaginably distant past.

'The rivets were white gold,' he said, turning to look at a photograph of the train on the wall of his alcove, flying in all its former glory. The caption read: *Maiden Voyage Of The Arkangel August 16th 1887.*

'A day to remember, it was. I was there, of course. But I'd been there long before that. Right back at the start, when the first weld was made, when the first bolt found its place.' He held his hand before Isabella's face. 'Come, child, remember with me.'

She felt her eyelids growing heavy. When she closed them, she saw a familiar foundry with an engine shed attached, and recognized it at once as the factory from her home town of Chelmsk. Inside, white-hot metal steamed and shrieked as it was plunged into vats of bubbling water. The clanging and hissing; forging and annealing. Iron plate and tempered steel, rods and bolts and blood red fire.

'The world of the engines was always like this,' said the Conductor.

Hammers rose and fell in unison, a hot steel choir. The engine

shed was filled with the town's workmen—there were no women here, and never had been. They stayed at home behind closed doors, washing and baking and raising children. Here in the foundry, strange rituals bound the men together as ancient symbols were pressed into the pliable metal.

'The whole town built trains,' said the Conductor. 'Men lived and died at the forges. Even before the *Arkangel* was finished, it had claimed its first victim.'

She watched in horror as one of the workmen dropped a rivet and fished for it between two great slabs of sizzling metal. Squeezed her eyes shut as he rolled up his sleeve and went deep in the way of the coupling, trying to grab it. Tried to blot the sound of his screaming as the engine's coupling joint closed, neatly shearing away the four fingers of his right hand, the heat cauterising the wounds so that he could not bleed to death. Screaming, he was carried off by men who had lived with such accidents all their working lives.

Behind this hellish scene, watching in silence from the gantry above them, shadowy figures smoked cigars, overseeing the construction. Well-fed men who wore crimson tabards decorated with masonic pentagrams and other ancient guild symbols. At the centre of their circle was the most corpulent of their number, the bloated Controller, in his stovepipe hat, embroidered silk waistcoat and chains of office. Isabella gasped in recognition of her uncle's silhouette. His face remained in shadow, as if light could not touch it.

The group had gathered around him in the great engine shed. Now he placed his meaty fists on the gantry rail and addressed everyone in the foundry. 'We are men of dark vision,' he called to them. 'It has taken us thirteen long years to complete construction of this mechanical marvel. And now our task is complete.'

Isabella watched as four engineers bolted the steel nameplate to the front of the train.

'The name is a reminder that Satan was once an angel of God,' said the Controller, looking proudly on.

Isabella saw that the name had originally appeared in a different form. The plate read *The Dark Angel*. The men looked up to their bosses with expectation. They had never been interested in the reasons for the train's construction. They were only concerned with the engineering problems it presented. If the train ran well, then others would be ordered and the foundry would remain in business. And if the foundry was busy, the town would become prosperous once more.

Outside, watching through a crack in the engine shed wall, was a little girl who saw everything. She recognised her uncle among the industrialists, and also the Conductor, as pale and straight-backed as he appeared now, but a young man of around seventeen summers. She watched through the splintered wood as engineers fussed around the locomotive, adding its final touches.

'Our train is a thing of cruel beauty,' said the Controller. 'The triumph of mechanical might over the human spirit.'

The *Arkangel*'s symbol, a V folded inside a circle to represent fury contained, had been pressed on a brand, and was being heated up in the foundry's largest forge. The members of the inner circle descended the gantry and passed before it, unflinchingly accepting the white-hot iron on the bare skin of their right forearms.

'I surrendered my life for the Angel,' intoned the Conductor. 'I was but a boy.'

'Why did you do it?' asked Isabella, who now remembered what she had for so long tried to erase from her mind, what was about to happen.

The Conductor could not bring himself to answer. The smoke-filled foundry. The impassive men. The great green engine on its turntable. The young apprentice being placed in a strange device of curved and oiled brass tracks some fifteen feet in diameter. The whole thing was shaped like the train's symbol, and lay angled on the factory floor. The clamps that pinned him down by ankles and wrists made it seem as if he

was an extension of the train itself, conjoined in the creation of its spirit.

Nobody moved from their places, but heads slowly turned towards the doors. Stony eyes followed a sleeping girl as she was carried into the engine shed by half a dozen middle-aged men. The only female ever to be admitted to the foundry in the last thirteen years. Many recognized her as the flirtatious dairymaid who had been long promised to Ivan. Where was her fiancé in her hour of need? Lying dead drunk in the inn run by Isabella's father, where he had been plied with powerful liquor.

The locomotive shed was laid with tracks that crossed each other. The engine stood at its centre, completing a pentagram in shining steel.

The girl had been dressed in a robe of rough white linen, symbolising purity. Her hair had been woven with tiny blue cornflowers. She was carried to the head of the train and set down before it. The men who had carried her in took their leave. They were not foundry workers, and this was no sight for them.

Incantations were made. The Devil was invoked in hushed tones, as if raised voices might incur his wrath. The girl was lovingly stripped and tied naked to the track. Her clothes were thoughtfully folded in a neat square pile.

The brass mechanism that held the compliant young Conductor was powered by steam. It began to saw at the pale insides of his wrists. Gashes appeared, and blood spilled into bored-out channels, down into the machinery, turning it.

The rails on which the girl had been placed rotated until they were arranged before the engine of the train. The workmen watched in silence. None dared turn away.

'Tonight,' said the controller, 'we witness the baptism of the *Dark Angel*.'

The young Conductor raised his eyes to the great roof of the engine shed, where pigeons shat and fluttered on the shadowed crossbeams. He cared only for the glory of his role in bringing

the *Arkangel* to life. As he was drained of blood, the train's brass cross-rods began to move. The great wheels turned, and the girl was drawn into the churning machinery.

It was an unfortunate time for the girl to awaken. She began to scream and struggle, to no avail. Nothing could prevent her from being slowly fed to the great mechanical beast. The wheels ran over her, tearing her sinews, crushing her bones, until she was wholly devoured by the great engine, and the ritual was complete.

CHAPTER FORTY-ONE
THE MAIDEN VOYAGE

THE LITTLE GIRL who had been outside the engine shed, watching the ritual, ran away in terror. She ran until she could find no more breath, collapsing in the wet graveyard at the edge of the town.

'But what about the maiden voyage?' asked Isabella, reaching up to touch the photograph on the wall of the Conductor's alcove—the same picture that had once hung in her uncle's house, the picture no-one would ever talk about.

'Well, of course, this was long before the war,' said the Conductor distantly. 'But even then, the world was changing. Borders were moved. Suspicions were rife. Every advance is beset by protestors. Something had to be done.'

'I don't understand.'

The Conductor raised his hands and pressed his fingers on either side of Isabella's head. 'See what I know about the *Arkangel*'s maiden voyage,' he said.

HER GRANDPAPA SHOULD have been proud to be selected for such an important position, but a sense of foreboding crept through his bones every time he hauled himself up onto the footplate of the *Arkangel*. Men had died building the train, and what was

this grand machine to be used for on its first outing? Ferrying the directors and a lucky handful of the town's best families on a pleasure trip to the seaside!

Food had been scarce in the town of late. Even the price of turnips had soared so much that people no longer fed shavings to the pigs. But no expense was to be spared on the train. The priests said it would bring new prosperity to the town, but lately they had been proven wrong every time they opened their mouths.

And still the great locomotive went nowhere. It sat in the siding at Chelmsk station to await its duty. Finally, when things got really bad, it was announced that the train would make her maiden voyage...

Sighing, grandpapa adjusted his cap and signalled to the driver. With an angry blast of steam, the shining behemoth rolled forward out of the station.

The first journey of the *Arkangel* took place on a day of glorious windswept skies. The engine was draped in fluttering red and blue flags: to many, a source of national pride, but there were others who gathered on the street corners at dusk to mutter darkly about its sinister origins.

The directors occupied the front carriage. Their respected guests spread through the second and third. As the train chuntered amiably out of the station, the parents proudly pointed out the Chelmsk Foundry to their children; this was where the carriages had been so expertly crafted.

Sandwiches and cakes were consumed as the train plunged on through dense forest. Lemonade and beer was drunk. Conversation became more sporadic. The fathers fell quiet while their wives tended to the children. It was only when the Conductor passed through the car with two officers at his back that the mood changed to faint uncertainty.

The papers handed out to the passengers had a strange request printed upon them. For the sake of safety, it was desired that all valuables were to be handed to the officers for safekeeping before the train's arrival at the Eastern depot.

This included all wrist and pocket watches, wallets, fountain pens, rings, brooches, necklaces, tie-clips, bracelets, earrings, cufflinks, money clips and loose change. Furthermore, any important documents, including all identity papers, deeds of covenant and documents pertaining to property or wills should be handed in at the same time. In certain cases, the gentlemen would be required to write a short note of explanation to their nearest relatives in Chelmsk.

The uncertainty turned to fear now, especially when one of the children saw his family's precious belongings being unceremoniously tipped into a leather station bag and carted away on a trolley.

The mood on board was suddenly very different. Even the children had begun to sense that something was wrong. A couple of them cried that they wanted to go home, but were sternly admonished by their parents. The countryside continued to roll past. The sun continued to shine down on the carriages. Some of the fathers continued to read newspapers. In one of the carriages, there was a mechanical doll of a young girl that moved its arms and sang pretty songs to keep the children amused. No-one could truly believe their worst fears. It was the modern world. An explanation would be proffered, belongings would be returned with profuse apologies, the day would end well enough. Calculations were made about how long it would take to reach the coast. The fathers attempted to jolly their wives and children into happier moods.

Then, as the *Arkangel* slowed across the windswept plain toward its final stop, they saw the great dark bulk of the terminus approaching and began to fear for their children's lives.

When the officers demanded that they strip their children and then themselves, a raw terror set in. Clothes were to be folded and left at the end of each compartment. From the windows they could see the passengers in the carriage ahead of them stumbling onto the platform. Their bare white nudity was profoundly shocking. The children were screaming and

sobbing now, their naked mothers pawed and prodded by the guards, the men sometimes punched with the butts of rifles if they questioned what was happening. Some of the older ones fell, and were trampled underfoot. An old man with bloody dentures hanging from his mouth lay screaming and clutching at the passing legs until one of the train's officers stuck a bayonet into his lower belly and dragged it upward, eviscerating him.

The directors felt that mistakes were made. No-one should have been killed on the concourse; it made the terrified passengers too difficult to control. Lessons were quickly learned in the management of the damned.

The train returned empty to Chelmsk. All those who waited for news of friends and relatives waited in vain.

And thus all those in the town who had expressed disapproval over the building of the *Arkangel* for the past thirteen years, all those bitter men who had whispered about the growing wealth of the foundry's directors, all those pious creatures who had gathered in the church to speak of the foundry's blasphemies, were removed in a single stroke. Generations of dissent were obliterated, and the children were taken to make sure that the seeds would never grow again. If there was nothing to remember, no voices could be raised against the evil they had bred in their midst.

The Conductor removed his hands from Isabella's head. She was crying. 'And now I think you understand the purpose of the *Arkangel*,' he said gently. 'It is a kind of great sieve, shaking out the righteous from those who sit and watch. Our purpose is more suited by inactivity in the population. All it takes for evil to flourish is for good men to do nothing.'

CHAPTER FORTY-TWO
THE DEAL

ISABELLA REMAINED BEFORE the Conductor as the memory came to an end, unable to move. 'Why?' she demanded to know, angrily wiping away tears. 'Why would you wish for this?'

'Our town was dying. The train was good to us.'

'But why this vessel of misery? How could you volunteer to be part of such an obscenity?'

'We have helped to create the modern age,' the Conductor replied. 'A world without a heart, as pure as a machine. There is no room for sentiment in this new century. There is no room for God.'

'But what on earth did you do it for?'

'To reveal the Devil to mankind. To prove the futility of the divine. To become a keystone of the future, instead of being a remnant of the past.'

'And I was there when it was born? I saw all this?'

'Yes, but you did not remember until now. You were six years old.'

'Is that why we are here? It was no accident we caught this train. We've done nothing wrong.'

'Young lady, I think you know the truth.'

'Josef—the man to whom I was promised—he was to become

a director at the foundry.'

'More than that. He will one day inherit it. And you were to bear his children. You were to be the mother of the foundry's future keepers. The train must always be maintained,' the Conductor added. 'There are big plans for the Chelmsk Foundry. A munitions manufacturer is required in Eastern Europe. Someone with the ability to precision-engineer new mechanised instruments of death. Instead, you derailed our plans. You used the foreigner to escape.'

'I used no-one! Fate took a hand—'

'We only wanted you, Isabella; you were the one to be tested and punished. You brought the others with you.'

Isabella saw it again. The moment they boarded the train. The hands of Thomas and Miranda connecting as she helped them to climb up into the *Arkangel*. The spark of conjunction. Destinies that entwined forever. The chain of fate, newly forged along a different path.

'No,' she insisted, you cannot use this as proof that I failed. I didn't know the result that my actions would bring. I had to get away, and Nicholas was there to help me.'

'Perhaps. People always profess to be unaware of the consequences of their actions. You have won, but you have passed your test alone. Nicholas is dead. It is time to decide what is right.'

'No! Dead!'

'He chose well but not wisely. And now it has all reached an end.'

'That's not fair!' Isabella cried. 'I thought the Devil loved to bargain.'

'And so he does. The train tries all who climb aboard. The ones found wanting are doomed to ride forever. You were each tempted, shown visions of your other lives, the worlds that might be, that might already have been. The rules of the *Arkangel* are very simple. If those who board it fail their test, their souls are taken and they remain for eternity. If they

succeed, they are free to return to their old lives. Everyone who boards the *Arkangel* must face this ordeal.'

'But how do you judge failure?' asked Isabella.

'That is the beauty of the process. You can only act in accordance with your nature. The vicar's wife revealed her greed. Her husband could not control his lust. Your adventurer—'

'You could not charge him with cowardice. He fought bravely. He returned to redeem himself.'

'He understood the nature of his test and chose the right solution, but that was also his undoing. I always knew that you would be our greatest challenge, for I could only find one flaw in you—your insatiable curiosity. You wanted to see the world beyond your town. You wanted to look inside the box.' He looked up and sniffed the air. 'Smell the brimstone? We're almost there now. So close. I felt sure you would fail.'

'But I prevailed. You know I did. I won, and now I want you to keep your side of the bargain. Let the others go, all four of us.'

'I'm afraid that's not possible. The others spoiled their chances, and they'll stay with me to tend the train. In place of the children you failed to deliver.'

'But I passed my test. I should be free to go.'

'Then perhaps I will make a proposal.'

Isabella stood her ground. 'It must be fair. You know as well as I that evil must be balanced by good. You have to let me go.'

'But suppose you could save your lover as well? How would you feel then?'

'What must I do?'

'I can bring him back.'

'And you would save him?'

'No, you would.'

'How?'

'I cannot tell you that. You know your adversary. You would have to find a way.'

'I don't know what to do.'

'The decision is yours,' the Conductor told her, checking his

pocket watch. 'Better hurry, though. The train is approaching its final destination.'

'Surely it should be slowing down.'

'No. It must reach its maximum speed to break through the wall.'

'The wall?'

'Between this world and the next. Between Heaven and Hell. You must decide whether or not to accept the wager, Isabella. We like wagers.'

'Then I take the challenge,' she said, trying to sound confident.

'Very well.' The Conductor clapped his hands together. Standing behind her in the corridor was Nicholas, dazed and bleeding badly from his chest wound, but alive.

CHAPTER FORTY-THREE
THE HORDE

SHE RAN TO Nicholas and took him in her arms. 'You are safe,' she told him. 'Tell me you're real and not one of the Devil's illusions.'

'I think I'm real,' said Nicholas. 'I don't know what happened. I feel bloody terrible.' He raised his bleeding wrists, chafed from the handcuffs, and touched the wound in his chest. 'I jumped from the train and lost consciousness. Someone helped me—a kind man. How did he get me back on board?'

'He brought you here on his horse. You survived, but by leaving the train you nearly forfeited your soul. You returned.'

'Oh, God, my son. I saw my son, Isabella, the little boy I was too selfish to stay with. I tried to save him but he was already dead. They tricked me into taking my own life. I should have joined him in the afterlife.' He dabbed at the chest wound. 'I'm losing blood. What happens now?'

'The Conductor has brought you back, on the condition that I beat the Devil.'

'Beat the Devil?' Nicholas tried to understand, but was struggling with the idea. He looked at her tattered undergarments. 'What happened to you? Where are your clothes?'

'We have each of us faced the Dark One. The Red Countess, Mr Scheffen, Mr Freely, Professor Io, all those who helped in their charades, they're all Satan's passengers, doomed to ride the train forever, enlisted to perform their roles in ensnaring us. The *Arkangel* is nothing more than a giant soul trap. But you've been given another chance. I survived, but your fate hangs in the balance.'

'Then what must we do to save ourselves?'

'I wish I knew. We'll soon be reaching our journey's end. There are no more stations on the line. I don't think there is anything we can do.' The wind from an open window was blasting their faces. The train was moving faster than it ever had before. The sky was turning purple above the treeline. 'The *Arkangel* will never let us off.'

'What about the Conductor? He could stop the train. Where is he?'

Isabella turned around. 'He was here a moment ago.'

'Come on, we know where to find him.' Nicholas led the way back along the corridor of the carriage, but the Conductor's alcove was empty.

'He said I would find a way to challenge my adversary,' said Isabella. 'What am I supposed to do?'

'I don't know,' Nicholas admitted, touching his bleeding chest with concern, 'but you'd better think of something quick. This wound is starting to open again.'

The *Arkangel* hammered over several sets of points, the entire carriage juddering. Outside, the purple clouds began to redden with hellfire. The fir trees at the horizon appeared to have small furnaces flickering among them.

'We're getting close,' said Isabella. 'I suggest we go through the train carriage by carriage. Perhaps I'll think of something and understand what I have to do.'

As soon as Nicholas and Isabella had left the corridor, the Conductor appeared and began opening the doors of the compartments.

'Time for you to earn your keep,' he told the dead passengers, forcing them to raise themselves. Slowly they stood throughout the carriage, answering his call. Farmers and foundry workers, housewives and shopkeepers, they shuffled toward the front of the train in anticipation of arrival.

'There is only one remaining traveller left alive on board. She has a chance—the slimmest chance—of beating us. You have to make sure that she does not have time to discover how.'

The undead passengers stared at the Conductor, awaiting his command.

'Do I have to spell it out for you?' he shouted at them. 'Kill her!'

'CAN YOU FEEL it?' said Isabella. 'The train is a living thing now. Hell is calling us to eternal damnation.'

'Thank you for that cheering thought. I don't know whether I ever mentioned this, but I'm not a Christian. Church to me is just a hard bench, a cold arse and a dim man in a robe spouting rubbish.'

Nicholas walked unsteadily through the rushing train. In the compartments around them, the dead passengers were slowly waking, responding to the Conductor's invocation. Nicholas realised that they were staring at him. 'Well,' he shouted, 'what are you peasants looking at? Yes, I'm English, sorry if my natural superiority offends you, you brainless shit-shovelling imbeciles.' He turned to Isabella. 'I don't like this, they're waking up. I think they may mean to do us harm.'

'We can't fight all of them, Nicholas. I have yet to come up with a plan.'

The first of the undead reached out to Isabella. Two farmhands in smocks and straw hats attempted to paw her. Clad only in her underwear, covered in blood and slime, she was hardly in a position to fight back. Slapping their hands away angrily, she wondered what she could use to fight them off.

'We need weapons, urgently. There are too many of them.'

'They're slow-witted,' said Nicholas. 'They shouldn't be too hard to keep at bay.'

'Nicholas, you can't kill what's already dead.'

'We have one advantage. We have our brains. We're still alive. And we're getting off this bloody train.'

'No, I'll find a way to do it. I got you into this. It's my fault. I'll get you out.'

'I don't see what you can do. Get away from her, cabbage-breath.' He swatted away an undead farmer's hand as it reached for Isabella's breast. The passengers were now filling the corridor and moving toward them.

'I know our final destination,' she told Nicholas. 'There was never any question about it. We're going into the mouth of Hell itself.'

Nicholas set his jaw. 'We're not going to Hell. We're going to London. We need something to fight them off with. The soldiers. They may have died but they were never meant to be on board. You heard what the Conductor said.' The nearest compartment housed several sleeping infantrymen. On the luggage rack above them were their officers' rifle-cases. He swung inside and pulled two down before they had a chance to wake up. 'Do you know how to use a gun?'

'If the target is a rabbit.'

'Fine. Think of them as big rabbits.'

Nicholas clapped his hands. 'Wake up, men, we are under attack.'

The soldiers snapped to alertness. Before they could question why one of their old compatriots had taken their guns, Nicholas pulled them to their feet and showed them the advancing horde. 'These godless creatures intend a hellish death for us. Will you help me fight them?'

'You have my gun,' one of the soldiers pointed out.

'Surely there are more?'

'Yes, of course,' said another.

'Then break them out.'

'Who are we fighting?'

'The undead. If it helps, think of them as Germans.'

The soldiers set to work without any further questions, tearing the lids from the crates in the luggage rack and pulling out rifles. The boredom and confusion of their unwarranted journey had now yielded a purpose close to any soldier's heart: the possibility of committing acts of violence.

Armed and ready, they advanced upon the undead passengers. Then they loaded, aimed and fired.

CHAPTER FORTY-FOUR
THE PLAN

THE TRAIN RACED on through the darkness, gathering speed, its great wheels heating on the rails, sparks flying, setting fire to the forest beside the tracks. At the treeline, Isabella could see the bonfires of Hades, fast approaching. From inside the train came flashes of light as the soldiers warded off the travelling dead.

The Conductor turned to his acolytes. The soulless were a trial; they rarely concentrated on anything for more than a minute or two, and forgot what you told them even more quickly. 'Remember,' he shouted to the ranks of peasants, 'there is a living soul on board the train. Keep her occupied. Let her try to hold out until we reach our final destination. You can overwhelm her allies. Go after them now and make her lose heart when she sees she is standing alone. Either way, she *must* lose.'

Among the resurrected passengers, Thomas and Miranda had joined the newly undeceased. At this early stage, they yet retained some small remnant of their former humanity, and looked about themselves in puzzlement, trying to understand what had happened.

'This is not fair,' Miranda said, bristling with indignation. Her wounds were truly terrible to behold. In time she would heal and bear a passing resemblance to her living self. It was

the smallest recompense for being doomed to travel on board the *Arkangel* for all eternity. 'I had high hopes for my life, and now it has been cut short.'

'If you think life's not fair, wait till you've tried living death for a while,' said the Conductor.

'Thomas,' Miranda snapped at her shuffling husband. 'Do something. Don't just stand there.' She studied him for the first time. 'You look dreadful.'

Thomas caught sight of himself in the window, a blackened bubo-riddled walking corpse. He looked at Miranda, who was missing most of her face. 'Have you seen yourself? You're not exactly the radiant bride I married.' he scoffed. 'Actually, you weren't even radiant when I married you. I'm not following his instructions.' He pointed over at the Conductor. 'He's got plenty of slaves to do his dirty work. Come on.' He grabbed her hand.

'Where are we going?' she asked.

'To the restaurant car. We may be dead but we're still English. I'd like a cup of tea. And some decent biscuits.'

NICHOLAS AND ISABELLA stood at the head of the soldiers, who were braced across the corridor of the third carriage, firing at all who came within range, but they were fast running out of shells. Besides, the bullets did little more than knock their attackers back a few feet at a time.

'We couldn't alight at the stations,' Nicholas reasoned, exploding a cowhand, 'but what about in between them? I jumped and survived.' He threw open the door of the train. Together, they looked down at the rushing ground.

'We can't jump. We'll be dashed to pieces.' Isabella's rifle recoiled violently as she blasted a hole through a yokel.

'And that would be worse than what exactly?'

'You know we would simply be reborn on the train. There has to be something else. I think there's another reason why there's no end destination on the map.'

'They wouldn't get many passengers if they put 'Chelmsk—Hell Express' on their routes, would they? It's over.'

'No it's not. I have a chance. I gave way to my own foolish curiosity, but I might still be able to make amends. I think I know of a way to save us. We need to find the map of the *Arkangel*'s route.'

Leaving the soldiers to hold the front line, they made their way back to the last framed corridor map and examined it. One route vanished into darkness and storms, the other appeared to lead to greener pastures. Set at the top of the map was a series of tiny sepia photographs of the Controller, the Conductor and the train.

'The Controller has been there all along,' said Isabella. 'Come on. We need to search the carriages behind us.'

Nicholas followed her, intrigued.

'Nicholas, where was the Red Countess?'

'Why?'

'I have to find her luggage.'

They pushed their way back to the first class suites.

'Here.' Isabella pulled back the red velvet drapes of the Red Countess's stateroom and began to search through her stacked valises.

'What are you looking for?' asked Nicholas, puzzled.

'Something like this.' She removed an elegant, sequinned scarlet dress from the Red Countess's case. 'Cover me for a minute.'

Nicholas raised his rifle and shot a few peasants until Isabella returned. She had wiped the blood from her face, corseted herself into the gown and tied her hair up. She looked battered but radiant.

'What on earth do you think you're doing?' he asked.

She checked herself in the Countess's mirror. 'I have a plan. I need powder and lipstick.'

'You're not going on a date.'

'Yes I am,' she told him. 'I'm going to beat the Devil.'

CHAPTER FORTY-FIVE
THE CONTROLLER

'THERE, WHAT DO you think?' She stood before Nicholas, resplendently dressed in the low-cut gown of lace-edged scarlet silk, her hair neatly arranged in ringlets. She had done her best to powder her face, and had sprayed herself with the Countess's most expensive perfume.

'Well, I suppose you look less indecent with some clothes on, but I really don't see the point in dressing up for your arrival in the bloody Underworld. Have you seen it out there? It's like a scene from a medieval painting.'

'Stay close to me, but don't interfere, no matter what happens. I need to find the Conductor.'

With Nicholas warding off the marauding passengers, they searched the train. The Conductor was in the next carriage, and had no wish to be seen supervising his rampant acolytes, in case Isabella accused him of cheating.

'Ah, sweet Isabella, the last to fall,' he said cheerfully. 'How beautiful you look. Have you come to confront me? Is that your response to the challenge?'

'I'm not going to fight you,' she told him. 'You're just a servant. And a dead one, at that. I demand to see your superior. My uncle.'

'Ah.' For the first time, the Conductor was stung. 'I wondered if you would decide upon that. Of course, it would be appropriate, seeing that your own family was complicit in the building of the *Arkangel*.'

'At first I could not recall my uncle's face, for he left us when I was young. I could only remember him in shadow at the engine shed. You were foolish enough to put his photograph on the map.'

'Well, I am afraid you cannot see him now. You can't go in there without going through me. There are no exceptions, not even for family members.'

He stepped aside to provide a glimpse of the private compartment behind. Isabella looked in and recognised the corpulent Controller in the stovepipe hat from his photograph, and vague memories of family gatherings when she was very small. He was sitting in a velvet armchair, enjoying an absurdly long cigar, entirely unconcerned with the lunatic behaviour of the train's occupants. She studied his sweat-sheened face.

She wanted to find a way across the threshold, but at the last moment her nerve had failed her. She remembered the last time she had seen him, the horror of the virgin sacrifice that had haunted her childhood. No-one had ever mentioned him again. Her father had eventually convinced himself that he had no brother, just as the town had convinced itself that there had been no train.

'Go. Turn around and walk away.' Angered by her hesitation, the Conductor shoved at her. 'Silly, arrogant little girl! Look at you, parading in a noblewoman's clothes. Did you think it would make you like her? Did you really think you could change anything?'

The Conductor gave into his anger and lashed out at her, knocking her to the floor. Yanking her to her feet, he gave her another hard crack across the face. Nicholas stepped forward to intervene, but as he did so the wound in his chest burned as if it was being pulled apart.

The Conductor slammed Isabella against the wall of the carriage, bearing down on her. 'You have no idea how much I hate the living,' he said. 'You always think you can make a difference.'

The soulless had broken through the soldiers' line of defence and were bearing down on them. Nicholas had used up all his ammunition, and had split his rifle stock on the head of a gurning farmhand. Now he looked up to see the Conductor raising his fist again. Nicholas tried to pulled him away, but it was like shifting steel. As the Conductor's fingers closed around Isabella's throat, he ignored the searing pain in his chest and searched for another weapon among the men he had just destroyed.

He spotted a pair of swords on the belts of two felled soldiers and pulled them free.

Isabella felt herself losing consciousness. Nicholas lunged forward and rammed the blades at the Conductor, but the pain in his chest was now so severe that he could barely see. Thrusting the sword points into the Conductor's startled wide eyes, he felt them come out through the back of his skull, pinning him to the carriage wall.

Although he was speared clean through the sockets, the Conductor continued to thrash about. 'Your world will burn,' he cried. 'Your world will burn!'

The Controller could hardly be expected to ignore the commotion outside his compartment any longer, particularly after a pair of bloody sword-tips had come through his wall. He slowly rose, tapped his cigar and came lumbering out of his cabin to see what the fuss was about.

As the leader of the Satanists who built the train, the Controller presented a grand figure. He was older and vastly more dissipated now, but his appearance still filled Isabella with childhood terror.

'Hello, Uncle. I need to speak to you,' said Isabella, trying to control the quaver in her voice.

The Controller admired her form. In her borrowed gown she appeared transformed, grown up and beautiful. He studied

her and sighed. 'Well well well, my little Isabella. You, of all people. Why must there always be a virgin?'

'I don't belong here, sir. And this man—well, he's not perfect, but he doesn't deserve to go to Hell.'

'But you will. Especially you. The virgins always go.' He checked his watch. 'I don't like the idea of you being abducted by a foreigner, going off and leaving the family without sons for the foundry. I was most surprised to hear you had boarded the *Arkangel*. The Conductor tried to tell me he had lured you here, but I think he was trying to make the best of the situation. Running away, though, it's not very loyal of you.'

'You disappeared when I was six.'

'I began my indenture to the *Dark Angel*. I followed my duty.'

'The sign above our inn had a painting of a sacrificed virgin. But that was standing long before the foundry was built.'

'Indeed it was, because there have always been rituals in our town, sacrifices to ripen the wheat, sacrifices to make the fruit trees abundant, sacrifices so that the midwives would bring more boys than girls. You should know that. Our family was involved in all of them.'

'So the building of the train—'

'—was the next logical step. We'll be arriving very shortly, my dear. A little behind schedule, but that can't be helped. There's nothing you can do to stop the *Dark Angel* now, I'm afraid.'

'But I haven't done anything wrong.'

'It's too late. Those who come this close to our final destination are doomed to stay on board forever.'

Anger replaced Isabella's fear. 'That's cheating!'

'What did you expect? Enjoy these last few moments. Let me look at you in this form, one last time. You were always my favourite niece. I never imagined you would grow up to be so beautiful. Come—have a drink with me.' He took her arm, leading her into the dining car.

'Is that it?' called Nicholas. 'Is that your big plan? We're about to burn for all eternity and you're going for *cocktails?*'

Disgusted, he turned and punched a coal merchant in the face.

Isabella and the Controller sat opposite each other. He pawed at her hand, a cat playing with a new toy. Outside, the sky was flickering with streaks of vermilion. Every few seconds the horizon erupted.

'We are approaching the final stop. I envy you, Isabella. The terrors you've experienced on this journey are nothing compared to those that await you. Don't be sad. All our passengers fail. We are only human, are we not?' He checked his pocket watch as it began to chime.

'Only human. So you are human too.'

'Yes, the only living human allowed to stay aboard the *Dark Angel* for each of its journeys between life and the underworld. I built it, after all.'

'But you must stay on board for eternity.'

'That was my end of the bargain. It's not such a hardship. Every voyage is different. No two passengers are ever alike. You'd be surprised what fun we have.'

'Then if I too have failed, I must accept my fate.'

Nicholas was watching through the carriage window, outraged. 'What? You're giving in, just like that?' he bellowed. 'You're the only one who could have saved me! Well, thanks a lot, Little Miss Virgin!'

Behind him, the dead passengers advanced once more. One soulless soldier reached out and dug bony white fingers into his shoulder.

'Join us...'

'And you can clear off, for a start.' Nicholas punched him in the eyes.

But he had a fight on his hands, holding back the damned while Isabella flirted with the corrupt Controller.

Outside, the sky was fully afire. The train was gathering speed, preparing for its arrival in the land of eternal torment. And although Nicholas fought back as bravely as he could, he knew in his heart that the real battle had been fought and lost.

CHAPTER FORTY-SIX
THE CATACLYSM

Nicholas had fired his first rifle in Algiers after being chased from an illegal camel race by a pair of angry Spanish gamblers, and the trenches had taught him rougher manners. Confronting the fears that had driven him from his comrades had brought fresh courage. Tearing a machete from the hands of a befuddled fieldworker, he wielded the dull, heavy blade against the heads of the attacking horde, splitting a considerable number of soulless skulls before it was finally pulled from his grasp. Soon the carriage was awash with gore, and his right arm was aching.

Even though he had been pinned through the eyes with swords, the Conductor was determined to make his announcements. 'We will shortly be arriving in Hell,' he called. 'The train terminates here. All change. Please remember to take all your belongings with you.'

And inside the Controller's apartment, seated opposite the grand Satanist himself, Isabella cast down her eyes, contrite.

'I could not imagine that I would be a match for you and your train,' she said sadly.

The Controller raised his wineglass to her. 'Don't feel bad, my sweet child. I hope you take it as a consolation when I tell

you that you got further than anyone else has in years. Take a look out of the window and tell me what you see.'

Looking through the glass, she watched a scene that would have made Hieronymus Bosch feel sick. Here and there, groups of men could be faintly discerned, employed in pointless, impossible tasks; the rolling uphill of a giant eyeball, the lowering into a pit of an immense ear, soaring tangles of absurdly complex machinery operated by hundreds, designed to cut a grape in half or tear the petals from a rose, men climbing human pyramids to redirect the stars or change the shapes of lightning bolts, and all the while a screaming, singing cacophony of voices, a reek of burning flesh, a sting of brimstone, a corrupt hint of perfume, a sense of all things spoiled, betrayed, poisoned and unforgiven.

'This is the Hell you expected, yes?' said the Controller. 'Suppose I was to tell you that it is not Hell at all?'

'It hurts my eyes to look upon it,' Isabella admitted. 'What do you mean, it is not Hell?'

'This is what your church would have you believe awaits poor sinners. Such images adorn the walls and windows of your places of worship, to frighten you into belief and obedience. But the underworld does not exist in any single frame of time. It flows continuously back and forth. And it is not a great land of fires and tortures. Let me show you the real Hell.'

He wiped his hand across the window and the landscape fell away, to be replaced by blank, silent blackness. 'Hell exists in no geographical landscape. It cannot be found with compasses. I will show you where Hell is.' He raised his index finger and touched his forehead. 'It is inside here, and only you control it. Hell is the sum of your greatest fears. The most precious gift of life is the acknowledgement of your existence. Hell has no memory and nothing to offer except the thought that nobody ever cared about you, or ever will. Hell is an absence, the Hell of men and women who are utterly indifferent. *L'Enfer, c'est les autres.*'

'Why would people dream of Hell?' Isabella demanded to know. 'We want what is good. We don't wish to suffer.'

'Bless you for your naivety, my little one. How little you know of the world. I only tell you this because you are family. And I would be proud to have you in the family business. Here, have your fantasies of Hell back.' He passed his hand across the window and the fiery landscape returned.

'The family business.' Isabella turned the thought over.

'Don't do it!' Nicholas shouted, hammering on the window.

'You would really have me?' Isabella asked, a smile touching her lips.

'Oh, yes,' said the Controller.

'Your proposal is something to celebrate.'

'I hoped you might see it that way.'

'I suggest a toast.' She held her glass high.

'You're a good sport. To your youth. And to your innocence.'

The Controller drank noisily. Then he stared at her. A sudden look of unpleasant surprise crossed his features.

'It's true,' Isabella admitted, 'I'm young and have not travelled before. But I'm not that innocent.'

The Controller appeared to be choking. He opened his mouth and found a pulsing white egg sac on his tongue. Isabella had slipped one of the eggs from *Coleoptera Freely* into his red wine.

'Try taking your own test,' she said, slamming his jaw shut with her fist and making him swallow.

The Controller began to cough and shake. His sweating jowls and stomach wobbled. There was a pop as the egg sac burst open and new-born beetles invaded his guts. Moments later, the hungry new bugs found the softest channels of escape, burrowing out through his eyes and back again, noisily eating his brain.

The Controller screamed as his head was devoured from the inside. The beetles burst out of his ears and took flight, heading into the corridor, and his headless body fell forward in a spectacular spray of gore, demolishing a bone china tureen filled with pork chops.

Without a controlling influence, the *Dark Angel* began to

shake itself apart. The walls around Isabella strained and creaked. Steel screamed and timber tore. Isabella rose and ran outside, where Nicholas was fending off a pair of dead blacksmiths with a broom.

The windows exploded in splinters of glass. Pinned by his eyes, the Conductor's body swung back and forth. 'All change! All change!' he managed to scream before his head came off.

The floor was buckling as the undercarriage began to break loose and the great wheels bounced about, unmoored. Sparks sprayed all around them. The walls split, and part of the roof was ripped away. The *Arkangel* was breaking up faster than a ship hitting an iceberg.

The undead passengers were thrown into a panic and all began to scream. The noise was appalling. The great train lurched and fell like a roller coaster.

Isabella screamed.

Nicholas yelled.

Everybody shrieked.

With its Conductor speared and its Controller beheaded, the *Dark Angel* fell back on the tracks, hammered over points and over a vast wooden viaduct, shedding its carriages as it went. Each was whipped away from the last as it dropped toward the empty, soundless void below, a Hell far more frightening because it offered nothing at all, the Hell of non-existence.

The remaining carriages were tearing themselves to pieces. Isabella clung to Nicholas, recited the Lord's Prayer and closed her eyes, hanging on for dear life.

With a final boost of speed, the *Dark Angel* left the tracks and hurtled toward the end of the line.

Ahead stood a vast dark terminus, black against black, almost invisible. Beyond them a wall of sound was rising, a cry of terror so dense and discordant that it seemed like one great voice. It broke over the train in waves, splintering into individual human cries, pleading, panicked, fearful, the voices of those who would do anything at all in order to draw one

more breath. It was the sound of Hell's damned, begging to be forgiven for their foolish, sorry, wasted lives.

Isabella opened her eyes and looked upon the mouth of Hades.

The terminus glowed with a million crimson pinprick fires, a vast dark landscape animated in hallucinatory hues. It was the antithesis of a starscape, the universe in reverse.

The buffers and the siding roared up to the train and smashed over it with a thunderous roar.

The *Dark Angel* ploughed right through, hurtling across the precipice. Isabella felt the cataclysm shake her bones, and saw the explosion as if from a great distance, as a volcanic flare in the night sky. The deafening grind of metal reverberated through the blackened countryside. The train sounded like a great dying beast.

And finally, all was quiet.

CHAPTER FORTY-SEVEN
THE GAME

THROUGH BLASTS OF steam and acrid coal-smoke Nicholas saw the nightmare vision roll back and fade like a scene fragmented by migraine.

When he was finally able to raise his head once more and look from the window, all that remained was the empty plain, the ancient meadowlands, and the approaching forest of silver birches. The sky was clear and cornflower blue. He reached down and touched his breastbone, pushing his fingers beneath the rags of his blood-soaked shirt. There was no wound.

He watched Isabella sleep on until sunlight dappled her cheeks, causing her eyelids to flutter. The train was still rocking and swaying, but gently now.

It was dawn, and they were coming into a station. There were buckets of primroses on the platform. The sky was growing brighter by the second.

The *Dark Angel* now looked like a rather shabby old train, brought out of engine-shed retirement for one last spin around the map. She had finally come home, to the place where she had been built.

Isabella yawned and sat up, looking about herself. She stretched and climbed to her feet, opening a window, letting

the breeze caress her. Shafts of sunlight fell all around.

Beside her, Nicholas flexed his aching arms and rose. Squinting and shielding his eyes, he peered out into the brilliant sunshine. The train now looked like any other, patched and tired, grey with dust, its empty corridors scoured with overuse.

Outside, everything was blue and yellow. Isabella opened the carriage door and stepped blinking into the light. She took stock of her surroundings and liked what she saw. The army had left the town. The platform was covered with flowers. She was home. Back in Chelmsk, where her father and friends were waiting to welcome her.

Josef approached her shyly and took her in his arms, holding her safe. The men were different versions of themselves now— the good people they should have been, if the foundry had never allowed the committee to conduct its Satanic ritual.

'Isabella. Thank you for coming back to me.' Josef hugged her close to him. In her lover's arms, Isabella looked up to Heaven and smiled. She felt that the spirits of Thomas, Miranda and all of the other undead souls who had been trapped on the train were looking down at her.

Nicholas stepped forward. 'Thank you, Isabella. Perhaps we'll meet again in another life.'

'What will you do?' she asked, knowing he would go.

'Paradise was always here waiting for you,' he said with a shrug. 'It's not my world. My home is among the fine ladies of London. But perhaps I'll stay for a few more days. I'll never forget that I owe you my life.' He blew her a kiss and walked away toward the sunlit lane that led to town.

THE TRAIN SMASHED across the room, blasting all the furniture to smithereens, then started to shrink, growing smaller and smaller, until it was a toy of battered green tin once more.

It fell onto its side, smouldering, its engine shorted out. The passenger-pieces had been thrown from the Damnation

section of the playing board, hurled from the path appointed by the cards, and had landed instead in Paradise. The train had scorched the board, obliterating the name of its destination.

It was time to put the damaged pieces away before she got into trouble again. Her mother had come home. The little girl looked down at the outcome and smiled to herself. She was six years old, and her conviction that the Devil did not exist except in silly games would last for just another three weeks, until the day she went to the foundry to look for her uncle.

'Isabella! Isabella!' called her mother. 'Wash your hands and come down to lunch right now, or there'll be hell to pay!'

Isabella wiped the pieces from the board and returned them to their boxes. Then she replaced the lid and re-knotted the string. On the lid was the picture of the *Arkangel*, accompanied by the caption: 'A Century Of Wonders Awaits!'

CHAPTER FORTY-EIGHT
THE DELIVERY

'THANK YOU FOR coming back to me?' said Emma. 'That's a bit rich, nicking the end line from *Brief Encounter*. That was a flop when it first opened, you know.' She lay naked on his bed, reading the final pages of the script as rain coursed down the Red Lion's windows.

'It makes an ideal end,' said Shane. 'Besides, *Brief Encounter* is a train movie, isn't it?'

'I'm sure Freddie Francis would love to direct it, but you've absolutely blown the budget. Michael will have a heart attack when he sees you're expecting us to build a vision of Hell. He'll be thinking, *now how can we re-use Dracula's Castle as Hades?* We're much better at suggestion, a whisp of sulphur here, a touch of brimstone there. It's cheaper that way. I suppose it could be done with miniatures, but they aren't our strong point, I'm afraid. We're terribly good at travelling mattes and glass paintings, though. We could probably cobble something together.'

'Well, don't sound too enthusiastic, eh?'

'No, your script is exactly the kind of fantastical thing we'd do, but that's sort of the trouble, isn't it?'

'What do you mean?'

'Well, there we are making these fairy tales starring middle-aged men, Frankenstein and Dracula and what have you, but the only reason the kids go is because they're gory—and they're not even that really, it's mostly red paint and ominous chords, suggestively acted by professionals. The stories aren't really about anything, are they? I mean, when you look at what's going on out there in the real world, the teenagers all fighting one another and getting worked up about pop groups, and there we are making films about the concept of good and evil, set in castles in Transylvania. In deadbeat towns across the country, the kids are waging war with their elders. I know we don't do social realism, you get enough of that on the telly now, but can you imagine anyone remembering any of this stuff in ten years' time? Oh, I know we're not creating high art or anything, but sometimes I wish we'd make something with more lasting appeal.'

'Thank you for that.'

'I'm just being honest. I think the writing's on the wall for us. The Americans are gradually severing ties with the company. It's getting harder and harder to enthuse our overseas partners. They're talking about turning television shows into films next, just because audiences will instantly recognise the actors.'

'That's a cheering thought.' He gave her a slap on the bottom. 'Come on, get dressed, we've a presentation to get to.'

They drove back to Bray and prepared for the meeting.

'WELL, GOODNESS ME, you have been busy.'

Michael Carreras turned over the final page and squared up the sheets. 'It's hugely enjoyable, of course. And there are some lovely roles. I can just imagine what Christopher could do with the part of the Conductor. He's always complaining that we don't give him enough to do in his films. I don't think he's quite forgiven us for making his role virtually mute in *Dracula, Prince Of Darkness*. And I'm sure Peter would jump at the chance to play both the undertaker and the chap who collects

insects. He likes the smaller parts. Terribly self-effacing, for an actor I mean.'

Shane waited for the *but*.

'But it's not cheap. I mean—Hell! Whoosh, there goes the budget right there. And all those undead passengers. I think we rather covered that sort of thing in *The Plague Of The Zombies*. I can't see much of a future for zombies, can you?' He patted the pile of pages. 'There's an awful lot of makeup and special effects work. We'd have to do weeks of experimenting with prosthetics. We've just done that with an Egyptian head while finishing *The Mummy's Shroud* and I'm still not really happy with it. The film will probably go out as the lower half of a double bill, but at least we've got the Milk Marketing Board doing a nice tie-in. And then there's all the soul-searching stuff. Too many abstract speeches. I can see the kids fidgeting about in those bits. So, all in all—' He patted the script again.

Shane caught Emma's eye. He held his breath.

'—I think we're going to pass. We're gearing up for another Dracula, a new Quatermass, and something from the black magic chappie, Dennis Wheatley, but I'm glad we took the time to investigate other avenues. I'm sure we can find something in the coffers to recompense you for your time. Emma, can you make sure Mr Carter is paid today? And see if you can't find him something nice from the wine rack.'

Shane went to take back the script, but Carreras seemed reluctant to part with it. 'Could I ask you a favour—as a gentleman—not to take it straight to Amicus? I'm sure they'd balk at the budget, but even so, you understand...'

'Of course. Entirely understood.'

Carreras breathed a sigh of relief and returned the script. 'I do hope you don't think this little exercise has been a waste of your time.'

'On the contrary. I think I learned a lot from it.' He rose and shook Carreras' hand. And then he was back in the corridor, heading for the wet green lawns and the countryside once more.

Emma walked with him to the studio entrance. 'I'll send a cheque over to the inn and we'll sort out the bill there,' she said. 'Don't feel too bad about it. They're trying to keep the company alive, and they just don't know what works anymore. What do you think you will do now?'

'I don't know,' Shane admitted. 'There's a lot happening in London at the moment. It feels like the place to be. If I stayed here, would you stick around?'

'Of course. It's my home. I'm like the girl in your script. You have to find Paradise where you can, but there's nothing like going home.'

Shane narrowed his eyes at her. 'Am I missing something? Why do you think Michael turned the script down?'

'I think he probably found it a bit too daunting. The risk was too great.'

'I feel like the guy in those Amicus anthology movies,' he said. 'I suppose I should be thankful that Michael didn't turn out to be the Devil.'

'Maybe he did. If you'd gone to Amicus first, they would probably have hired you for an anthology film. Instead you came to us, and now you've promised not to go to them.' Emma laughed. 'Actually, Dr Terror didn't turn out to be the Devil, did he? He was Death. The death of your script.'

'Damn, you're right. I should have remembered that. I think I've been had. In the nicest possible way. Can I ask you something? Were you a part of the deal?'

She smiled sadly. 'We had to make sure you produced a script, so that we could stop it. You accepted a paid commission, which makes it our property.'

'I could write another. It was just a story. Characters live and die. They're saved or damned. All very black and white. No moral, just entertainment value. Not like real life. It's all so much more complicated out here, isn't it?'

'Not that much, and not from a distance. You'll look back on this and laugh. Besides, I don't think you'd have got on

with Amicus. They'd have found your script a little too—questioning.'

'I'll never know now, will I?'

'I can understand that you're probably feeling a bit angry at the moment. If you ever decide to forgive me, you have my telephone number.'

'I'm not angry, Emma. I think I learned something.'

He kissed her and left, reluctantly.

Climbing into the red MG, Shane took one last look back at the girl, the studio, the white crenelated walls closed in by the avenue of dense dark trees.

SOON AFTER, BRAY shut its doors for good. It was never used as a studio again. Emma had been right. After *The Mummy's Shroud*, Hammer left the studio, embarking on a desperate jumble of ill-conceived projects that killed their last hopes of ever regaining their unique position in the film world.

Less than a decade later, after promises of a rebirth with grand new projects like *Nessie* and *Vampirella*, the company crumbled in the harsh light of economic reality and died, and the family of Hammer finally disintegrated. The carpenters and seamstresses, the designers and riggers, the writers, artists, cameramen and producers went their separate ways.

Hammer's ashes were blown to the four winds, to await fresh blood and rebirth.

ABOUT THE AUTHOR

BORN IN LONDON, Christopher Fowler has written for film, television, radio, graphic novels, and for newpaper including *The London Times*, for more than thirty years. He is a regular columnist for both *The Independent on Sunday*. Fowler is the multi-award winning author of more than thirty novels, including the lauded *Bryant & May* mystery novels. In the past year he has been nominated for eight national book awards.

For more information visit

www.christopherfowler.co.uk

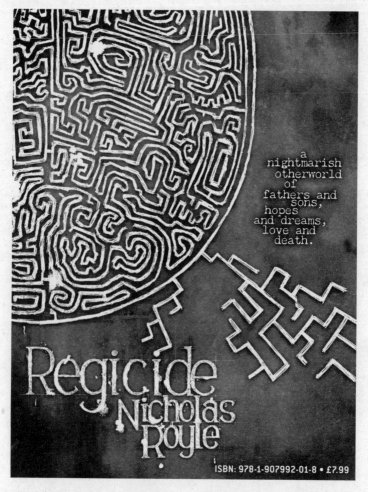

a
nightmarish
otherworld
of
fathers and
sons,
hopes
and dreams,
love and
death.

Regicide
Nicholas
Royle

ISBN: 978-1-907992-01-8 • £7.99